SHE WOULDN'T GIVE IN.

Carrie took a deep breath of country air. No matter what, she was going to keep it together from here on out. But when Tyson came up behind her, holding two glasses, and said "I've got a special new Pinot I'd like you to taste," the prim and proper voices in her head gave way.

Standing right in front of her was a man who oozed raw, masculine sex appeal. And somewhere within Carrie, there was a powerfully sexual woman dying to get out.

Sweet lord, she wanted to sleep with Tyson. Only a foolish woman would deny herself such pleasure. She surprised them both with, "I'd rather taste you instead."

Praise for the erotic fiction of Bella Andre

"Andre writes a wonderful story filled with lovable characters and steamy sex. Anyone looking for a funny and intelligently written read should definitely give [Andre] a try!"

—*Romantic Times*

Tempt Me, Taste Me, Touch Me is also available as an eBook

Turn the page to read rave reviews of Bella Andre's irresistibly hot and sexy novel *Take Me.* . . .

An appetite for sensual pleasure must never be denied . . . and in the beauty of Tuscany, curvaceous Lily Ellis will get her fill—of the lover of her dreams. . . .

Don't miss Bella Andre's sizzling national bestseller

TAKE ME

"Oh my! Bella Andre's *Take Me* is wonderfully sexy—a big, fun fantasy with an equally big heart. You'll cheer these characters on as they find each other . . . and themselves!"

—Emma Holly

"Emotionally charged and deliciously erotic. A must-read from cover to cover."

—Jaid Black

"A story with a woman who isn't model perfect is a refreshing change in *Take Me*. . . . A delightfully engaging tale of erotic contemporary romance."

—Romance Reviews Today

"A terrific book. . . . The sex scenes . . . are hotter than molten lava. . . . Lily and Tavis are wonderful characters. . . . Ms. Andre is a gifted author with a knack for penning stories about realistic women and the sexier than sin men who fall in love with them. . . . I loved this book!"

—Just Erotic Romance Reviews

"It's easy to be seduced by this story. *Take Me* is most of all hot, sexy, lush, hungry, and sweaty. Lily and Travis burn up the pages, but there is a story to go with all the wonderful sex, and it's a good one."

—A Romance Review

"A fine contemporary romance. . . . A fun, often amusing tale, with a serious theme of 'to thine own self be true.'"

—Harriet Klausner

"Andre's vivid descriptions of her characters' physical and emotional relationship engage the senses from the start. . . . There's an overall message of hope and empowerment."

—*Romantic Times*

"Packed with sizzle, but also contains a good balance of emotional pull."

—Round Table Reviews

"The chemistry between Lily and Travis is powerful. The love scenes are passionate and sensual with a romantic appeal that readers will love. Bella Andre has done an outstanding job creating a heroine who is not average and a hero who loves her just the way she is."

—Romance Junkies

Also by Bella Andre

Take Me

Tempt Me, Taste Me, Touch Me

Bella Andre

POCKET BOOKS

New York   London   Toronto   Sydney

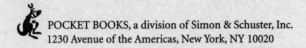

POCKET BOOKS, a division of Simon & Schuster, Inc.
1230 Avenue of the Americas, New York, NY 10020

Library of Congress Cataloging-in-Publication Data
Andre, Bella.
    Tempt me, taste me, touch me / Bella Andre. —Pocket Books trade pbk. ed.
      p. cm.
    ISBN-13: 978-1-4165-2417-5 (pbk.)
    ISBN-10:   1-4165-2417-7 (pbk.)
    1. Napa Valley (Calif.)—Fiction. I. Title.
  PS3601.N5495T46 2007
  813'.6—dc22

                        2006051399

This Pocket Books trade paperback edition January 2007

10 9 8 7 6 5 4 3 2 1

Manufactured in the United States of America

For Paul, the very best part of living in a wine-country paradise

ACKNOWLEDGMENTS

Thanks again to Jami Alden and Monica McCarty, the two best friends and critique partners a girl could have. And thank you to Jessica Faust for always picking up the phone when I call (rather than running screaming in the opposite direction) and to Selena James for all of our enjoyable phone calls. Big hugs to everyone in the San Francisco RWA chapter. And to the Fog City Divas (Candice Hern, Barbara Freethy, Carol Grace), thank you for not only giving me my very own Diva crown, but for saving my sanity over lunch more times than I can count.

Tempt Me

1

*T*ONIGHT WAS THE NIGHT the world would say good-bye to Carrie Anderson, single-girl-in-the-city, and hello to Carrie Anderson, deliriously happy woman-engaged-to-a-wealthy-hunk.

Ever since her boyfriend, James Carrigan, had asked her to dinner at Farallon, San Francisco's most elegant restaurant, she'd taken to staring at her bare left hand with a secret smile. She'd have bet the contents of her 401(k) that, come Thursday night, a sparkling diamond was going to be weighing down her left ring finger. Farallon was their special place. It was where they'd dined for their first date, the night they'd first slept together, and their one-year anniversary.

Dinner had been lovely. Although, to be honest, she hadn't really tasted the butternut squash soup. And she'd barely been able to swallow her grilled salmon on a bed of polenta. With every moment that had passed, her stomach had twisted into a tighter, tenser knot. And when the waiter had asked her if she'd like to see the dessert menu, she'd nearly bitten his head off. *No, I don't want flan,* she thought. *I want an engagement ring!*

At long last, the waiter cleared their plates away and brought over two snifters of warmed B&B. Carrie had never been a huge fan of the potent after-dinner drink, but as it was James's favorite, she gamely took a sip. It burned her tongue and stung her throat, but she didn't mind, because James was finally reaching into his pocket. For a ring!

Her very own Prince Charming was about to bend down on one knee and ask her to become his wife. She'd run through the scene at least a hundred times. Her eyes were going to be filled with tears as he popped open the Tiffany's box; her hands would be trembling slightly as he slipped the engagement ring on her finger. She would whisper yes, and then they would kiss passionately to a backdrop of applause.

But James didn't bother getting down on one knee. Instead he simply put the open ring box on the place setting before her and said, "It's finally time for you to become the next Mrs. Carrigan." Carrie's breath left her chest in a whoosh of disappointment.

She knew she was supposed to gasp with glee, to offer James her hand so that he could slip the ring on at the very moment she said "yes." Carrie worked to swallow her dissatisfaction at James's unromantic proposal. She tried desperately to get her lips to form the one word that would ensure her position as newly crowned Princess of the San Francisco elite. She pushed her tongue into her molars and opened her mouth. She could do it, she could say it. "Yes" was a one-syllable word. Even her one-year-old niece could say it. But all that came out when she forced the air up from her lungs was, "Yeourgh."

What was wrong with her tonight? Of course she was going to marry James and live happily ever after. They were going to have 2.4 children and live in a large ranch house in the wealthy suburbs of Palo Alto behind a remote-activated iron gate. She was going to drive a HUMMER with booster seats in the back, and she'd drop off her kids for swimming lessons in the summer, piano in the fall. They'd play tennis every Saturday with the Williams gang, winter in Hawaii at the family beach estate, get their teeth whitened twice a year by his uncle John. They'd have the perfect life, the perfect kids, the perfect marriage.

It was all so perfect that Carrie's head swam. She felt nauseous. This perfect life was what she had always wanted. Wasn't it?

Evidently, a badly mangled "yes" was good enough for James. He reached for her clammy hand and slid the enormous, square-cut, canary yellow diamond onto her ring finger. The huge jewel sparkled in the candlelight, but Carrie felt like it was mocking her, telling her she'd never fit into his world of society galas and charity lunches. Of gray-haired moguls with barely legal, silicone-enhanced second wives. Sure, during the past two years she'd learned to play her part to perfection. She went to the right hairdresser, used the right personal shopper at Neiman's, made the right witty remarks at exactly the right time. But could she do everything just right for a lifetime? And, she couldn't help but wonder, did she really want to?

James's voice cut through her reflections. "The minute I saw this ring I knew it would look perfect on you, Carolyn. And I was right."

A silent "as always" hung in the air between them.

Carrie looked up from the blindingly gorgeous jewel. James was better looking than any other man she'd ever met, let alone dated. Too bad his smug grin seemed to say marriage proposals were only a formality for a catch like him.

And why did he insist on calling her Carolyn when he knew she much preferred Carrie? She'd always thought it was charming, the way he was so formal, but now she wondered if it was simply a way to change her into his image of perfection. For her to be the perfect addition to his already perfect life.

On paper, James was Prince Charming come to life. His staggering wealth and his Harvard MBA, combined with his classic blond, blue-eyed good looks put him at the top of any list of eligible bachelors. One of her residential landscaping clients had set them up, and Carrie had been shocked, and terribly pleased, that he'd wanted to see her again. On their second date, he'd hired a classical quartet from the San Francisco symphony to serenade her with Tchaikovsky's *Romeo and Juliet* Overture. For the next two years he'd showered her with gifts and weekend trips to Paris.

And yet . . . something was missing. None of her other lovers had treated her like a porcelain doll in bed. At first, she'd felt cherished when James had insisted on taking things slow. But as the weeks had rolled into months, she couldn't help but wonder if there was something wrong with her, if she wasn't sexy enough to drive her boyfriend wild.

She felt like she was seeing the real James for the first time. Even though she hadn't agreed to marry him yet, he'd already closed the deal.

Ring, check. Fiancée gaping at size of diamond, check. Now all he had to do was iron out the details.

"We will use Grace Cathedral for the wedding, of course. Mummy will have a word with the pastor for us. They're quite close, you know. The Olympic Club for the reception. And then—"

"James," Carrie said, trying to stop the train before it picked up enough speed to smash into a brick wall. And flattened them both.

"Carrigans have always honeymooned in Bora-Bora, so of course you can spend a month on the beach while I play golf."

Carrie cleared her throat and tried to steel her nerves. Could this be any more awkward? Somehow, some way, she needed to avoid a scene.

"James," she tried again, "maybe we should discuss this at your—"

But James had already clicked open his cell phone and speed dialed darling Mummy. "Guess which great-looking San Francisco couple just got better-looking thanks to a two-hundred-thousand-dollar diamond?"

Agnes's grating squeal came through the earpiece, and something inside Carrie snapped in two. It was one thing to deal with the idea of waking up next to a gorgeous man who didn't really listen to her every day for the rest of her life, but the thought of having to do Sunday brunch with his mother fifty-two times a year (not to mention countless family dinners and parties) was truly vile.

She could no longer avoid the horrible truth: She didn't love James after all. She couldn't marry him. She was going to have to give the four-carat ring back.

And just like that, the fairy-tale love story she'd been trying so desperately to hold on to shattered into a million pieces.

"No!" she shouted, yanking the beautiful ring off her finger. Well, she should have yanked it, but she couldn't. It was too beautiful. Instead, she slowly slid it off, fighting back tears at the thought of willingly giving up such beauty. Even if it was the right thing to do. Could she help it if turning down six-figure engagement rings made her a little weepy and shallow?

She tried to hand it to him across the table, but he was still holding the cell phone to his ear and frowning at her. Before she could close her fist back around it, the ring dropped onto the table. It bounced off the pristine white tablecloth and rolled beneath the stiletto heel of the woman sitting at the table beside them, who looked to have undergone one face-lift too many.

Clearly irritated with her, James said, "Sorry, Mummy. I'll have to call you back," then scooted back his chair to retrieve the precious ring.

But Carrie felt that it was her responsibility to be the bigger person here. To act like a lady, one last time. Besides, she wasn't angry with James. She just didn't want to marry him. The least she could do was give him back his ring in a civil manner.

A moment later, she was on her knees, with her butt way up in the air and her hair hanging in front of her eyes. She reached for the ring just as Ms. Extreme Makeover's stiletto pierced the back of her hand.

"Ouch," she cried, smacking her head on the bottom of the table as she sat up too quickly.

Suave as ever, even in the midst of an embarrassing situation that involved approximately one hundred strangers, James held out his hand to Carrie. All out of options, she allowed him to escort her back to their table. He slipped the ring back on her finger and said, "Why don't you hold onto this until Monday, when your PMS isn't quite so bad."

At that moment Carrie knew without a shadow of a doubt that she was making the right decision. She stifled a scream and fled the restaurant into the streets of Union Square. She was desperate to put as much distance between her and her ex as she possibly could.

Thank God she was leaving tomorrow for a weekend of wine tasting in the Napa Valley with the girls. If there was ever a time for late-night wine and chocolate-inspired advice, it was now.

CARRIE WAITED to spill the news until her two best friends, Rose and Vanessa, were buckled into her silver Mustang convertible and the wind was whipping through their hair en route to Napa Valley.

"James proposed."

Vanessa, unromantic to her very core, cut right past congratulations. "Where's the bling?" she asked, tucking a few long, red strands of hair that were flying around her face back into her chic black cap and kicking off her Manolos.

"I'm not wearing it," Carrie said as she reached into her beige linen slacks for the ring that was burning a hole in her pocket. The ring that had haunted her all night long. "I didn't know what else to do with it."

"My God," Vanessa said as she grabbed the ring and stared at it with big eyes. "I've got to try it on." The band was a perfect fit on her left hand, the yellow diamond nicely offset by her deep tan. "I can't believe you get to wear this ring every day, you lucky bitch! Which begs the question, why the hell aren't you wearing it? Afraid you'll blind the other drivers when the sun sparks off it and they crash into the center divider?"

Carrie laughed. "Yeah, that's exactly why," she said, wondering if they were going to think she was crazy when she told them how she'd panicked at the thought of a life sentence as a perfect little society lady.

Rose held her unruly black curls down, having lost her scarf five minutes into their drive, and yelled from the backseat to be heard over the engine noise. "Does that mean you said yes?" Her oversized white blouse flapped in the wind, and her blue eyes were full of concern.

The song "I Will Always Love You" came on the local pop station, and Carrie temporarily avoided answering Rose by fiddling with the tuner. In the best of circumstances this song made her want to puke. What she needed right now was a female power song. Something like Aretha Franklin's "Respect."

Despite her moment of clarity at the restaurant, she'd been up all night wondering if she was making a mistake snagging the catch of the decade and then, in the eleventh hour, deciding to throw him back. Which was why she'd tucked the ring into her pocket before leaving the house. Maybe her friends would make her see the light and she'd want to slip it on her finger.

The digital tuner landed, ever so helpfully, on "Ironic."

Carrie gave up. The radio programmers were out to get her. Over Alanis Morissette's catchy, but so awfully appropriate tune, Carrie finally replied.

"I didn't exactly say yes."

"Under any other circumstances I'd encourage you to play hardball for a bigger ring. But in this case," Vanessa said as she held her left hand up and salivated over the diamond some more, "even I'd say that's going too far. This baby is big. Nice and heavy. Just the way a girl likes it." She winked to send home her none-too-subtle double entendre.

Carrie playfully smacked Vanessa on the shoulder. "Holding out for a bigger diamond is something only you would do."

Vanessa sniffed. "That's because I'm the only one with the panache, not to mention the balls, to carry it off."

"You said no?" The shock in Rose's voice was strong enough to carry over Alanis and the road noise.

Heat flooded Carrie's face. "I didn't say no, I yelled no." Now that the dam had broken, everything came spilling out. "He was talking about Mummy and Bora-Bora and I wanted to smack him. He didn't even wait to hear if I said yes before he was naming our children."

In a show of solidarity that Carrie couldn't have predicted, especially since she knew firsthand how difficult it was to take the diamond off, Vanessa slipped the ring off her finger and shoved it back into Carrie's pocket.

"At least now you don't have to give up your career to be a trophy wife," Vanessa said, in her characteristically blunt manner.

Carrie's mouth fell open and she spun around to face Rose, putting their lives in jeopardy for several seconds. "Vanessa just called me a trophy wife. A trophy wife! Aren't you going to make her apologize?"

Rose bit down on her lip. With great reluctance, she finally said, "She's right, Carrie."

Vanessa reached across Carrie to take the wheel as they swerved into the fast lane and Rose let out a high-pitched yelp of fear.

"Sorry I'm almost killing us here," Carrie said, turning back to the road. "I just can't believe this. Why didn't you guys ever say anything?"

Vanessa shrugged. "James was rich and successful and good looking, and you seemed to like that."

"And this was your 'Year of Marriage,'" Rose said, an embarrassing reminder of Carrie's drunken New Year's resolution. "We didn't want to mess that up for you."

Last December 31 she'd decided that nearly two years with James and no wedding ring was long enough. Plus, she'd been thirty-two, and time had seemed of the essence. Babies, the next stage of life, the whole nine yards. Which meant it had been time to get her boyfriend to make the big move. And so she'd declared her "Year of Marriage" resolution to her friends in a private, well-liquored embrace and had dropped numerous hints to James for the past nine months, not to mention leaving dog-eared copies of *Bride* magazine on the coffee table at her apartment.

"I still don't understand why neither of you went out on a limb to tell me what you really felt about James. If I'm too blind, too stupid to save myself, isn't it up to my best friends to save me?"

Vanessa pressed her lips together, making it clear that she didn't appreciate having to defend herself. Rose stepped in to smooth things over. "You always said how perfect everything was with James, so we kind of figured things were just how you wanted them. That they were good enough."

Carrie looked at Vanessa for the full, unvarnished truth. "And?"

"You never want to hear anything negative. You convinced yourself that he was wonderful, and if we'd said anything you would have blown us off."

"We didn't want you to have to choose sides," Rose said, trying to soften Vanessa's harsh, but honest, statement. "No matter who you marry, we'd always want to be your friends. But if we'd said we didn't like him . . ." Rose didn't say any more, didn't say how Carrie might have given up her best friends because she hadn't wanted to face the truth about the man she'd been dating.

Carrie felt tears welling up and was glad she had her sunglasses on. "You're right."

"Don't be mad at us, Carrie," Rose said.

Carrie shook her head. "Of course I'm not mad at you guys. How can I be? I'm just upset that it took me so long to face up to who James really was. To what our relationship was all about. I wanted him to be perfect, and he was on paper, so I pretended that he was in real life too. But all along, he was only good enough. And I was just as bad as he was, because last night I realized that I never truly loved him. Even though I tried to convince all of us that I did."

While Rose rubbed Carrie's knotted shoulder muscles gently from the backseat, Carrie wished she could rewind the last two years and start over.

In a shaky voice, she said, "Well, now you know the whole sad story," hoping that they could drop the subject for now. But, of course, she knew there was one more question on everyone's mind. And she could trust Vanessa to ask it.

"So, since you said no, what are you doing with his ring in your pocket? Shouldn't that be on its way back to Tiffany's so that one of my überthankful lovers can buy it for *moi*?"

Carrie sighed. "He told me to think it over. He thinks I'm going to say yes on Monday."

"What an idiot." Vanessa rolled her eyes. "Any guy who gets turned down with a ring like that should know that it's going to take a hell of a lot more than a weekend to change a girl's mind."

Sensing that Carrie would welcome a change of subject, Rose poked Vanessa in the back. "Speaking of breakups, Elliot dumped me."

Carrie's head whipped to the backseat again. "Oh, honey, I'm so sorry."

Vanessa grabbed the wheel and straightened out their weaving course. "You want to watch the road already? I'm not going to be too happy if we roll into Napa in an ambulance." She shifted in her seat again to see Rose better. "What happened?"

Rose shrugged. "The usual, I guess. He went thinner. Younger. Have I mentioned thinner yet?"

Vanessa snarled. "I don't get it. So what if you're not an anorexic stick? You're lush. You're curved in all the right places." She looked down at her own slim hips and small breasts. "I hear butt implants are the new breast implants. When I was sleeping with that plastic surgeon, he gave me a great price quote on some work and I briefly toyed with the idea."

Rose groaned. "Don't tell me that I've been trying my whole life to look like you and even you're not happy with what you look like." She closed her eyes, and when she opened them, her blue orbs were bleak. "I'll tell you a surefire way to get some curves. Right after your boyfriend dumps you, eat every cookie, piece of chocolate, and ice cream bar in your house. I always get a nice five-pound bonus with the 'it's not you, it's me' speech."

Carrie couldn't believe the bad turns their relationships had taken this week. "You know he didn't deserve you, Rose. And one day you'll find a man who loves you for the gorgeous, wonderful woman you are." Rose pinched her lips together, and it was clear that she didn't believe a word of it, so Carrie barreled on, saying, "Seems like at least two of us desperately need this weekend to unwind."

Rose shook her head. "I don't need to unwind. I need to diet."

"Bullshit," Vanessa said. "You need to get flamingly drunk with me and Carrie by the pool while we pick apart all the women's haircuts and drool over the men. Elliot was a boring, balding loser with a roving eye. You deserve better. Both of you do."

"Which brings us to you," Carrie said, pointing a finger at Vanessa. "Any traumas come your way lately? Any losers to lose?"

Vanessa pulled the black cap off and let her striking red hair blow free. "You know I don't do boyfriends. Or trauma. I do sex. And fun. This weekend is all about the girls, the booze, and, if all goes well, an uncomplicated, wine-country fling." The corner of her mouth curved up. "For all of us."

Carrie shook her head. "I can't. I mean, I've hardly broken up with James. There's no way I could jump into bed with a stranger."

"I'm with Carrie," Rose said. "I can't imagine sleeping with someone I don't know or have feelings for."

"Your problem is that you think Prince Charming actually exists," Vanessa said pointedly. "Because he most certainly doesn't."

Rose protested immediately. "Don't say that, Vanessa. Lots of people find true love." She paused for a moment, frowning. "At least I think they do."

Vanessa pounced on that small seed of doubt. "Haven't you ever wondered what really went on behind the scenes in all those fairy tales? All the things they don't let little girls know about."

The conversation was hitting far too close to home for Carrie's comfort, but Vanessa had a way of drawing people into her world, whether they wanted to go there or not.

"Behind the scenes?"

Vanessa shifted slightly in her seat to better address her grudgingly captivated audience. "I never bought into those fables my mother read to me. I couldn't help but wonder how many of the princesses-to-be had trouble saying 'yes' when the princes rode up on their white chargers and kissed their cherry red lips. What if they had a crush on the stable boy? Or a different prince from another country? A better-looking one? A prince with more money? A bigger penis?"

Carrie chuckled, feeding Vanessa's fire. "And why was it that every princess in every story had pale white skin? What about all the redheaded, dark-skinned princesses out there? Because we all know that red lipstick would clash terribly with a complexion like mine."

"Oh, Vanessa," Rose sighed. "You're taking all the fun out of it."

Strangely, for the first time, Carrie could see Vanessa's point. "I don't know, Rose. She might be on to something. What if the girls were so desperate to get away from their evil stepmothers that they hopped into the arms of the first prince that came along?"

Just like I almost did, she thought, *and I didn't even have a good excuse like an evil stepmother to justify my stupidity.*

As Carrie made a right turn into the entrance to the Napa Valley Hotel & Spa, Vanessa took one look at the hunky bellboys and her mouth curved into a come-hither smile, fairy tales already forgotten.

Carrie handed her keys to the young valet, wondering if there wasn't something to Vanessa's love-'em-and-leave-'em attitude. Since college, as she'd watched her friend go through men like cigarettes, she'd always questioned Vanessa's behavior, certain that she'd been missing out by not opening herself up—emotionally anyway—to the opposite sex. But both she and Rose had opened themselves up, and here they were, battered and bruised.

Maybe Vanessa was right. And true love didn't exist after all.

2

CARRIE GRATEFULLY TOOK THE GLASS of champagne she was offered inside the lobby. The luxurious hotel, with its marble floors, mustard yellow walls, and old wood ceiling beams, reminded her of a trip she'd taken through Tuscany in college.

"Now this is something I could get used to," Vanessa purred as she ravenously eyed the closest bellboy.

Carrie grabbed her arm and pulled her to the check-in counter. "It's called statutory rape. Forget about it."

After getting their room keys, Vanessa said, "I'll see you both at the pool in five," already en route to her room.

Carrie tried to muster up the proper enthusiasm for an afternoon of drunken splashing. And failed. Turning to Rose she said, "I'm feeling restless after the long drive. You don't mind if I go out for a walk and meet up with you two later, do you?"

Rose pulled her into a warm hug. "Take all the time you need. I'm sorry about how things turned out with James."

"It's okay. I'm okay," she insisted, even though she wasn't. She kissed Rose on the cheek and stepped out of her embrace. "I'll meet up with you both in a bit. And I promise I'll be all smiles." Carrie said, then hurried off to her room. The hallway was as cool and soothing as the lobby and if she had been in a better mood she would have taken the time to admire the lush paintings of ripe grapes on the walls and the magical spun-glass light fixtures that hung from the ceiling. After slipping her key into the slot on the door, she entered the room. As she closed the door behind her, she caught sight of a boring-looking beige woman in the mirror. She dropped her weekend bag to the floor in dismay. Was this what she'd let herself become? She'd always loved color, reds and yellows and greens. Over the past two years, she'd slowly but surely become colorless, thinking that's what she needed to do to please her boyfriend. To get him to become her husband. She would have changed clothes, but the contents of her suitcase were just more white and beige and brown. Maybe a little gold to spice things up.

Impulsively, she headed back into the lobby. "I need to buy some clothes," she said to the woman behind the front desk who had checked her in. "Right away."

Behaving as if Carrie wasn't a complete lunatic, the woman said, "We have a wonderful boutique in the hotel, around the corner from the concierge."

"Great, thanks," Carrie said, not caring that she was about to pay way too much for a new outfit. She needed out of her beige prison, stat.

A mannequin in the window of the boutique caught her eye. The tank top it sported was a low-cut swirl of color with a print that would have looked more at home on a canvas than a cotton shirt. Carrie loved it. She charged the top and a pair of yellow Capri pants to her room.

Five minutes later, she left the store wearing her new outfit and a pair of fun flip-flops. There were no recognizable labels on anything, and she felt freer than she had in a very long time. She didn't plan on ever wearing beige again, so she'd left her old clothes at the boutique to donate to charity. She was halfway through the lobby when she remembered the ring. In the pocket of her dull linen slacks.

Uh-oh. That was an expensive mistake. She half jogged back to the store, her palms already sweating at the thought of losing the ring. She'd have to put a second mortgage on her house to pay James back if she lost it.

"Um, hi again. I forgot something in my pants," she said. When she pulled the enormous diamond ring out of the pocket, the owner gave her a funny look.

"Strange thing to forget," the woman said.

Carrie nodded. "I know. It's a long story. Thanks again."

Her heart was still pounding overtime as she walked back through the lobby, desperate to get out of the hotel. She walked down the main street in a rush, trying to escape her thoughts. The smell of freshly baked bread and pastries from a charming bakery wafted out onto the sidewalk, but she hardly noticed. She sidestepped several florists' buckets, filled with blooms of every color. She increased her pace past the restaurants and boutiques that lined the streets, walking so quickly that her breath came in puffs and droplets of sweat formed between her breasts. She veered off the sidewalk onto a dirt path between vines, a fine layer of dust covering her French-manicured toenails. By the time she stopped to catch her breath and look up, she was surrounded on four sides by vineyards.

The splendor of the vines took her breath away. She'd been wine tasting in Napa before, but apart from getting out of the limo to taste Cabernets and Pinots and Chardonnays at each winery, she'd never explored the area. The grapevines stretched before her, creeping up the mountains on both sides of the valley. She hadn't been immersed in beauty like this for a very long time.

She breathed in the sweet-smelling air, glad for the new surroundings—and her spontaneous outfit change, she thought with a sudden grin as she looked down at her bright clothes. She was going to donate the rest of her all-beige wardrobe first thing Monday.

It all seemed so obvious now how wrong she and James were for each other. If only she could have figured this out a week ago. Before the proposal at Farallon.

She sighed deeply. It was time for her to face the cold, hard truth. Time to admit that she'd been ignoring the warning signs for the past year. She'd let her landscaping business drop off because James had needed her to attend more events with his mother during the day. She hadn't seen nearly enough of Rose and Vanessa and had only been able to schedule this weekend with them because James was busy with a men's-only golf tournament on Saturday.

Little by little she'd allowed him to take over her life. She'd always thought of herself as an independent woman, but now she wondered—if she'd really been self-sufficient, then why had she let her life be taken over?

If she'd grown up poor, if her parents had struggled to clothe and feed her, if she'd had to scrape her way to the top, she might have had some excuse for having fallen so hard for James. And all his stuff. But her upbringing had been comfortably middle class, her parents were still married, and neither she nor her sister had been the least bit traumatized by their childhoods.

The truth was, until he'd popped the question, until she'd really had to take a long hard look at becoming Mrs. James Carrigan, she hadn't let herself think clearly about the reality of spending the rest of her life with him. Thank God she hadn't done all the wedding planning and then jilted him at the altar.

She looked up again to get her bearings, but she had no idea where she was, no sense of how to get back to the hotel. This vineyard looked exactly like all the others. Beautiful, green, lush with ripe grapes, but indistinguishable.

She was lost.

TYSON GREEN LIKED TO END every day in his wine cave. Especially when it had been a grueling one—his afternoon having been all but wasted with a near-miss labeling debacle for the new Petit Syrah. One of the best ways to revive his spirits and his passion for winemaking was to shove back from his desk, don his well-worn cowboy hat, and disappear into the cool serenity of the underground cave. His ex-wife, Kimberly, had called him a living, breathing version of the caveman, but frankly, her opinion no longer mattered.

He pushed open the thick oak door and inhaled the scent of fermenting grapes. A man couldn't ask for more than this, his own underground castle beneath the award-winning grapevines of Napa Valley.

If only that were true, he thought as he adjusted the brim of his hat to examine a hairline crack in the bottom of a barrel of Pinot. A man could ask for love, real love that lasted. And he had. But for all the success he'd had as a vintner, he'd failed miserably at being a husband.

Tyson made a mental note to send his foreman in to check the cave's temperature and to see if there were any other cracks that needed dealing with, then he turned and pushed back through the thick wood door into the rapidly darkening evening. He was going to take his bad attitude, and worse memories, out of the cave and turn them around with a juicy, grilled steak out on his porch.

His long, muscled legs ate up the quarter mile between the winery and his ranch house. On a good day, when he was able to forgo paperwork for the joy of working with the vines, his jeans and denim "Green Vineyards" work shirt would end up covered in dirt. Today, unfortunately, his shirt still had the dry-cleaner's lines on it. Still, he pulled the button-down shirt off as soon as he walked inside the foyer, preferring to relax with a glass of wine out on his covered porch in his well-worn T-shirt. He poured himself a large glass of fruity red wine and opened the French doors that led from his kitchen out to the porch to let the warm, end-of-summer air in.

Walking to the rail of the deck, he surveyed his land. His vines. Everything he loved was out there. The dirt, the trees, the grapes, the mountains. He'd given his heart to winemaking, and it had rewarded him a thousand times over. Not only with money but also with satisfaction. He'd grown up comfortably middle class, and he had no complaints about his parents or brothers. They were engineers and bookkeepers, and he'd always thought to follow in their footsteps. But then he'd taken an agriculture class at the University of California in the small farm town of Davis and discovered viticulture. He hadn't been old enough to drink back then as a nineteen-year-old sophomore, but he'd been hooked. He'd worked his ass off, and fifteen years later, he called a small part of Napa Valley his own.

With nightfall, the vineyard was silent, save for an occasional wildcat on the prowl for mice. So when he heard the sound of dried grape leaves crunching, he sharpened his gaze. And saw a gorgeous blond walking through his vines.

In the moonlight, the woman's hair glowed like a halo. And where the ends brushed against her breasts, well, that was a beautiful thing. A small waist and great legs rounded out the exceptional package.

For the first time in six months, Tyson found himself wondering what it would be like to sink into a woman. To have her naked and slick beneath him, crying out as she came.

It was a relief to feel desire again. He'd worked to push away the image of his vineyard manager, a man he'd believed to be loyal and steadfast, pumping in and out of his wife. On their bed. His bed. Even when Kimberly had seen him standing in the doorway, she hadn't been able to hide the pleasure of being in Rogelio's arms.

He'd thought her betrayal had stolen his heart. But when he'd examined their relationship from all angles, he hadn't been certain that they'd ever truly been in love. Just a powerful lust that had burned out in less than a year.

Which meant that what she'd really taken from him was his pride. And he had no intention of ever allowing a woman to rip his pride to shreds again.

But as he stood on his covered wraparound porch, watching the tall, curvy blond hike across the land he was more proud of than anything else, Tyson decided he was sick of letting his ex-wife's transgression ruin his sex life. Sure, lust had sucked him into a bad marriage, but he knew better now than to confuse sex with love.

Every weekend women came to his tasting room for wine and the hope of a weekend fling. And every weekend he turned them down. But not this time.

Tyson straightened his well-worn cowboy hat and headed down the stairs into the field. He'd go say hello, and if it turned out that his trespasser was looking for a weekend of wild sex in the wine country, well, he'd just have to oblige her, wouldn't he?

CARRIE HEARD A RUSTLING to her left, but the rows of vines that surrounded her were so tall she couldn't see anything. Didn't mountain lions come out to hunt at dusk? Her heart jumped in her throat as she remembered a recent article in the *San Francisco Chronicle*. This year's rainfall was so low that the pumas were coming down to the lowlands for water. And, if she wasn't mistaken, the wine country was rife with rattlesnakes. How could she have been stupid enough to off-road in flip-flops?

She'd never longed for the relative safety of the city more than she did now. At least in San Francisco she had a chance of kicking a mugger in the groin or yelling for help. Whereas if a mountain lion was hungry, she was going to be a Carrie sandwich. And if a rattler got her, she'd have to fashion a tourniquet out of her tank top and they'd find her poisoned and topless in the field the next morning. Neither was a pretty picture.

The only good thing about her predicament was the certainty that turning down a marriage proposal paled in comparison to being eaten by a three-hundred-pound lion.

The rustling grew louder, and Carrie didn't know whether to scream or run or stop breathing and stay completely still. She knew from hiking in Yosemite that if she saw a bear she was supposed to jump up and down and wave her arms and holler to fool the bear into thinking she was bigger than it. But what if a mountain lion simply thought that made her a better target? More fun to kill and all that.

Holding her hands out to protect herself, Carrie took a step backward. A loud snapping sound that seemed to come from beneath her right foot had her leaping forward, clinging desperately onto the nearest thing in her path.

Which just so happened to be an incredibly hard, tall cowboy.

For a long moment, Carrie was so thankful to be spared from the fangs of death that she hardly noticed, or cared, that she had her legs wrapped tightly around the man's waist. Or that her breasts were smashed against his hard chest. Or that she was clinging onto his neck for dear life, pressing her face into his neck.

As her heart rate slowed, she realized he had an incredibly nice smelling neck.

That's when it hit her: This man who had saved her could just as easily rape her. Oh, God, why had she ever gone for a walk? If only she'd taken Vanessa up on the offer to lounge poolside.

Heart in her throat, Carrie told herself not to show any fear. If she acted like everything was perfectly okay, she might get the chance to disappear into the night by running away as fast as she could in some random direction that hopefully led to her hotel. But before she could do much more than send up another prayer for help, the man said, "Does every vineyard in town get to have a trespasser as pretty as you, or is it just my lucky night?"

His rich, low voice rumbled down her spine. All at once, every nerve in her body came to life. Especially the ones at the tips of her breasts and in the vee between her legs. It was the oddest thing, but the sound of his voice, the way the words wrapped over her like a warm blanket, made her feel completely safe.

What was wrong with her? Hadn't she gotten enough of the fairy tale yet? Prince Charming wasn't going to show up at sunset in the middle of a vineyard to sweep her off her feet and show her perfect, endless love.

As if he could read her mind, he said, "Don't worry. I'm not going to hurt you. I saw you from the house and wanted to make certain that you were all right."

Her city-girl-training told her not to believe him. She should knee him in the balls or poke his eyes out and run for her life. But for some crazy reason, she felt that he was telling the truth, that she could trust him not to hurt her. At the same time, she became aware of how ridiculous the situation was. Like some crazy, trespassing slut, she was clinging onto a man who'd simply come to see if she needed his help. And to think, just yesterday she was on her way to having her engagement photo in *Town and Country*.

I should really get off him, she thought, but her limbs wouldn't obey. Probably had something to do with the way the cowboy's heat burned through her, scorching her breasts where they pressed against his large, wonderfully hard chest.

Pulling her face back from his neck, where, frankly, she wanted to hide forever—partly because she was so mortified, but mostly because he smelled like an intoxicating blend of bonfires and sugar—Carrie forced herself to make eye contact.

His eyes burned into hers, and she forgot how to swallow. The cowboy was the most gorgeous man she'd ever set eyes on. His face was all hard planes, and the only word she could think of to describe his mouth was rugged. Mouthwateringly rugged. How could she have ever thought that James was good looking, with his whitewashed, featureless face? This, here, was a real man. Mr. Marlboro come to life.

She opened her mouth to thank him for coming to her aid, but instead she found herself saying, "I'm so glad you found me."

His eyes crinkled slightly at the corners, and a bolt of lust burned through her. "I'm glad I found you too," he said, and her nipples hardened.

Good Lord, she was practically having an orgasm from the sound of his voice. She'd never felt this hot, this ready. This completely devoid of social skills. She couldn't think of anything to say, apart from, *Could you take me right here, right now, hard and fast and hot? On the ground is fine, thanks.*

She was shocked by her utterly inappropriate thought. Had Vanessa taken over her body? Her mind? She struggled to remind herself that she was barely out of a relationship, that she wasn't a casual-sex kind of girl. But none of that could keep her from blurting the first silly thing that popped into her head.

"I thought I was going to die out here tonight." Why couldn't she keep it together? And why were her legs still wrapped around a stranger's waist?

The cowboy's large hands seared her butt cheeks as they held her firmly up against his body and his gorgeous mouth turned up at the corners, all the way this time. "Die? From what? Eating too many grapes?"

Carrie had never felt more stupid. "I thought you were a mountain lion," she said in a tiny voice.

This time, the cowboy flat out laughed. With his head thrown back, his neck exposed, Carrie saw the allure of being a vampire. For one wild moment she wanted to sink her teeth into his dark, lightly stubbled skin.

She wondered if sex was different with a man who used his hands, his strength for a living. Her other lovers had all been businessmen and engineers. Never hard, muscular cowboys who could last all night long, and then some. Never magnificent strangers who could hold her up against them without so much as breaking a sweat.

Yet again, Carrie was stunned by her wanton thoughts. She'd never, not once in her life, considered having a casual fling. Sex had always meant love. Or so she'd thought. For the first time, Carrie wondered what would happen if she had sex for sex's sake. It couldn't possibly hurt any less than finding out she'd been lying to herself for two years, could it?

"You're worrying for nothing," he finally said through a grin.

"Mountain lions rarely come down to the valley floor. It's too hot. Not enough trees."

"Thank God," she said, amazed to find herself fluttering her eyelashes in a come-hither way.

His grin turned into an intense look that made Carrie's rapidly fluttering eyelids still. "Tell me your name," he said.

"Carrie. Carrie Anderson."

"It's nice to meet you, Carrie. My name's Tyson," he said, as if holding a woman against him was his usual greeting, rather than a handshake. "Hungry?"

Something in her stomach flip-flopped, but not from a hunger for food. "Starved," she said.

"Good." He grinned again, and it was all she could do not to lean her mouth into his. "Because the boss says he'll forgive you for trespassing if you have dinner with him."

Oh God, she was such an idiot. She'd been caught trespassing and the cowboy had been sent out to bring her in to have her hand slapped. Or have dinner. Whatever. The point was, he didn't want to make mad, passionate love to her under a silvery moon. She'd read him all wrong. Could she do any more to embarrass herself?

Turning from flirt to prim stranger, she dropped her legs from his waist, unwound her hands from his neck, and put a good two feet between them. "I apologize for trespassing. I assure you it was an accident. I'll leave at once."

The cowboy shook his head and whistled. "I don't think I've ever seen anyone go from scared to friendly to downright frigid that quick before. Got any other tricks up your sleeve?"

Carrie felt her cheeks flame. She wished she could throw a bucket of ice water over the lusty beast that had emerged from within her. Trying to act normal, she said, "It's been a long day. I went for a walk and got lost. If you could point me back toward the Napa Valley Hotel, I'll get off of your boss's land. And if you could tell him it was an accident, I'd appreciate it."

He took a step closer, and everything in her wanted to leap back into his arms again. Leaning down so close that she felt his breath on her earlobe, he said, "I don't think he'll like that much."

Her heart raced another thousand beats per second. "And how do you know that?"

He looked down at his dirty clothes, then back up at her. "Because I am the boss. And I never take no for an answer."

3

ⵌⵌⵌ

CARRIE SAT ON THE LANTERN-LIT PORCH, a glass of cool Syrah at her lips. On their short walk to the house, she had learned that the cowboy was Tyson Green, founder of the very well respected Green Vineyards. While he made small talk, and she pretended to listen, she studied his features. And drooled.

He was tall and lean, and his well-worn jeans outlined every delicious inch of his butt and muscular thighs. He wore a T-shirt that had seen better days, and Carrie admired the tendons on his arms, his large hands. Beneath the wide brim of his cowboy hat, his dark eyes flashed with humor and his prominent cheekbones caved to deep laugh lines. And his wide, full mouth made her heart race even faster than the thought of an impending mountain lion attack had.

Once they'd arrived at his lovely Craftsman-style ranch, Tyson had lent her his phone to call her friends. She'd left them messages letting them know that she was having a bit of a wine-country adventure but that she was perfectly okay and would tell them everything tomorrow morning at breakfast. She'd felt a twinge of guilt at bowing out of their evening plans, but she'd known they'd understand.

For the past ten minutes, while Tyson had been busy bringing things out from the kitchen to the grill, she had been trying to decide whether her motives for staying for dinner were purely innocent or completely carnal. Having wild sex within an hour of jumping on this big, gorgeous cowboy was a ridiculous, laughable thought. Or was it? Because she'd never met anyone as tempting as Tyson. She couldn't stop thinking of him naked above her, saying, "I never take no for an answer," right before he slid into her, so thick and hot and . . .

Tyson closed the lid on the grilling tri-tip, grabbed his glass of wine, and sat down next to her on the thick cushions of the outdoor sofa. More than a little nervous now that she'd nearly decided to take temptation up on its offer, Carrie fumbled for something witty, yet seductive, to say.

"I still can't believe that this vineyard is yours." Okay, so that was neither clever nor alluring. "I read an article about Green Vineyards in the *Chronicle* last weekend. They said you make the finest Syrah in California. I'd have to agree."

She tried to sound sexy but it was difficult to pull off while parroting newspaper headlines.

Tyson looked far more pleased than aroused by her compliment. "The finest? I don't know about that. How about top five?"

Carrie grinned, forgetting for a moment that she was on a path of seduction. She liked that he was modest. But not too modest.

"But I'm glad you like it," he said. "Very glad."

Wow. He should give lessons on seductive infusing. Because the way the words "very glad" poured from his lips made her wet. Very wet.

Her brain scrambled, along with her hormones, and she babbled on about the article. "Don't you use organic farming techniques?"

"I don't care for pesticides," he said, and it was clear he didn't want to talk about wine anymore. Maybe, she wondered wildly, he didn't want to talk at all anymore.

Feeling way out of her league—if only she were as brazen as Vanessa—she took another sip of the fruity Syrah. The smooth wine softened her fears enough to let her relax herself into the cushions.

"But organic farming has got to drive your profit margins down," Carrie mused while reformulating her approach at seduction.

Something in his face changed, hardened at her words. "Some. But enough wine talk. Tell me about you."

Carrie took a huge gulp of wine. She couldn't exactly say, "*Up until yesterday I thought I had landed the perfect man who would give me the perfect life, but when he proposed I freaked out and yelled no at him. For some reason the ring's still in my pocket. Do you want to see it? It's really big. Oh, yeah, and even though I've never had a one-night stand, I'm really thinking that the two of us should give it a whirl because you're so incredibly hot I can't think straight.*"

"Not much to tell," she eventually said. "I live in San Francisco. I own a landscape design business. And I'm up for the weekend with some girlfriends. We're going to do some wine tasting." There, that was all safe territory. She tried to think of something sexy to add to her incredibly dry self-portrait, but nothing came. She swallowed another huge mouthful of wine to cover the fact that she was at a complete loss for polite conversation.

She polished off her glass in record time, and Tyson obligingly refilled it, saying, "Got a boyfriend stashed away in the city?"

Carrie flushed. "No," she said in a wimpy little voice.

He raised an eyebrow. "No?"

She shook her head. "Not me," she said more emphatically.

"Not you," he repeated, almost as if he was laughing at her.

"I'm single. Free. On the market."

The words flew out of her mouth in rapid succession before she put a sock in it. She sounded like a complete loser. A desperate, hard up, I-need-to-have-sex-with-the-first-available-hard-penis loser.

"Great," Tyson said. "I'd better check on the meat. It's probably ready."

Carrie had never felt more like a bumbling fool. What had happened to the cool, poised woman who could effortlessly entertain a party of one hundred and make each one feel like the guest of honor?

Frankly, she wished a mountain lion had eaten her, thereby saving her from being a complete idiot all night. So much for convincing Tyson to have a dirty weekend with her.

She put her glass down on the pine coffee table, walked to the rail of the deck, and took a deep breath of country air. Dried hay mixed with newly crushed grapes was a heady, sweet scent. She decided that no matter what, she was going to keep it together from here on out. But when Tyson came up behind her, holding two glasses, and said, "I've got a special new Pinot I'd like you to taste," the prim-and-proper voices in her head gave way.

Here was a man who oozed raw, masculine sex appeal. And somewhere within Carrie, there was a powerfully sexual woman dying to get out.

So Carrie turned to him and said, "I'd rather taste you instead."

A LOUD ROAR filled Tyson's head as all the blood in his body rushed to his cock.

Had she actually said she wanted to taste him?

It was obvious with just one glance, one word from her incredibly seductive mouth, that Carrie Anderson was wealthy, polished, and sophisticated. Her nails were perfectly manicured, her fingers so long and graceful that he couldn't help picturing them gripping his cock. He grew another inch behind his zipper and shifted to get comfortable, looking away from her hands. But that brought him right back to her mouth, to her red lips, just made for sucking—

His penis was running away with itself. Hadn't he learned the hard way that a guy like him, with dirt under his nails, who preferred being outside in the fields to sitting in a stuffy theater suffering through a symphony, had no business being with a woman like Carrie?

And that comment about lower profits due to organic farming . . . it was exactly what his ex had said. For three years she'd tried to convince him to abandon his meticulous planting techniques, his organic pesticides, in favor of more grapes, more cases, more money. Marriage was forever, and Tyson had figured that every couple had things to work out, so he'd tried to see her point. Heck, he'd considered planting an acre of quick-to-profit Merlot to make Kimberly happy, but the only thing she'd been happy doing had been sleeping with his right-hand man.

He'd made the mistake of dating, and marrying, a money-hungry, status-concerned woman before. And it had bit him in the ass. Hard.

Then again, he didn't want Carrie for marriage, did he? And he was betting that a woman like her might want to slum it for a weekend with a guy like him, without ever contemplating a relationship on Monday morning.

All in all, a perfect arrangement.

He'd gone long enough without a woman. So when Carrie

deftly plucked the stems of the balloon wineglasses from his hands, put them on the porch rail, and looked back up at him with a wicked gleam in her beautiful eyes, Tyson gave in.

He was going to let her have her way with him. And maybe later, if things went really well, they could play out some of the increasingly elaborate scenes in his head where she was the naughty grape stealer and he was punishing her with the flat of his hand against her soft, round ass. He wasn't the same man who'd once confused lust with love. He'd never make that mistake again.

4

CARRIE DIDN'T WANT TYSON to know that her hands were shaking with nerves. She wanted him to think she ate men like him for dinner. The truth was she had never called the shots with a man. If a boyfriend liked his steaks rare, she sucked down bloody meat. If he was a well-done kind of guy, she chewed burned beef for hours. God forbid she actually impose her will on anyone.

But the new, sensual Carrie wanted to know: Would sex with a stranger be better than sex with a boyfriend?

How hard could he make her come?

Would he use his hands? Or his tongue?

Would he be satisfied with missionary position, or would he tie her wrists to his bedposts?

She'd never had naughty thoughts like this before. They made her feel wicked and, well, wonderful. No wonder Vanessa always seemed to be having so much fun.

Her hands now steady, she licked her lips and grabbed the soft cotton of Tyson's T-shirt.

"May I?" she said in a husky voice.

Tyson didn't say anything, he simply looked at her hard, his eyes burning straight into her core. She held her breath, willing herself not to run as fast as she could back to the hotel if he said, "No thanks. Let's just eat dinner." The seconds ticked, by and she was about to drop her hands from his shirt when he said, "Go for it."

Letting out her breath, she pulled the faded red fabric out from the waistband of his jeans. Relishing every second of the foreplay that she was actually instigating, Carrie pulled the soft cotton up his stomach, revealing his impressive six-pack. Holding the fabric halfway up his chest, she gave in to the irrepressible urge to kneel down at his feet and gently press her lips against his hot, tanned flesh.

Tyson groaned and threaded his hands through her hair. His thigh muscles tensed against her forearms as her tongue shot out of its own accord to taste him, falling into the lower groove of his abdomen. Her hands slid up beneath his shirt as she tried to memorize every inch of his chest and stomach by touch.

As she stood back up, she pulled his T-shirt off, past his broad shoulders, over his head. He didn't smile, he didn't move to kiss her. Instead he let her take charge of the dance.

When she was finally face-to-face with him, she stepped back and ran her hands over him, watching his chest rise and fall. He was beautiful, so beautiful that she was practically melting with need. They hadn't kissed, he hadn't so much as touched her, yet she was on the verge of falling apart.

She brushed the tips of her fingers up the side of his neck, and several taut cords sprang to the surface. His skin was so warm, so silky. As she got closer to his jaw, his skin grew rougher with a faint five o'clock shadow.

Before she was aware enough to stop them, the words "I want to feel your stubble against the inside of my thighs" were out of her mouth. Tyson's eyes lit up, and that gorgeous half grin emerged across his full lips again.

Carrie's fingers stilled on the hollow of Tyson's cheek. "Did I say that out loud?" she whispered.

One large, callused hand covered hers as the other moved around to the small of her back, pulling her closer. "You did. And I was thinking exactly the same thing."

Her insecurity was replaced with a rush of lust, but before she could reach for him, he leaned his head down and Carrie was tasting the most delicious mouth in all creation. His tongue swept into her mouth, brushing against hers, branding her as no man ever had. The kiss grew wild as she sucked in his lower lip, devouring him, unable to get as close as she needed to be. And then his lips were moving across her jaw to the tender skin of her neck. She called out his name, wanting him to keep doing that thing he was doing, but needing to taste his lips again.

Reading her mind, his mouth was on hers again, punishing her with addictive kisses. Then, somehow, her tank top was down around her waist and those magical lips were on her nipples, sucking and pulling until she was crying out, more desperate for release than she had ever been before.

A cloud moved in the sky and moonlight fell across them, illuminating Tyson, who had changed places with her and was now kneeling in front of her, loving her breasts like he'd never seen or touched anything so beautiful in all his life. The scene was so erotic, so reckless, that a shiver shot through Carrie.

Tyson looked up at her from between her breasts, the heat in his eyes taking what was left of her breath completely. She swayed on her feet, and in an instant he was standing again, holding her, their naked chests pressed together. Steady again, safe in her cowboy's arms, she wrapped her arms around his waist and rubbed the tips of her taut nipples against him.

"I want you naked," he said as he reached for the snap on her Capri pants.

But she had started as the aggressor and wanted the arousing reins of control back.

"You first," she said as her hands dropped to the waistband of his jeans. His erection pushed against the zipper, and it took a long moment to get it open, to pull down his boxer shorts.

Never before had Carrie wanted to touch a man so badly. Her fingers fairly itched to wrap themselves around him, her mouth wanted to know how round, how smooth his penis would be against her tongue. She shoved his jeans and boxers to the deck and gasped when his glorious shaft emerged.

"You're beautiful," she whispered. At her words, a drop of pre-come emerged on the tip of his penis. Kneeling down again, her fingers stroked, squeezed, and explored his entire length.

The thought of having his hard, huge length pumping into her made her groan with ecstasy as she sucked him into her mouth, down deep in her throat. He pulsed once, then twice, in her throat. God, he was delicious. She'd never wanted to give a man as much pleasure as she did this one, but somehow, at the same time, all she cared about was how good touching him, licking him, sucking him was making her feel.

With his erection in her mouth, she felt like a goddess who had just come alive.

She moved her hands to caress his balls, and his growl echoed off the porch ceiling. He scooped her up off her knees into his arms and carried her inside, past a state-of-the-art kitchen, through a large, high-ceilinged living room, and back down a dimly lit hall to his master suite.

Laying her on a down-covered bed, he said, "You're so beautiful, Carrie."

Her heart nearly burst with it all. It was the most wonderful thing anyone had ever said to her.

And then he said, "I love what you were doing to my cock, but I need to be in you. Right now," and romance turned into out-and-out hunger.

"Why are my pants still on?" she wondered wildly, and was answered with a lusty grin from Tyson, who opened his bedside table and quickly rolled on a condom.

"You keep taking the words out of my mouth," he said, and she realized she'd spoken out loud again, but it didn't matter because seconds later, her yellow Capri pants and panties were on the floor and his head was between her legs.

His tongue. His fingers. My God.

She knew she sounded like a wild animal, but no man had ever licked her like that, plunged his thick fingers all the way inside. And then, as the first wave of an absolutely enormous orgasm struck, he was filling her with his cock, sinking in and out, rocking against her, pulling her into him. She was out of control, wanting him closer, wanting it harder.

Again and again he bucked into her, and everything went black as wave after wave of intense pleasure rocked through her.

"Carrie," he groaned, his penis growing harder and bigger with every thrust. She felt a delicious pulsing inside her as he exploded.

For a long moment, they lay panting together on the duvet. Carrie had no words for what had happened. She'd never had such incredible sex with a virtual stranger before. With anyone, for that matter.

The only unfortunate thing about it was that Vanessa hadn't schooled her in one-night-stand etiquette. The only thing she could think of to say was, "I wonder if the meat is ready."

Fortunately, Tyson wasn't turned off by her mundane musings. He simply rolled over, pulled her on top of him, and said, "Personally, I'm only hungry for one thing right now. What do you say to shower first, dinner later?"

A wide smile split Carrie's face. "This time you took the words right out of my mouth."

TYSON LOVED THE WAY she shimmied off him, the way her breasts, her hips, were so soft, so round. He'd never been with a woman like her before. Proper on the outside, wild on the inside.

He had a feeling that if he let the fire between them cool for much longer than it would take to turn on his shower and pull her in, she'd start to regret what had happened between them. He didn't want her turning back into a prim and proper society girl just yet.

He followed her to the bathroom and stepped into the shower, fully comfortable with his own nakedness. As he pulled Carrie into his arms, the beginnings of worry, of doubt, crept into her blue eyes.

"Carrie?" he said, letting her name be a question on his lips.

"I've never done this before," she whispered.

He couldn't help his grin, even though he was so aroused that he could hardly think straight. "You've never been wet and slippery as you came?"

She shook her head. "No. Yes. But it's not that. I've never been so intimate with someone I didn't . . ."

He bent his lips to hers and gently kissed her. He'd already known she wasn't the one-night-stand type. She didn't need to say anything more. "Me, either. So I guess we'll have to keep making it up as we go, won't we?"

The sparkle came back then, the glow that was hers alone. "Mmm," she said as he reached for a bar of soap. Maybe he should be going slower, maybe he should be working harder to keep his desire from spiraling out of control. Maybe he should quickly soap her up, spray her off, and go down on her before taking her back to bed for some missionary-style loving.

Screw that. He wanted to do things to her that would blow both their minds.

He turned her to face the wall. "Put your hands on the tile," he said, and he was pleased when she didn't hesitate. "Now open your legs for me."

She pushed off the wall and spun around to face him. "What are you going to do to me?" she asked, her voice so soft he almost couldn't make out her words above the spray of the water.

He knew she was waiting for an answer, but he couldn't speak. She was all wet now as the showerhead soaked them both, and her hair was slick against her head, a darker color now than the gold it had been dry. Her eyes, her high cheekbones, the red flush across her lips stood out in sharp, stunning relief. Drops of water ran into the curve of her neck and down over her shoulders. Her breasts were high and proud, and he envied the water as it poured over her nipples. Already, the sight of her naked in the shower rivaled any naked-in-the-water pictures *Playboy* had ever published. Every memory he had of other women naked—in the shower, in his bed, in the back of a car—was erased as his eyes followed the streams of water down past her rib cage to her waist. Heading straight toward her pussy.

He got lost there, staring at her sweet mound, and his cock grew big. Bigger than it had been out on his porch twenty minutes ago, even.

He felt her fingers under his chin and he looked up at her eyes, finally realizing that somewhere along the way he must have dropped the thread of the conversation. Fortunately, the look in her eyes told him that was just fine.

"I'm not scared anymore, Tyson," she said, then slowly turned to face the tiles. She placed her hands up high on the granite, one at a time, and her fingers were elegant as they splayed out to support the weight of her upper body. She shifted her legs until they were spread apart for him, and she looked back over her shoulder.

"I'm ready now. For you to do whatever you want. Anything you want."

The images that hurled through his brain, one after the other, nearly knocked his feet out from under him. She didn't know what she was saying, did she? Anything? Jesus. He needed to get a grip or he was going to shoot his load before he so much as laid a finger on her.

Blocking the spray with his back, he moved in behind her, pressing the head of his penis into the small of her back. Any closer and he wasn't going to be able to keep from plunging into her wetness. She sucked in a breath as the front of his thighs met the soft skin of her ass. They were good, so damn good together. He'd never had this kind of immediate satisfaction with a woman before. As if they'd been designed specifically for each other.

"You must have been hot out there, walking as far as you did," he murmured behind her ear. His hand, and the soap, found her shoulders. Lightly he massaged her skin with the bar. "Dusty too."

"Mmm," she said again as she shifted her hips back into him. "Get me clean, Tyson."

He put the soap down and let his hands rub bubbles into the base of her shoulder blades until the tight muscles loosened, then down her spine to the flare of her ass. He moved his hands around to her belly, and although her muscles were tight beneath his fingers, her skin was soft. So soft. He massaged the foam into her flesh, increasing the pressure of his palms.

Up or down, that was the question. But he already knew that if he let himself touch her between her legs, he'd never resurface. And that wouldn't be fair to either of them. Holding his breath in anticipation, he ran his fingers up her rib cage until he felt the bottom swell of her breasts against his knuckles.

"You're so soft," he said as he covered her breasts with his large hands. "I know my hands are rough," he said by way of an apology for the calluses that were a part of his livelihood.

"They're perfect," she said, her words a moan of pleasure. "You're so gentle."

She turned her head and he captured her mouth in a deep, hot kiss. His thumb and forefinger found her nipples, and she gasped into his mouth. His tongue slid between her teeth so that he could taste her more fully, and he finally let himself slide his hard, thick shaft against the silky skin at the small of her back. She rubbed her tight, round ass into his thighs and it took everything he had not to explode right then, there, rubbing against her soft skin.

But he wasn't ready to lose it yet. He had the rest of her body to explore first. Forcing himself to pull away from her sweet mouth, her perfect ass, he let the water course down her back, watched it wash the bubbles away.

He picked up the bar of soap again and bent down to run it up the alluring curve of one leg, from her ankle, up and over her strong calf muscle, into the valley behind her knee, and finally, up the back of her thigh, to the luscious curve of her bottom. Carrie's breath was ragged as he laved her other leg with the soap. She opened her legs wider for him, and the temptation was more than he could take. He dropped the bar of soap to the floor and sat down on the granite tiles, sliding between her open thighs, his back against the same wall that her hands were on.

He looked up and knew, with absolute certainty, that they'd

been made for each other. Because her clitoris, her wet, plump lips, were right there for him to take into his mouth.

So he did.

Her hands found him, curving around his skull as he ran his tongue in long strokes up the length of her labia. Fluid escaped from the head of his penis, but he was too focused on Carrie's sweet pussy to notice, to care anymore if he shot into air. He sucked her clit in between his lips, pushing one finger, then two into her tight canal, feeling her squeeze him tight.

Her inner muscles clenched and pulled at his fingers, and she was panting now. She was so close to coming, so close to breaking apart with his mouth on her clit. Her legs were shaking, and he used his free hand to hold her up. And then a soft scream echoed off the granite walls and all of her muscles went loose as she found her pleasure in his mouth, with his hands on her, in her.

He licked and sucked and stroked and loved every moment of her orgasm. Before. During. Even after. And the way she looked as she fell onto his lap was nearly the best part of all.

Flushed and sated and perfect.

5

CARRIE WAS STUNNED by the force of her orgasm. A part of her wanted to weep. Another part, a bigger part, wanted to shower Tyson with thank-yous for showing her a wild streak she hadn't known she possessed.

Even so, even after the best climax of her life, she knew that what Tyson had done to her in the shower had been more than just a fantastic sexual experience.

It had been emotional too.

He had been surprisingly tender, paying attention to her desires, to every part of her. He'd taken the time to figure out what she liked. What she craved. How she wanted to be touched.

And now, he was still hard, still waiting for his turn, but not in a rush to get inside her. He wasn't trying to figure out how long it was going to be until he got to come.

She'd never been with anyone like Tyson. In less than an hour, he had already paid more attention to her sexually than James had in two years. And she'd never known, not until tonight, that she'd needed, desperately needed, to be made love to like this.

Shamelessly.

Forcefully.

She was so grateful that she would have done anything right then to make him feel as good as she already did. Before she could sink down onto his thick shaft, he helped her up and wrapped a plush towel around her waist.

The cool air outside the shower rushed over her body, making her shiver as they moved back into the bedroom again. Tyson reached into a bedside table for protection, but she couldn't let him do all the work. It wouldn't be fair. Not after the way he'd given her an all-over, full-contact orgasm in the shower.

She dropped her towel to the oak floor and picked up the condom that fell from his fingers to the ground. No one had ever looked at her like that, like she was the most beautiful thing he'd ever seen. His gaze made her feel powerful, bold, and she pushed him down, damp and warm, onto the bed as his huge cock pulsed toward her again.

"I want to taste you again. But," she said as she ripped open the condom wrapper, "I need you inside me more."

He grabbed the rubber from her and slid it on, and then his hands were rough and wonderful as he pulled her on top of him, all the way onto his throbbing shaft. She braced herself with her hands across his chest, just as she had against the tiled shower wall. Feeling wild, free, and so much happier than she could ever remember, she rode Tyson as his hands slid up from her breasts, tangling in her wet hair. He pulled her mouth down to his, and his kiss robbed whatever breath remained in her lungs. With every passing moment, she fell deeper and deeper into this sexy cowboy who had been a stranger mere hours before.

LATER, IN TYSON'S BED, with his big, strong arms wrapped around her, Carrie's stomach rumbled. His laugh was warm and soft as it reached into her. "How about I make good on that dinner I promised you out in the vineyard?"

Five minutes later she was sitting on his porch, relaxing with that glass of Syrah she'd put aside several hours earlier.

"No surprise, the steaks have burned to an unrecognizable crisp," Tyson said when he checked the grill. "Why don't you enjoy the wine and the evening for a few minutes while I go scrounge up some more meat?"

He disappeared into the kitchen before she could offer to help, and she was glad for a moment alone to think, warm and cozy in one of his flannel work shirts and some seriously baggy jeans.

She had plenty to think about.

A handful of orgasms in her pocket, Carrie found herself with new answers to questions she'd never thought to ask. Yes, she'd known that something had been missing with James, that he could be arrogant and pushy and elitist. But she hadn't thought to question their sex life. She'd figured that coming on a regular basis had meant their sex life was good.

How wrong she'd been.

When Tyson so much as stood near her, or gave her that look that promised more pleasure than she could bear, she went up in a mass of flames.

When he kissed her, when he stroked her, when he was in her, she felt complete. Strong. Sexy.

But even though her newfound sensuality helped her more tightly shut the lid on her relationship with James, it sent her reeling off in a scarier direction. Hadn't she just decided that she was only in the market for a light, sexy fling?

She was already blowing it.

Somehow, some way, she had to protect herself from falling for another man for all the wrong reasons. She certainly wasn't going to deny her lust for Tyson. That would be a joke. But this time, she was going to go out of her way to make sure her head was on straight and her emotions were on hold.

Great sex, she reminded herself firmly, was merely great sex. Even if, in Tyson's case, the term "great" took on a whole new meaning.

Like stupendous. Staggering, even.

"Thinking about world peace?" Tyson teased when he came back outside and threw two more tri-tips on the grill.

Carrie blushed as he slid a delicious-looking feta, walnut, and tomato salad in front of her. If only he knew how far her thoughts were from world peace.

"Something like that," she said, and when she glanced up at him, from the laughter in his eyes, she knew he knew.

She'd been thinking about sex. With him.

Her inner hostess got to work making small talk to relieve the sexual tension that hung in the air like a fine mist.

"I know you've heard this a million times already, but this really is an incredible Syrah."

"Thank you. When you own a winery, you never get tired of hearing that people enjoy your wine. Every vintner worries about someone taking a sip from a new batch and getting that look."

"What look would that be?"

He grinned. "The one that says they'd spit it out if they weren't so polite."

"You're kidding, right?"

He shook his head. "Trust me, I'm speaking from painful experience."

"I can't begin to imagine," she said, sinking back into the cushions, letting the wine flow through her veins, the warm evening breeze carry the bulk of her anxieties away. "It's bad enough when a client doesn't like one of my drawings or thinks I should dig another five-gallon hole to move a mature tree. But at least I haven't spent a year growing grapes for them."

"Don't feel too bad for me," he added as he stood up and flipped the steaks. "I'm doing just fine."

"I'm amazed that you've done everything organically. Please, tell me more. I've thought about incorporating natural pesticides with my clients, but I'm not sure if it will work for me. Or for them."

"What about the lower profit margins?" he asked, and she wondered at the new edge in his voice.

"I'm not worried about that," she said, "just whether or not organic methods can really keep the bugs away."

Something that looked like surprise lit his gaze. "It's been working out. I've got better vine strength and soil quality. My grapes are more resistant to hot spells and frost."

"What about pests, mold, disease?"

"I've seen much less damage on my plants than on neighboring vineyards. Plus, I've been able to use less water. So I spend my time composting and covering crops, not spraying."

All this talk about composting was making her hot for him again. She'd never thought to find a guy with whom she could make love one moment, then discuss crops the next.

"What about the mustard that grows between vines in the spring?"

"It's all part of what feeds the vines. I've added in some oats, some winter peas to the mix."

She looked at him over the rim of her glass. "Seems to me you've given up most of your secrets tonight. How do you know I'm not going to sell them to the highest bidder?"

His eyes shuttered, and she had a feeling that her teasing had been way off the mark. Or, worse, too close to it.

SHE MADE HIM COMFORTABLE. Too comfortable. If he wasn't careful, he'd be baring his soul. No matter how intimate they'd been on the porch, in the shower, in his bed, he needed to remember that she was a society girl from the city who was having fun with a farm boy who'd done good.

"Looks like dinner's ready," he said, knowing her big, blue eyes were on him, not trusting himself to look in them just yet.

He had to give her credit for keeping the conversation light and fun. She had an arsenal of humorous stories about working with wealthy residential landscaping clients, not to mention a few tales about the volunteer work she'd recently done at an elder care center.

His ex had done a lot of charity work. That is, if you considered throwing lunches and gala dinners work. Frankly, while he was glad for the money raised, he'd never sympathized with Kimberly's whining about how hard it was to be on fund-raising committees. She'd loved the power, the prestige that had come with her position as the wife of a winery owner. And if he had let himself become the man she'd really wanted—slick, impossibly wealthy, willing to sell his grapes out to the low-budget commercial wine sellers—they'd likely still be together.

Maybe Kimberly had done him a favor by sleeping with his foreman. She'd taken a broken marriage and shattered it to pieces.

He let himself look back into Carrie's intelligent eyes. Throughout their meal he worked to read between the lines of her stories. Was she trying to impress him with how giving she was in working with the elderly? With how successful she seemed to be at her profession? Amazingly, she managed to look put together in his ragged shirt and oversized jeans with her hair still damp and wild from their impromptu shower.

Nonetheless, he couldn't escape the feeling that no matter how classy she was, how different her upper-class life might be from his middle-class upbringing, she wasn't out to screw him over. Or anyone else, for that matter.

Hell, it was just one weekend. That was the important thing to remember here. She was gorgeous and intelligent and great in the sack. And if he didn't know better, he'd say she was exactly the kind of woman he'd been searching for.

His divorce had forced him to think about what he wanted from a girlfriend. From a wife. The second time around he wanted forever. Most of all, he wanted a partner. He wanted the woman he loved to support him, to be excited about his passions, even if she didn't share them. And he wanted to support his partner in exactly the same way. He wanted to be there for her, to boost her when she was low, to celebrate with her when she was on top of the world. Of course, he wanted the icing on the cake too. He wanted great sex with his future wife. Phenomenal sex.

But he wasn't going to let great sex cloud his judgment again. This was simply one weekend of the best sex he'd ever have. With the hottest babe this side of the Golden Gate Bridge.

"Ever thought of using vines in your designs?" he asked as they carried empty dishes into the kitchen.

"Honestly, no. But it might work for some of my clients in the sunnier locations in the city."

"I agree. Why don't you join me tomorrow and I'll give you some pointers."

She turned to him, a naughty gleam in her eyes. "Is that all you're planning on doing with me tomorrow?"

"Not a chance," he said, scooping her up in his arms as the clock struck midnight. "Looks like tomorrow just started."

CARRIE HELD ON TIGHT as he carried her into the bedroom for the third time in as many hours. She'd never had so much sex in such a short time—she'd had five orgasms already. Or was it six? She was losing count of all the ways Tyson had made her come, and it was wonderful.

To her surprise, he carried her past the bedroom door and out through a back door. "Where are you taking me?" she asked as her eyes slowly adjusted to the darkness.

"Someplace special," he said. "To a place where you can scream as loud as you want—"

She finished his sentence. "And no one will hear me."

His eyes gleamed with lust in the moonlight. "Smart girl."

A shiver ran up her spine and her nipples hardened in anticipation as he walked down a short flight of stairs, then pushed a large wooden door open with his foot. The first thing she noticed was the smell of fermenting grapes, so sweet, so strong, so heady. The darkness sucked them in. The old Carrie would have been scared, frightened of the untold things that a cowboy could do to her body in a place like this. The new Carrie wanted to lock them both inside the deserted wine cellar for the rest of the weekend. Tyson would be hers to endlessly tempt, taste, touch.

He set her down, and her legs were unsteady. Desire did that to a girl, she thought with a grin as she supported herself against the cool cement wall. He lit a match, and the glow from two lanterns on the wall lit up the wine cave.

"It's so beautiful down here," she breathed, knowing that "beautiful" didn't cut it. She'd done winery tours before, she'd been in the caves where the grapes ripened into wine, but her breath had never been taken away. The love Tyson poured into his passion was more apparent than ever here. "Your cave is magical," she said, and he moved behind her, wrapping his arms around her waist and pulling her against his hardness.

"Magical," he repeated, and the fine hairs on the back of her neck stood up. She pulled his hands up to her mouth and pressed a kiss to them.

"I want to do something for you," she whispered. "Something

I've never done before." He growled as his hands moved up to cover her breasts. Blood rushed to her nipples, to her clit, and she moaned, on the verge of giving in to Tyson's plan. But no matter how ready she was for him to sink into her, to make her scream with pleasure, she needed to do this. She needed to prove to herself that she was brave enough to own her own sexuality.

She forced herself to move out of his arms, then pointed to a bench in the middle of the cave. "Sit," she ordered, and she could have sworn the corner of his mouth curved up. Slowly, he moved across the cave to the bench and lowered himself down. He bent one leg and crossed his ankle over his knee.

Her legs started that awful trembling again, and she bit her lip. What was she thinking? She didn't know how to do a striptease. She was going to make a fool of herself. Or pass out from embarrassment.

As her thoughts rammed into each other in her brain, something in her broke. She was sick and tired of being the good girl.

She was going to strip for Tyson. And then she was going to touch herself. While he watched. And when tomorrow came, she'd know that she didn't have to let the good girl win all the time. Because the bad girl had finally been given free rein.

TYSON WATCHED UNCERTAINTY and doubt flit across Carrie's face. Even if this was just an incredibly hot weekend fling, he couldn't stuff away the part of him that wanted to hold her, to comfort her. He couldn't help but like her, and he wanted her to win whatever battle she was fighting. And so he stayed where he was on the bench, his hard-on pulsing against his zipper, his heart pounding with desire, his blood racing.

"Ready whenever you are," he said, purposely taunting her to break the hold her thoughts had on her.

Her head snapped up and she narrowed her eyes. Glaring, she said, "Good. You'd better be. Because I'm going to have to chain you to that bench before I'm through."

"Big threats for such a little girl," he mocked, playing along, hoping that riling her up would only serve to make things hotter.

Unexpectedly, she smiled, and her expression held so much feminine mystery, so much power, so much sensuality, that Tyson wished for chains. Otherwise, he was going to leap off the bench and take her on the cement floor.

Slowly her fingers moved to the buttons on the plaid work shirt he had given her to wear after their sexy shower. She unbuttoned the second button from the top, and he swallowed. Noisily. Oh, shit, she was going to strip for him. Carrie was a wet dream come to life. Her fingers moved down the shirt, unfastening one button and then the next. Finally it was open and she shrugged, letting the shirt fall back on her shoulders. The curve of one breast was bathed by the light from the lantern, and he felt himself pulse in his pants. He was going to come, just sitting here, looking at her, even though she wasn't naked yet.

Her blue eyes found his and her lips curved up as she pushed her breasts out and let the shirt fall to the ground. He'd seen her in the shower, but still, he wasn't prepared for this. For her jaw-dropping beauty. For the perfect curve of her breasts, where the soft flesh met her rib cage. For the tightly puckered areola, the same rosy red of her lips.

"Carrie," he groaned, unable to keep her name from his lips.

"Was this worth waiting for?" she asked, and he nodded like an idiot schoolboy being given a sweet treat. Her fingers moved to the button on the top of the jeans he'd loaned her, and he tightly gripped the wooden slats on the bench until his knuckles went white. The sound of the zipper opening reverberated against the walls of the cave.

The jeans dropped to the floor, and she stood naked and glorious before him. He started to get up, to come to her so that he could lick her and touch her and drive into her, but she put her palm up. "Stop," she said. "I want you to stay there. On the bench. Across the room. Until I'm done."

What the hell? Was she crazy? But he knew better than to argue with a woman, especially one this intoxicating, so he sat back down without taking his eyes from her.

And then she was running her hands over her breasts, pinching her nipples between her thumb and her middle finger, and she was throwing her head back and moaning with pleasure. His cock pulsed again, then he forgot all about himself as she moved one hand from her bountiful breasts down her stomach. Past her waist. Over the golden thatch of hair. Straight for her pussy.

She buried her fingers there and then, on a gasp, widened her stance and started masturbating. Right in front of him. In his cellar.

He leaped up off the bench, closing the space between them, unable to take it anymore. He needed to be in her. Now. He turned her, and she bent over a low barrel, propping herself up on her hands as he undid his zipper, rolled on another condom, and gripped her hips. All it took was one thrust and he was exploding, his shouts of satisfaction echoing off the walls and merging with her screams.

His cave was never going to be the same again.

6

IT WAS THE RECIPE for a perfect Saturday. Wake up to slow, wonderful lovemaking from the man who could make you come with just a look. Eat the fabulous gourmet breakfast he insisted on dishing up for you. Head out onto his property—his Napa Valley vineyard, no less—and immerse yourself in one of the subjects you are most fascinated by, which he happens to know inside and out.

Again and again throughout the day, Carrie was distracted by Tyson's fine butt. His work-hardened hands. His toned, buff torso as he lifted heavy rocks like they were marshmallows. Nothing about him fit her previous version of the perfect man. He wasn't polished or refined. He would rather be outside covered with dirt than wearing Prada.

So then why did he seem so perfect for her? She'd been sixteen the first time she'd gone out on a date, the first time she'd been kissed. Was it possible that all this time she'd had her sights on the wrong kind of man? Had she always fallen for shine over substance? For smooth words versus honest ones? And would she ever learn to trust her instincts again, when she'd been so far off base for so long?

She suddenly realized that her hair must be sticking up in a hundred different directions. Not to mention that her Capri pants and one of Tyson's old T-shirts were pretty much covered with dust and sweat. James had never seen her this untidy. For two years, she'd made certain that she didn't sweat, or smell, or have a hair out of place in his presence. Then again, she'd never done anything strenuous with him, save an occasional handball game at the gym.

She could see herself spending more days like this with Tyson, working in the sun together . . . "I know you didn't intend to spend your whole weekend with me," Tyson said.

Carrie stood upright so fast that she bonked her head into one of the wires that held the vines upright. Her stomach sank to her knees as the implication of that comment sank in. Here she was wondering if Tyson was her perfect match, while he was trying to figure out a nice way to get rid of her.

"Ouch," she said, rubbing her head. Of course he had better things to do than babysit some tourist all weekend. One thing she'd learned during the past two years was that the perfect guest never outstayed her welcome. Tyson was running his own vineyard and prestigious wine label, for God's sake. She handed him her clippers and took off the gloves he'd lent her.

It shouldn't have hurt so much, but it did.

"I really shouldn't have monopolized your time like this. Thanks so much for everything you've taught me today. I'll be sure to get this T-shirt back to you once I've washed it."

She turned to make a hasty, mortified exit, but he grabbed her arm before she could get away and spun her into him.

"You know, I think this hot-cold thing you do is really a turn-on, but what I was trying to get at is that I want you to be my date tonight."

"Your date?"

"The Napa Winemaker's Dinner is tonight. If you don't come with me, I'll be forced to make small talk with the single, desperate woman they always seat me next to."

She grinned at his joke, even though she wasn't sure she felt much better about being invited merely to save him from a worse fate.

"That didn't come out right. I want to be with you, Carrie. Plain and simple. But I've got this industry commitment tonight and I hope you'll have a good time too. If you agree to come, that is."

"I'd love to be your date," she said softly, turning her face up to his and pulling him down for a hot kiss. "But there's only one problem. I don't have anything to wear."

"How about this? I'll drop you off at your hotel so that you can clean up. Even though I think you look amazing dirty. And you're so much fun to wash." He ran his thumb over her lower lip and she shivered in anticipation for what she knew would come later, when his big, hard body was hovering over hers. "I'll find you a dress. A great one."

TYSON DROPPED HER OFF at her hotel, and she let herself into her room in a dreamy daze. She was stripping off her clothes— too bad Tyson hadn't been able to stay for another soap-up session—when she saw the blinking light on her hotel telephone.

"Rose and Vanessa must be worried sick," she said aloud. She should have called and left them another message today, but she'd been so swept up in Tyson that she hadn't thought of it until now.

She was startled when the voice on the line didn't belong to either of her friends.

James had called. His words swam in her head and she sat down, hard, on the edge of the bed.

"Carrie, it's James," he said, as if she could have mistaken his cultured, precise tones for anyone else's. "I've called your cell phone several times, but you haven't picked up. I hope all is well." She heard him pause, as if he'd realized he needed to say something more personal than that. "And that you're having a good time with your friends."

His words didn't ring true, and now that she thought about it, he'd never really made a secret of the fact that he thought Vanessa was a slut and Rose needed to lose some weight. The jerk.

He cleared his throat, preparing to bring out the big guns. He didn't like to lose. Her refusal of his proposal must have burned a hole in his pride.

"I know you needed a few days to get used to the overwhelming idea of joining the prestigious Carrigan family. I'm confident that it will be everything you've ever dreamed of."

He was confident that marrying him would be everything she had ever dreamed of?

She could hardly believe he had said that. Or that he seemed to actually think he knew one whit about her dreams. Dating James for two years had been her first big mistake. Keeping his ring for the weekend instead of insisting he take it back to the jeweler for a refund had been her second, bigger blunder.

She was happier wearing Tyson's old T-shirt with dirt under her fingernails.

James was in her past, whether he liked it or not. She didn't know what her future would hold, but Tyson was her present.

And it was time to grab for real happiness with both hands.

She took a long shower and spent ages on her makeup and

hair. She wanted to blow Tyson away tonight. He'd dropped her off at the hotel an hour ago and already she was missing him. Craving him.

Just then, there was a knock on the door. Her heart went to her throat. It couldn't be James, could it? But when she looked through the peephole, she saw a man holding a large box. And a gorgeous bouquet of oversized mustard flowers.

She grabbed a wad of bills to tip the man and placed the stunning arrangement on the table by the window. She opened the card, smiling as she read, "'A beautiful wildflower for a beautiful wild woman.'"

Tyson thought she was a wild woman? No one had ever called her that or, so far as she knew, ever thought the word "wild" in reference to Carrie Anderson.

She turned and looked at herself in the mirror above the table, wondering if something tangible had changed about her. And then she remembered her striptease in his wine cave, and her cheeks flushed. Not out of embarrassment. Rather, remembered pleasure.

Turning back to the box, she gave in to the unbridled urge to rip it open. Beneath a thick layer of tissue lay the sexiest dress she'd ever set eyes on.

She picked up the green silk with trembling hands and slipped into the dress. Twirling in front of the floor-to-ceiling mirror on the back of the bathroom door, she'd never felt so pretty before. Or so daring. James had always told her that less skin was better, classier, so she'd never worn something strapless, or tight, and had certainly never had a dress slide open all the way to the top of her thigh.

Suddenly insecurity threatened to overtake her. But she had great shoulders, didn't she? Her thighs weren't bad either, and she couldn't deny that there was something naughty about the idea of flashing her gams at people when she walked by.

She needed a glass of wine to calm her nerves before Tyson came to pick her up. She wanted him to be proud of her tonight. But before she left for the hotel bar, she wanted to share her joy with her best friends. In lieu of hunting them out via their cell phones or by the pool, she made a quick call to Rose's room.

"Rose, I hope you haven't been too worried about me. I've met the most wonderful man. His name is Tyson and he owns a vineyard and he's just gorgeous and incredible." She sighed. "I know, I need to talk to James to tell him it's definitely over between us, but I just haven't had time. I'll probably be gone until Sunday when we check out and I feel really bad about leaving you and Vanessa, but he's amazing and I know you'd kill me if I didn't spend this last night with him. Although since I haven't heard from either of you, I'm going to assume that you're both having a great time too. Love you." She left a similar message for Vanessa, then grabbed her purse.

Last night had been Fairy Tale Evening, Volume One. Volume Two was about to begin.

7

$\infty\hspace{-0.2em}\infty\hspace{-0.2em}\infty$

CARRIE WAS WAITING FOR HIM in the bar, and when she stood up, he stopped breathing. He'd never seen anything so beautiful in all his life. He'd known the dress would look good on her, but the vision before him was so far beyond good . . . from her gleaming blond hair that fell to her sun-kissed shoulders in soft waves, to her deep blue eyes and her fantastic figure, she was a goddess come to life. *How am I going to let her go on Sunday night?* pushed to the front of his brain, and he was too thrown off his game to force it away.

She worked the green silk between her thumb and forefinger, and he knew she was waiting for him to say something. "You're stunning," was all he could manage.

"I never wear green," she said, and he hated the nervous lilt to her voice.

"You should. Wear it, I mean."

"James always told me that blue was my—" She caught herself and dropped the rest of her sentence, but Tyson was so mesmerized by the curve of her breasts that he didn't process her words.

"I'm going to be fighting men off with a stick."

Carrie's sweet smile hit him right in the gut. "Really? I'm used to wearing, well, more clothes than this, I guess. I wasn't sure I could carry it off."

"You can," he said as he brought her hand up to his lips. He pressed a kiss onto the back of her knuckles. "And you do. So well, in fact, that I'm not entirely certain we're going to make it to the dinner after all."

"I want you too," she said, just loud enough that he could hear her but no one else in the elegant cocktail lounge could. "Maybe we can figure out a way to go to the dinner"—she paused, reaching up to adjust his tie, a movement that went straight to his cock—"and . . ."

She didn't finish her sentence. She didn't need to. He could see the faint outline of her hard nipples beneath the thin silk of her dress, and he had to close his hand into a tight fist at his side so that he wouldn't rip it down to her waist, right then and there in front of a room full of strangers. He needed to get them out of the hotel in the next thirty seconds or they'd be no-shows at the Winemaker's Dinner.

"I like the way your mind works," he said, then leaned down to whisper in her ear, "all through cocktails, all through dinner, you're going to have to make small talk, appear interested in meeting local vintners and their wives, knowing that later, I'll be making love to you in the vines."

SHE WANTED HIM. Now. Here. In the car. She wanted to tell him to pull over. She wanted to unzip his slacks, take his hard length in her mouth. She wanted to scramble into the backseat like a horny teenager, fumbling with clothes and zippers and seat belts.

How had she lived for thirty years without knowing how insatiable she was? Without knowing that the word "horny" was actually in her repertoire? It had been wonderful to discard her inhibitions in his cave, to strip for him, to watch his penis harden with lust. For her. That kind of feminine power was addictive. Tyson's touch was too. And she wanted his hands on her, needed them on her in the next sixty seconds or she'd lose it.

"Find a dark road," she said. "Quickly."

She'd already kicked off her heels and was shifting in her seat to reach her zipper.

He didn't so much as look at her, but after a quick right turn, he swerved into a black patch beneath an enormous oak tree and turned off the ignition. The headlights ricocheted off the trunk, illuminating it for a brief moment before he flipped them off. She was certain her desperation showed on her face, but she didn't care. The only thing she cared about was having him inside her.

Before he got a chance to do it himself, she'd unhooked his seat belt and was working on his zipper. And then his shaft was free and in her hands. She couldn't see anything in the darkness, but she felt how hard he was. How hot he was. Her hair brushed against his chest, against his penis as she bent over and took him into her mouth. He tasted sweet and salty at the same time. She laved his head with her tongue, gently, slowly, and when she couldn't take it anymore, she gave in to temptation, sucking him all the way down her throat as far as he would go.

"Carrie," he groaned, and she knew that he was as desperate as she was. He bucked into her mouth, into her throat, and she drew him in deeper. She felt so powerful, so sexy. His wicked whispers in the hotel had made her grow wet, so wet, but now, with every thrust of his hips against her lips, she grew more aroused, more ready for him.

She wanted him to explode in her mouth, but Tyson had other ideas, because in an instant he had pushed the seat all the way back and pulled her on top of him. Her silk dress rode the tops of her thighs. His hands were rough, hurried, as he shoved aside her damp panties. The steering wheel pressed hard into her back, her rear, but she didn't care. He rolled on a condom in record time and she took him in, one inch at a time, and there was only the sound of their panting, the sound of her thighs rubbing, frantically, against the wool of his tux.

The pressure was more than she could bear and she was close, so close to exploding when he threaded his hands into her hair and pulled her mouth down to his. She took her breath from him as he lifted her up and down. He grew huger, thicker, and then she felt his orgasm begin seconds before her own spiraled out of control. They stayed like this for a minute, maybe two, catching breath, letting heart rates return to normal.

She lifted a leg and slid back to the passenger seat, pulling her skirt back down, smoothing out the wrinkles she couldn't yet see but knew had to be there after their wild romp. In the front seat of his car, no less. Could her life be any more exciting? Any more reckless? She felt like a ball of abandonment, and it was wonderful. She heard him tuck in his shirt, zip up his pants.

"I hope I didn't make us too late," she said as the first smidgeon of propriety came back to her.

His grin, satisfied yet still hungry, forced her anxieties away. "Nothing like having a good reason to be behind schedule."

She smiled back, and as he returned to the road, she touched up her makeup and tamed her hair in the mirror above her seat. If ever there'd been a good reason to be a few minutes late, making love to Tyson on a dark street was it.

ONE BY ONE, Tyson's initial impressions of Carrie were fading away. On first glance he'd thought she would be stuck-up, caught up in a web of impressions. He knew she'd been surprised by her hunger for him on Friday night. He'd wondered, even as his desire for her had grown so big he'd hardly been able to think straight, if his was the first cock she'd ever licked, sucked, with such passion. He hoped so. Her astonishment had radiated off her in waves every time they'd made love. And even though she'd let go, given herself up to him and the pleasure they'd given and received each time they'd made love before now, she'd been holding something back.

Five minutes ago, in the front seat of his car, she'd held nothing back. She'd wanted to take him in her mouth, into her sweet pussy, so she'd done it. He'd simply been along for the ride. And what a ride it'd been.

After the huge blow his ex had dealt him, and the mess of divorce proceedings, he'd instinctively built an impenetrable wall around his heart. Somehow, Carrie was breaking through. And he'd only known her twenty-four hours.

They pulled up to the Meadowood Resort in the hills of St. Helena, just north of Napa. He opened her door, and when she stepped out, he marveled at her poise. No one would ever guess she'd been riding him in wild abandon, screaming his name, minutes before.

He raked his gaze up and down her tall, perfect figure. Her dress was as immaculate as it had been on the hanger. Only it looked so much better covering her luscious curves. He took her hand and they walked inside, where cocktail hour was already in full swing. He was proud, honored really, to have Carrie on his arm. He'd bought the dress with the specific intention of showing her off, but as one set of eyes after another raked her up and down, he wondered if he would have been better off sending her a muumuu.

He knew, via the grapevine, that a few of his colleagues pounced on anything with breasts, but none had ever looked at his woman like this. Even his ex-wife, who would have dearly loved the attention, had never sparked so much male interest. Not to mention envy on the part of every woman in the room.

Jo and Will Korbum approached. Will had started a Rhone wine consortium five years ago and had done a great job spreading the word about Syrahs, Viogniers, and Muscat Blancs. Will grasped Tyson's hand and pumped it hard.

"It's been too long, Tyson. Nice to see you back out among the living."

"Been busy at the winery," he said, deliberately misinterpreting Will's words, the undertone that asked, *Are you finally crawling out from that post-breakup rock you've been living under?*

"Jo, Will, I'd like you to meet Carrie Anderson. She's a landscape designer based in San Francisco. Carrie, not only do they do great things for Rhone wines, but on many occasions I've found them to be a husband-and-wife comedy team."

Jo's eyes twinkled. "Tyson thinks we should take our act out on the road." She wrapped an affectionate arm around her husband. "I guess when you've been married thirty years, everything becomes an excuse for a punch line."

Will waggled his eyebrows and squeezed his wife. "Among other things," he said, and everyone laughed at the blatantly sensual undertones between the happily married couple.

"It's wonderful to meet you," Carrie said as she shook their hands.

"We're so glad you could join us tonight. Tell me, how do you manage to live in San Francisco with all that fog? Every time I go to Neiman's I need to wear my mink to stay warm in Union Square." Jo grimaced. "I just put my foot in it, didn't I? I'm so good at that, I should buy shoes for my mouth."

Carrie laughed. "The weather certainly is beautiful in Napa. I have to admit, I've found everything about the wine country to be wonderful."

Jo's eyes brightened, and she leaned in close to Carrie. "What brought you to Napa? Did our Tyson reel you in?"

No matter how well meaning and motherly Jo was, the way she said "our" Tyson put a very bad taste in Tyson's mouth, but again, Carrie seemed utterly unperturbed by the conversation.

"Actually, I came up for a girl's weekend with my two best friends. But I'll let you in on a little secret." Her eyes sparkled with wicked intent. "I haven't seen my friends since we checked into our hotel."

She flicked a quick glance at Tyson and he nodded almost imperceptibly, giving her permission to continue.

"You see, I've barely been out of Tyson's bed since Friday night." A beat later, when the Korbums' mouths still hung open, she winked and said, "It was nice to meet you both. I hope we'll get a chance to talk more later this evening." Her tone was gracious and charming, and Tyson couldn't help but chuckle as she deftly led him toward the balcony.

They stepped through the French doors and she turned to him, concern marring her brow. "I shouldn't have said that. I don't know what's wrong with me tonight. I don't have any self-control."

He pulled her against him and let his chuckle turn into a full-blown laugh. "Have I told you yet that you constantly amaze me? The look on their faces was priceless. I didn't think anything would ever cause Jo and Will to be speechless. I underestimated you and your multitude of talents."

A relieved breath left her body. "Oh, thank God you're not upset with me. I just couldn't wait to brag about being ravished by you. And they seemed like exactly the sort of couple who would appreciate it." She bit her lip. "But you do know that by the time we sit down, everyone's going to know about us. About what we've been doing."

"We don't have to stay for dinner. I can think of a dozen other ways to pass the time."

"Very tempting," she said, but her eyes were flashing and he knew that backing down wasn't an option. "But right now we've got a dinner to attend."

He brought her palm to his lips and pressed a kiss to the tender skin on the inside of her hand. "Ready when you are."

She threaded her fingers through his, and together they walked back inside. The murmurs dropped away and then, just as quickly, rose to a crescendo.

"We should get paid for our performance tonight, maybe think about taking it out on the road," she murmured, and his laughter came from somewhere down deep.

CARRIE COULDN'T REMEMBER the last time she'd had so much fun. Sure, there were thinly veiled questions about her relationship with Tyson left, right, and center, but there was no malicious intent to any of it. More the way of small towns, where everyone knows everyone else's business. Or hopes to. And she'd certainly made that easy for tonight's crowd, what with her "haven't gotten out of Tyson's bed" comment.

Knowing he was beside her, the heat of his thigh burning through her silk-clad leg, was enough to make it a perfect evening. So much better, in fact, than any one of the parties she'd ever attended with James. Even her own birthday party.

Inwardly she shuddered to think of the engagement party James had likely already planned. It was an awful reminder of the ring she'd left in the pocket of her Capri pants. A cloud descended over her good spirits.

She was halfheartedly listening to Tyson's conversation when the mention of a woman's name made her ears perk up.

"Kimberly says hello."

Tyson's posture changed from relaxed to on edge in an instant. Who was Kimberly? she wondered.

"Okay," he said to her, then turned to Carrie. "Why don't I take you for a tour of the property?"

But the woman was persistent. "She'll be very interested to know about your date for tonight. And what your date said earlier." Tyson's face was carefully blank, but tension radiated from him as the woman continued, "You two seem awfully close for just having met on Friday."

Carrie wasn't exactly sure what was going on, but the one thing she did know was that it was time to nip it in the bud. Good thing she had experience with this game.

"We haven't met yet," she said, extending her hand. "I'm Carrie."

The woman had no choice but to reply in kind. "I'm Lizzy. Kimberly is one of my best friends." She pointed to Tyson. "And his wife."

Carrie didn't blink at the bomb that'd just been dropped. After all, she and Tyson hadn't exactly discussed their pasts with each other. Because if they had, she would have had to come clean with Tyson about James. But still, she had to admit that a wife would have been a good thing to mention somewhere during the past twenty-four hours.

"That's nice," she said. "Are you in the wine business?"

The girl shook her head. "My husband owns a cork factory."

Carrie smiled. It had been hard to miss the older man with the very young wife on his arm when they'd been mingling before dinner. It was time to go for the kill.

"He must be very generous. That's a lovely ring you've got on."

Flustered by the way the conversation had changed course, but also flattered by the compliment, Lizzy held up her left hand for Carrie to get a better look.

"Three carats. Flawless color and clarity."

Carrie nodded. "I can see that your husband has a fine appreciation for the finer things." She looked pointedly toward the floating bar, where Mr. Appreciation was having an engrossing conversation with a brunette's double Ds.

The girl's face flamed. She turned back to Tyson. "Kimberly's going to take you for everything you're worth in the divorce." And then she was gone, although her cloying perfume lingered.

Carrie shook her head, more glad than she could say to hear the word "divorce." She turned to Tyson, whose face was a hard mask.

"Let's go," he said, no inflection whatsoever in his words.

"Aren't you forgetting something?" She put her hand on his wrist to emphasize her words. He finally met her eyes and she said, "Something about making love to me in the vines?"

He seemed to be warring with himself, so she took the decision out of his hands. She turned and left the dining room, headed out the French doors and down the steps to the garden. She didn't look to see if he was following her. She didn't need to. She could feel him.

She wound around a rose garden, stepping over a small rock wall into the vines. Her heart was pounding with desire when she finally reached the base of a large oak tree and turned to face Tyson.

"I should explain," he began. "What she said in there, it's true. I was married. The divorce is almost final."

Carrie took a step closer and placed one finger over his lips. "I don't want to share you with your ex-wife. Not tonight."

He picked her up so quickly that she gasped with surprise. She enjoyed the feeling of being carried through the vines as if she were weightless. "My Prince Charming," she sighed.

Moments later, he let her body slide down his until her feet barely touched the ground. He pressed her back into the wall of a small shed as he said, "I'm pretty sure Prince Charming never did to Snow White what I'm about to do to you."

Moisture flooded her pussy, and she swallowed even though her mouth had gone bone dry. With lust.

"And what is that exactly?" she asked in her primmest, most proper voice, even as she was coming apart at the seams with the force of her desire for him.

Instead of telling her, he showed her. Within seconds her skirt was bunched at her waist again and her panties were on the ground. "Lift your foot." She complied, more thrilled than she could have ever imagined at being so out of control. At being controlled.

In the time it took her to kick away her panties, he'd thrown off his jacket, unzipped his pants, and rolled on a condom. His cock was thick and perfect, and she wondered if there was ever going to come a time that she'd see his penis and not want to drop to her knees to taste him.

He cupped her butt cheeks with his big, rough hands and lifted her up. She wrapped her legs around his waist and he slid into her. It was better than anything she'd ever felt, better every single time he thrust into her. She clung to him, levering herself up and down on his cock, tilting her neck back so that he could bite down on her.

"Come for me, Carrie," he said, and as she dropped her chin to look at him, she wondered whether it was possible to fall in love with someone you barely knew. He filled her again and she thought of his tenderness, his intelligence, his lovemaking, and thought "YES!" just as her world shattered into a million beautiful pieces.

8

CARRIE WOKE IN THE CROOK OF TYSON'S ARM, snuggled tightly against him. She could hardly believe how wonderful last night had been. How passionate and gentle he'd been when they'd returned to his house, how he'd cradled her in his arms, how she'd fallen asleep lulled by the sound of his heartbeat below her ear.

Sleeping entwined like this had been a first for her. James hadn't liked to touch in bed beyond sex. He'd said he needed his space to sleep, and she'd respected that. Now she felt more intimacy wrapped in Tyson's arms as he slept than she'd ever had during sex with James.

Why hadn't anybody pointed out that she'd been settling? Had her parents settled for each other? They'd always seemed happy enough together, but maybe "enough" wasn't, well, enough.

They'd encouraged her relationship with James, been enthralled by his money, his connections, his family's standing in the community. Admittedly, though, so had she, so she couldn't exactly blame them for anything, could she?

But after last night, she knew she could never settle for good enough ever again. She was in love with Tyson. He was her fairy-tale prince.

She was a believer again. Even though she'd known him less than two full days. True love did exist. And its name was Tyson.

Her parents, her friends, everyone would have to accept her choice. Not that she was worried about anyone not liking Tyson. He was funny, smart, gorgeous, and successful. And he made her body tingle all over every time he touched her. Every time he looked at her.

The tingles started all over again. She opened her eyes and saw that Tyson was already awake and staring down at her. "I had a wonderful time last night," she said softly, as she nestled in closer to his warmth.

His hand rubbed small circles on her back. "I'm glad." He didn't say anything more, but she knew what was coming. "I should have warned you about the potential minefields when you agreed to be my date for the evening. If anyone offended you, I'm sorry. It was about me, not you."

"No," she said, "Lizzy's comments didn't bother me. Believe me, she wouldn't last an hour at some of the parties I've been to, where even the compliments are backhanded slaps."

"What kind of crowd have you been hanging with?"

She sighed. "It's a long story." It was time for her confession. One she didn't want to make.

"I want to hear your stories. I want to hear all about you," he said. "But first, I need to explain what last night was all about."

She pressed a kiss into his chest. "I know exactly what last night was all about. You just wanted an excuse to get me naked in a moonlit vineyard."

He reached for her and kissed her, hard. "Can you blame me?"

he said once they came up for air. Her lips tingled and her cheeks burned from his stubble. God, he was delicious. But as much as she wanted to explore his muscles some more, watch them flex beneath her as she rode him, she knew he needed to get his past off his chest.

"How long were you married?" she asked, opening the door.

"Three years. We began divorce proceedings five and a half months ago. It takes six for the divorce to be final." He brushed her hair away from her face, and she thought she saw uncertainty cloud his eyes. But then, just as quickly, it was gone. "You're the first woman I've been with. The first that I've wanted to be with."

"I'm glad," she said. "Not that you were hurt, but that I'm special."

She realized how that had sounded after the word "special" had left her mouth, and she nearly groaned. Nothing like telling a guy how he felt about you to totally freak him out.

Flustered, she blurted, "Why did your marriage end? What happened?"

He laughed, a mirthless sound, and ran a hand over his face. Suddenly, he looked exhausted.

"Never mind, you don't have to tell me."

"No. You're the one person who needs to know."

He closed his eyes, and she knew he was at war with himself again. Carrie didn't know if she'd given him enough of a reason, beyond great sex, to confide in her. After all, he didn't know she loved him.

"I haven't told anyone about that night," he said in a low, troubled voice. "The night my marriage ended. And no one has asked. I don't know, maybe they don't want to pry. Or maybe it's more fun to speculate."

She nodded, her expression grim. "I'd have to vote for speculation. Gossip tends to take on a life of its own." She touched his lips with her finger. "I already know you didn't cheat on her. You couldn't have. It's not who you are."

A flicker of guilt worked its way up her spine. She wasn't cheating on James, but then, she hadn't given him his ring back yet, had she?

But this was about Tyson, not her. "She cheated, didn't she?"

"It was as much my fault as it was hers," he said, and although Carrie disagreed, she kept quiet. For now. "Kimberly knew exactly what she wanted from me. From marriage. From her life. She was up-front. At least I think she was. She loved that I was in the wine business, but as she got friendly with the competition, she started wondering why I wasn't bottling more. Why my production wasn't on par with the big guys. She blamed my methods."

Carrie cut in. "She didn't support you being organic, I take it."

"She did at first. Thought it sounded New Agey, or something. But the reality is that it's expensive. And time consuming." He shook his head. "All of this is the long way of saying that I found her in bed with my vineyard manager. She wasn't the least bit upset to see me standing in the doorway. From what I hear, Rogelio didn't last long, so my sense is that she used him to get to me. To end things with me."

"I don't get it," Carrie said, enraged at this woman who had treated Tyson so badly. Even though her rage was at odds with the fact that she wouldn't be with him had his ex-wife not been an utter skank.

"Why would she want to leave you? You're intelligent, you've created a remarkable business, and on top of that, you are beyond amazing in bed."

She clamped her mouth shut, but she was a moment too late.

"Beyond amazing, huh?"

She blushed. "Can we forget I said that?"

He laughed. "Nope. I'll be remembering that one for a good long time. Beyond amazing applies to you too, you know. It's something I don't get, actually."

"What's that?"

"How come you haven't been snapped up yet? Us men aren't really that stupid, are we?"

"I'll plead the fifth on that one," she said in a teasing voice, but inside, even as she thrilled at his compliment, she was cringing. She should have already told him about James. Friday night, during dinner, when he'd asked her if she was seeing anyone, she could have made a joke about being on the rebound with a ring still in her pocket. And again, last night at the dinner, she'd had her chance out in the garden to say, "You're not the only one with a past," but she'd been too wimpy, too afraid of spoiling her fairytale evening to come clean. Now, it felt too late. Her timing was terrible.

Tyson's words broke into her jumbled thoughts. "I was that stupid, actually. About Kimberly. I should have known we weren't a good fit. But I wanted to be married. Have kids. It was time. Another thing to check off my list. Sounds stupid, doesn't it?"

"Not at all. I know all about lists. I think I invented them." He grinned at that, but she knew he wanted her to say more. To let him in. "I was in a similar situation. Not married," she said, wanting to be clear, still trying to find a way to tell him about James without making herself look bad, "but, I guess, trying to cross some things off of my list. Getting married was one of them. Kids would have been another if I'd ever made it to the altar."

They were sitting up in bed now. Tyson's back was propped against the headboard, she was sitting cross-legged, covered in blankets and sheets. She felt so comfortable with him, here, like this. She felt like they belonged together.

Please, God, she silently prayed, *don't let me mess this up.*

She took a deep breath and said, "It's a funny story, actually, has a lot to do with that horrible crowd I hung out with for too long," but just as she was about to admit the worst, a telephone rang and he shifted his attention away from her.

"That's my emergency line." He looked torn. "I wouldn't think of getting it otherwise. I want to finish this conversation. I want to learn more about you, Carrie. I'm hoping I'll get the chance."

She swallowed hard. Partly from relief. Partly because he wanted to see her again. He wanted to get to know her better.

"You will. Get the chance, I mean. Don't worry. Go deal with your emergency."

"You won't leave town before I see you again, will you?"

He was already out of bed, pulling on jeans and a T-shirt. He looked rugged and rumpled and gorgeous. Naked, she stood up and wrapped her arms around him.

She gave him a long, thorough kiss, then said, "Not a chance."

He gave her one last, hot kiss and told her to take his car back to the hotel, then he was gone. She felt silly putting the fancy dress back on, so she opened the door to his walk-in closet and tried not to feel like a snoop as she reached for a pair of sweatpants and a T-shirt. Everything in his closet smelled fresh and clean and wonderful. She wanted to stay in his house forever. Instead, she reached for the self-control that she'd been such a master of until Friday night, pulled on his clothes, carefully folded her dress, and grabbed his keys from the foyer table. Hopefully she could slink back into her room at the hotel without anyone seeing her.

∽ ∽ ∽

A FEW MINUTES LATER she pulled into the parking lot, wishing she knew of a back entrance. She took a deep breath, plastered a confident smile on her face, and walked barefoot through the lobby, holding her dress in one hand, her shoes in another, feeling more like a teenager who'd snuck out a window the night before than a grown woman.

She held her head high and met strangers' stares and inquisitive smiles with self-assurance. By the time she locked the door behind her and finally let herself breathe again, she felt as if she'd run a marathon.

She closed her eyes and let her weight rest against the door. She couldn't put James off any longer. A formal "I'm giving you your ring back as soon as I get home because we're completely over and never should have started in the first place" call to her ex was long overdue.

But first, she needed to clean up. The thought of facing James, even over the phone, made her want to look her best. Almost as if he'd know what a mess she was without seeing her and it would put her at a disadvantage.

She took her time in the shower. Somehow it seemed vitally important that she shave her legs, moisturize, pluck her eyebrows. She chose her outfit with undue care, slipping into a black tank top that she knew James hated (black was a big no-no in Mummy's book, of course) and a short denim skirt that Vanessa had insisted she buy last month. Carrie felt sexy and naughty.

She tried his cell, his house, and his office before she remembered that it was Sunday. Which meant church, first, lunch at Agnes's Nob Hill showplace, second. She was hardly able to believe that she'd forgotten the weekly ritual she'd endured for two long years.

Great. She was going to have to tell him they were officially over with his mother listening over his shoulder. It was almost enough of an excuse for Carrie to put the call off a few more hours. But she was sick to death of being a wimp.

Of being a good girl who never rocked the boat.

It was time for a tidal wave.

Her heart pounding hard, she dialed Agnes Carrigan's home number, cringing at her almost-mother-in-law's overly precise words. "Carrigan residence."

"Agnes, hello, it's Carrie." There was silence, and for a moment Carrie wondered if Agnes was thinking, "*Carrie? I don't know any Carrie.*"

"Is this Carolyn?" Agnes asked.

With only three words James's mother had managed to reduce Carrie to an uncultured shmuck who should have known better than to use the abbreviated version of her name.

"Yes, that's right," she said, refusing to give the woman the satisfaction of hearing her fumble. "Is James available? I need to speak with him."

Carrie realized, with utter certainty, that she was doing dear Agnes a favor by refusing James's proposal. Her heartbeat returned to normal. Not only did she not have anything to fear from Agnes, she was practically expecting a Thank You card to come in the mail next week.

She smiled at the thought, but then Agnes said, "I'm afraid he couldn't join us for brunch this morning." Carrie's smile disappeared. Not because the subtext was, "*And it's all your fault, you little tramp,*" but because a sense of foreboding had just hit her. Was strangling her, actually.

James never missed Sunday brunch with Mummy. Never.

Unless he thought he was going to lose a deal. Like, say, an engagement.

The message light on the phone started blinking, and she was sweating as she said, "I'm sorry to have bothered you, Agnes. Good-bye."

She hung up and dialed the message retrieval number. It was Tyson.

"You left something important at the winery. Could you please come and get it?"

His voice was curt, and he hadn't said anything about missing her already or wanting to be with her again soon. His voice had been all business, and not in a good way.

She took a deep breath. There was no point in freaking out over what was, in all likelihood, nothing but her imagination playing tricks on her. Fighting off the insane urge to speed straight into Tyson's arms for reassurance, she picked up her purse and headed out to the farmer's market to get their picnic lunch together.

SOMEWHERE BETWEEN MAKING LOVE with Carrie in the car last night and waking up in his bed with her long, supple limbs pressed against him, he'd stopped denying his feelings. She wasn't just a weekend fling. From that first moment out in his vineyard, she'd been special. Different. He hadn't been sweet-talking her when he'd said he wanted to learn more about her. He'd meant it.

Because Carrie was the partner he'd been looking for. He felt, deep in his gut, that what they had was a good thing. That it would continue to get better and better. That it would last.

As soon as he'd learned that the call on his emergency line hadn't been an emergency after all, just a new employee in the tasting room who couldn't locate a recent VIP shipment, he'd rushed back to the house to see if he could catch Carrie before she left. Maybe he could pull her into the shower again, maybe make a picnic and take it up to the top of the mountain. Sunday had never seemed so full of promise.

But he'd been too late. By the time he'd gotten back home, she'd already left. Then he'd seen it, beneath the legs of his media cabinet. A huge diamond ring.

An engagement ring.

What had to have been Carrie's engagement ring, likely having fallen out of her pants pocket when they'd been ripping each other's clothes off Friday night.

The name "James" had backhanded him as he'd picked it up. She'd mentioned him a couple of times, hadn't she? She'd seemed preoccupied the night he'd found her in the vineyard—because she'd been contemplating having one last fling before she tied the knot? Before she checked the marriage box off her list?

He didn't know how she could have slipped the ring into her pocket in the vineyard on Friday night without him noticing. It was too big to miss, although the sun had already set. Maybe she had done it earlier. Maybe, all along, her plan had been to reel in some sorry sucker, to screw his brains out, then go back home to another sucker. A filthy-rich one, judging by the size of the diamond.

Carrie had seemed so pure, so honest. Too bad those were the assumptions of a lovesick fool. "Fool" being the word of the hour. Hadn't he learned anything about women?

What really killed him was that he'd known Carrie less than forty-eight hours but she'd already stolen his heart. He'd been certain that being with her wouldn't hurt him. And now, this.

What was it she'd said this morning about hanging with gossips, fakes? The ring, heavy in his fist, told him a truth he couldn't deny. She was one of them. And he hadn't wanted to see it.

He left her a terse message at the hotel, then headed back to the main tasting room, hoping business would help him keep his head on straight until he saw her. Until he returned the ring.

And made her tell him the truth.

So when one of the wine pourers called back into his private office, saying there was someone to see him, he expected to see her beautiful face, to want her even though she was no better than his ex.

"James Carrigan," the man said, holding out his hand to shake Tyson's. "I'm looking for my fiancée. The hotel clerk said to look for her here."

9

ON HER WAY OUT OF THE LOBBY, Carrie left a quick message at the front desk for Rose and Vanessa, letting them know that they could reach her at Green Vineyards and that she'd call them soon to arrange their trip back home to San Francisco.

Home.

Funny how much at home she felt here, in Napa, in the country. She'd grown up in the suburbs, she lived in the city, and she had never once thought about moving out to a place like this, surrounded by tall mountains and rows of green vines. A town small enough that everyone knew your name—which, she supposed, could be both good and bad, based on the dinner last night.

She drove Tyson's car two blocks to the farmer's market entrance. Everything was alive—the people, the vines, the delicious aromas wafting from many of the small booths. She smiled as she picked out a couple of nectarines from an organic farmer who was set up under an umbrella. At the next booth, she selected a mouthwatering local Brie and some artisan sourdough bread. No question about it, she could get used to life in the wine country.

Tyson was the best part of the fantasy, of course.

Waking up with him. Going to sleep next to him. Or not at all if they were too busy with, well, other things.

She forgot her worries and took her time trying samples of pastries and peaches. She listened to a local rock band play hits from the sixties while toddlers danced in circles around them. She admired the painting a local artist was creating before a crowd of onlookers. She couldn't help but notice how handsome the painter was. Hey, she was hooked on Tyson, but she was only human. And this guy was hot.

Something about the painting he was creating made her think of Vanessa. She smiled again. She couldn't imagine Vanessa with a guy in paint-splattered jeans. She was more the CEO, drives a Jaguar, type of gal.

Finally, Carrie's bag was full and her arms were tired, so she hopped back into Tyson's car and headed over to his winery. She sang along with the radio, feeling carefree and happy as she drove up the long driveway to Green Vineyards. The parking lot was full of tourists on the wine-tasting prowl.

That could have been me, she thought, *just another random tourist going from winery to winery.*

Instead, she'd met Tyson and her whole weekend had been a blur of passion and laughter. He was the best thing that had ever happened to her, and she wasn't going to screw things up.

They were going to have to figure out the details. His business was in Napa, hers was in San Francisco. Maybe they could do three nights a week at her town house and four here for a while. Until she could build up a client base in Napa.

Okay, so she was really jumping the gun on their relationship. But as she got out of Tyson's car and headed inside her mind swam with the possibilities of the new, wonderful life they could share together. She was utterly confident about her feelings for Tyson and had high hopes about his feelings for her.

But then she looked up, and all her visions of a perfect afternoon, a perfect life together with Tyson, shattered to the ground. As did her bag of fruit and cheese and bread, which fell from her lifeless fingers to the gravel parking lot. But she didn't notice anything other than how cold, how distant Tyson's eyes were as he watched her from the shaded front porch of his winery.

With James standing right beside him.

Oh, God. Her knees nearly buckled.

Tyson thought she'd lied to him. Just like his ex-wife. He'd never forgive her.

She wanted to run to him, to beg him to listen to her explanations that things weren't how they looked. But she never got the chance. James was already heading for her, his arms open wide, as if he expected her to run, gratefully, into them.

"Mummy told me you called the house, baby. You sure missed me, didn't you?"

"'Baby?'"

He smiled at her, a smile so full of itself that she could hardly believe she hadn't really seen it for two whole years. "That's what a man calls the woman he's about to wed."

Her eyes shot to Tyson, and she knew they were wild. Horrified. But Tyson's expression hadn't changed. It was still grim. Worse, it was impartial. Almost as if he was doing nothing more than watching two strangers hash things out after an argument.

Carrie was desperate to clarify things, lest the man she loved with all her heart think she'd been playing him all weekend.

Directing her words at Tyson, she said, "We're not about to be—"

"I told Tyler all about our engagement on Thursday night at Farallon. He thinks I'm the luckiest guy on the planet."

"It's Tyson, not Tyler," Carrie said, feeling things spin more and more out of control by the second.

James threw one of his smooth smiles over his shoulder. "Sorry about that, buddy. Must have heard wrong."

Tyson didn't respond. Didn't take his eyes off Carrie. They burned through her, and she would have given anything in that moment, anything at all to have him look at her like he had a few hours ago in his bed.

Acting as if everything was perfectly normal, James said, "I drove all the way up to Napa to be with you. To show you that we belong together. You should really keep your cell on when you're traveling," he chastised, "so that I can get a hold of you. Mummy said the same thing."

Oh, God, he had to bring Agnes into it, didn't he? As if it wasn't bad enough that with every word out of his mouth she was losing her chance at real love. With Tyson.

She opened her mouth to tell James to go away, that she wasn't marrying him no matter what, but her tongue refused to work right. Besides, he was quicker, wilier than she could ever be.

Tyson finally spoke from up on the porch. "I found your ring, Carolyn."

Her heart stopped beating.

The huge yellow diamond lay in his palm, sparkling in the daylight, and she hated the expensive jewel more in that moment than she'd ever hated anything in her life.

"You lost the ring?" James said, the censure and disbelief in his voice loud enough to make several heads turn in the parking lot. Making an obvious effort to tamp down on it, he turned back to Tyson with an insincere smile. "I'd like to pay you a reward for finding my fiancée's ring. I know how heartbroken she would have been if anything had happened to it."

Carrie barely resisted the urge to punch him—maybe she had it in her after all—as Tyson said, "Seeing you two together is reward enough."

He threw the ring to her, and she watched it arc through the air as if in slow motion. She caught it as he walked away. Every muscle in her body screamed at her to run after him. To deal with James later.

But when James said, "Don't worry, Carolyn. I forgive you. You'll need to be less careless with your things in the future," she finally snapped. She had to clean up the bad things in her life before she could build better ones.

She shoved the ring at James, into his chest, and watched it slide down his Prada blue-striped button-down shirt to the gravel.

"A, I am not careless. Ever. I wasn't wearing your ring because I didn't want to wear it. I tried to give it back to you at the restaurant but you wouldn't hear of it. Wouldn't let me break up with you. Which brings me to B. There is no future for us. None. I'm not marrying you. Period. I'm breaking up with you, once and for all."

The words flew out of her mouth in a rush, and when she ran out of breath, she felt a pang of guilt. Just because he wasn't the right man for her didn't mean he was a bad person, did it?

She opened her mouth to apologize for breaking things off, for realizing in the eleventh hour that forever wasn't meant to be for them.

But again, James beat her to the punch.

He reached down and picked up the ring. He blew the dust off and slipped it into his pocket, then said, "Mummy never thought you were good enough for me. I can see, now, that she was right. Good-bye, Carolyn."

He turned to walk away. A better person might have let him go, might have let him get the last word in. But Carrie had finally come to realize that she didn't need to be that better person every second of every day.

"Oh, yeah, I almost forgot C. My name is Carrie. Not Carolyn. Next girl you ask to marry you, you might want to get her name right first."

10

Over James's shoulder, she'd seen Tyson heading into the fields. She took off, running, through the vines. And then she saw him. Hacking at an unruly bush. That might as well have been her head.

He was dripping with sweat, and he'd never looked more beautiful.

She'd never been so scared.

"Tyson," she said softly, not wanting to startle him when he had an axe in his hands. But he didn't stop slashing at the bush, so she raised her voice. "Tyson?"

"Don't worry, the underwear you left on my bedroom floor will be our little secret."

Every word hit her like a knife. All she could do was apologize.

"I'm sorry," she said, willing herself to be strong enough to face the man she loved, to tell him that she loved him. She regretted so much, but she wouldn't regret that. "I'm sorry I didn't tell you about James. About his proposal."

Another wall went up in Tyson's eyes, and Carrie hated how she'd caused him this pain. More pain.

"I don't know what he told you, but I didn't say yes. I said no."

"Most people don't keep a ring they don't want."

"You're right. They don't. I tried to give it back to him, I should have refused to take it." She fought back tears. "You want the truth, Tyson? Here it is. I'm not perfect. Not even close. The ring was big and beautiful and I thought, what the heck, what if I keep it for a couple of days? Who will that hurt? I didn't know I was going to meet you, out here, in your vineyard. I didn't know that you were going to take my breath away, make me forget about everything, including a man who'd just asked me to marry him."

Tyson didn't say anything, didn't reassure her in any way, but he put the axe down. He looked at her. Really looked at her for the first time since she'd driven into the vineyard.

A small seedling of hope took root in her chest. "I know you're afraid to trust me. I know she hurt you." His eyes shuttered again, and she inwardly cursed herself for screwing this up so badly.

"But this isn't about your ex-wife. It isn't about my ex-boyfriend. This is about us. Only you and only me." She stopped, took a deep breath. "I love you, Tyson. I love you in a way I didn't know I could love. I know it's completely insane to feel so much after just one weekend, but I feel like you're the other half of me, the one I didn't know was missing. I know I left some things out this weekend, I know I should have come clean about my past, but I hope one day you'll see that that's all it is. My past. You're my future. The only one I want to have."

She waited there, for him to say something. Anything. But the only sound came from a crow barking on the power line above them.

There was nothing left for her to do now but go.

ဢ   ဢ   ဢ

TYSON PICKED UP THE WOODEN HANDLE OF THE AXE, and it slipped out of his grasp. Love had always been his biggest mistake. He'd thought he'd found it with Kimberly. He'd been a fool. It had never been there. The only thing that had been lost when he'd found her in bed with another man had been his pride.

He didn't want to risk his heart again. But he knew that the pain of losing Carrie would be a thousand times worse than losing his ex-wife ever had been.

Like hell if he was going to let the only woman he'd ever really loved walk out of his vineyard and out of his life. Then he'd really be a fool. It was time for a leap of faith. Straight toward the woman who was worth that faith. And more.

"He called you Carolyn."

She whipped around to face him. "He didn't like Carrie. His mother didn't like it."

"What were you doing with a fool like him?"

She took a step closer. "I thought he had everything I wanted."

"And now?"

"Everything I want is standing right in front of me."

He forgot he was drenched with sweat as he pulled her into his arms. "I loved you from that first moment I held you in my arms when you thought I was a mountain lion coming to eat you. I'd never felt like that, like this, about anyone. I tried to convince myself over and over that you were playing me, some city tourist having fun in the country. But I knew, I always knew, that was a lie."

Carrie brushed her mouth against his. "You don't need to say anything else."

He wanted to devour her right there and then, in broad daylight, in his vineyard, beneath the old oak tree. And he would, but first he had to finish what he'd started.

"I know you're nothing like my ex-wife. I always knew it. And when I saw James, if I'd been willing to keep my eyes open, I would have seen that he meant nothing to you. I almost lost you, Carrie."

"No," she said, shaking her head, "you didn't."

"I've been tempted by you since the first moment I saw you walking through my land."

She jumped up to wrap her legs around him, and his hands came around to catch her, to cradle her butt.

"That night on your porch, I couldn't help it," she said. "I had to give in to temptation. You smelled so nice. Right here. I wanted to bite you."

He was already hard against her as he carried her into the shade, and she gave in to temptation again, lightly sinking her teeth into his skin.

"I was so wet already, just thinking about you touching me. You licking me."

"I've never wanted anyone the way I wanted you, Carrie. The way I'll always want you." Together they dropped to the ground, and he lay back to let her straddle him. "You were so hot. And so well-mannered. Even before you got down on your knees to taste me. May I?" he asked, reminding her of her polite query as he reached for the hem of her tank top.

"You'd better."

She held her arms straight up as he dragged her shirt up and off. He ran his hands over her bare breasts, watching her breath come hard as her arousal grew.

"Now it's my turn to taste you," he said as he pulled her down closer and sucked a nipple into his mouth. She moaned. His stubble rasped and scraped against her skin, and she pressed her breast further into his mouth.

Thanking God that she was wearing an easy-access skirt, he ran his hand up her thigh, past the thin barrier of her panties. She was so wet, and he knew all it would take was one small stroke across her clit, along her plump lips, into her tight vagina, and she'd be screaming with pleasure.

But Carrie was a woman with a mind of her own, thank God, and she had already undone his jeans and was sliding them down his hips. He was utterly impressed with her foresight when she pulled a condom out from the pocket of her skirt and slid it down his massive hard-on. But he didn't have time to start listing all the reasons why he loved her—there'd be sixty years for that—because he was sinking into her wet heat, sliding into his base, holding her there.

"Love me, Carrie."

Her smile was as good as yes, and then she threw her head back and rode him fast and hard. Her tight muscles contracted around him as she loved him.

Somehow, someway, he'd found his fairy-tale princess.

Taste Me

1

ROSE PUSHED THROUGH THE DOUBLE DOORS of the Napa Valley Hotel & Spa and sighed with pleasure. In contrast to the hot, dry air outside, the lobby felt cool and luxurious. She took in the terra-cotta swirls on the marble floors, the oversized canvases of vineyards on the walls, and knew that a girl's weekend in the wine country with her two best friends, Carrie and Vanessa, was just the balm she needed to soothe her raw nerves.

Carrie's big engagement drama had been the main focus during the drive to Napa, and Rose had been perfectly happy to let her breakup with Elliot—the jerk—fade into the background. It had been so embarrassing. So humiliating. She hadn't wanted to confess that she'd almost canceled on Carrie and Vanessa to go to a monster truck rally with Elliot instead. She hadn't wanted to admit that she'd apologized to him for having other plans and had planned to surprise him Sunday night with his favorite meal of fried chicken, gravy, and mashed potatoes, even though her hips couldn't afford more than a bite of it.

Because although Carrie and Vanessa now knew that Elliot

had dumped her on Thursday night, she'd left out some details. Like how he'd dropped by her apartment Friday morning to pick up a shirt he'd "forgotten about" with an emaciated blond on his arm. Rose cringed at the memory of how she'd stood there in her doorway, her coffee sloshing in her shaking hands, as the two of them had pushed past her. Like she didn't count.

A bolt of pain hit her square in the gut, and she reached into her purse for a roll of Tums. She popped one into her mouth, and as she chewed she chastised herself for being such a wimp that she hadn't kicked Elliot and his teenage Barbie out.

Vanessa had called Elliot a "boring, balding loser with a roving eye." But Rose felt like the biggest loser of all, because she was the one dating the losers, wasn't she? And then she couldn't hold on to them. Nobody would ever think that a short, round accountant was exciting.

Vanessa turned from the check-in desk and waved her room key at Rose and Carrie. "I'll see you both at the pool in five." Although lying on a chaise lounge next to her slim friend was the last thing Rose's ego needed, the allure of the sun on her skin was too much to resist. Maybe she'd take a little nap and finally catch up on the sleep she'd lost Thursday night when Elliot left.

Thinking about being dumped made her crave something fatty and sweet, like cinnamon buns. Which was exactly why she was going to stick to the low-calorie spa menu for the next three days. This weekend was all about detox. From bad food. And worse men.

She felt more pure, more virtuous, already.

Carrie finished checking in and turned to her, saying, "I'm feeling restless after the long drive. You don't mind if I go out for a walk and meet up with you two later, do you?"

Rose instantly felt selfish for wasting so much energy feeling sorry for herself when Carrie was hurting over her situation with

James. Wonderful, brilliant, gorgeous Carrie could have had any man she wanted. Too bad she'd chosen one who'd been more interested in how she looked on his arm than what was in Carrie's heart and mind.

Rose pulled her friend into a warm hug. At the very least, her softness was good for offering comfort. "Take all the time you need," she said. "I'm sorry about how things turned out with James."

"It's okay. I'm okay," Carrie insisted. But Rose could see the sheen of tears in her friend's eyes. "I'll meet up with you both in a bit. And I promise I'll be all smiles," Carrie said, moving quickly toward her room.

Rose's top priority this weekend was to boost Carrie's spirits. Which wouldn't leave her any time to feel sorry for herself.

She stepped up to the counter to check in. "Hello. I'm Rose Morgan. I've reserved a nonsmoking queen for the weekend."

The woman's face lit up. "How wonderful to meet you, Ms. Morgan. And congratulations! You're our grand-prize winner for the weekend."

"I won something?" she asked, pleasantly stunned by the unexpected news.

"Private lessons with Jack Gerard." At Rose's blank stare, the woman said, "He's one of the top new chefs in Napa." The woman fanned herself and leaned forward to whisper, "Not only is his food to die for, but he's gorgeous. What I wouldn't give to be alone in a kitchen with that hunk."

Food? With a hunky chef? The very last thing she needed was cooking lessons. Clearly, the Universe was out to get her.

The woman mistook Rose's horrified expression for confusion, hurrying to explain, "The Napa Valley Visitors Bureau automatically entered every hotel guest checking in throughout the valley this afternoon into the drawing. I know you're going to have a fabulous time. Spending an entire weekend with Jack Gerard and eating his food. It's truly a dream weekend." The woman winked. "He's the hottest bachelor in the valley, if you ask me."

Pasting a smile on her face as the woman quickly typed something into her computer, Rose said, "Thank you so much, but I really can't accept the prize. I'm here for a weekend with my girlfriends, and we've got a lot to catch up on. Would it be possible to swap the cooking lessons for a session with one of your personal trainers?"

The woman frowned and looked at her computer. "I just sent the Visitors Bureau an email telling them that you'll be meeting Jack at his restaurant in thirty minutes to arrange your lessons. It's all set."

Rose opened her mouth to say, "*Send another email saying there was a mistake,*" but the words sounded horribly rude in her head. For the rest of the weekend the staff would probably gossip about the ungrateful and bitchy frumpy woman with the gorgeous friends from San Francisco. They'd spit in her soup and give her wet towels by the pool. It really wasn't fair that the one time she won a prize it was something she absolutely couldn't indulge in.

She pasted a wide smile across her lips. "Well, um, this is great. Thanks. Wow." Now she was going to have to meet with the chef and somehow grow enough of a spine to turn him down in person. At his restaurant.

"Gerard's is one block down, on your right. You can't miss it. There will be plenty of people waiting out front tonight, vying for one of his coveted tables."

Rose nodded and turned away from the counter, dragging her bag behind her. She was going to have a quick drink of no-calorie seltzer water with the chef and then she'd politely decline the prize. In all likelihood, turning him down would be far easier than saying no to the perky woman behind the front desk. She probably wouldn't get a chance to finish her seltzer water before he escorted her out the door so that he could go have wild sex with a size-two tourist. He'd probably thank her for canceling. She slipped the key card into her door and walked inside the luxurious room, but before the door latched shut behind her, Vanessa breezed in wearing a tiny white bikini that left nothing to the imagination.

"Ready to head out to the pool?"

"I can't."

Vanessa shook her head. "One complaint about appearing in public in a bathing suit and I'll smack you. I don't care what that idiot you were dating said, you've got the curves of an old-school pinup. Besides, once we get enough of these into you," Vanessa said as she held up a freshly topped up glass of bubbly, "you'll forget all about him."

"It's not that," Rose said, wondering for the millionth time where everything Vanessa scarfed down went on her slim body. "It turns out that I won a weekend of cooking lessons with Jack Gerard and—"

Vanessa whirled so fast from the window that some of the bubbly spilled out of the top of the glass and onto the carpet. "Jack Gerard? Of Gerard's Restaurant? Are you kidding?"

Rose eyed her friend warily. "No. I'm supposed to meet him at his restaurant in a few minutes."

"You lucky bitch," Vanessa exclaimed. "I saw an article about him in *Food & Wine* last month, and not only did they say that he's the biggest thing to hit the restaurant world since Thomas Keller, but the man is gorgeous. Forget about eating his food, I want to eat him."

Rose felt her face flame. She was used to Vanessa's insatiable appetite for sex—and how much she liked talking about said appetite—but it was embarrassing when targeted at a man she was about to meet face-to-face in a matter of minutes. Rose pulled a brush out of her bag and dragged it through her out-of-control, dark curls several times, finally giving up when she realized she was mostly ripping her hair out, rather than taming it. She wished everyone would stop going on about how good looking the chef was. All it did was make her more nervous about meeting him.

Rose had a stroke of genius. "Go in my place."

Vanessa's eyes lit up for a moment, but then she shook her head. "Nice try."

"I'm going to turn down the lessons anyway, so you might as well go instead of me."

Vanessa advanced on Rose. "You're kidding me, right? First Carrie says no to the biggest diamond ring I've ever seen, and now you're turning down a weekend of pleasure"—she made the word "pleasure" sound naughty enough that Rose blushed again—"with a hot hunky chef?" Vanessa shook her head fiercely and wagged a long, slender finger at Rose. "Carrie did the right thing by dumping that prissy boyfriend of hers, but if you think I'm going to let you mess this up for yourself, forget it. You're going to meet Jack Gerard for more than a drink, but like hell if you're going dressed like that." She took in Rose's baggy T-shirt and jeans with a look of disdain.

Before Rose could stop her, Vanessa was pulling one outfit after another out of her bag. "Nope, too frumpy. Nope, too boring. Yuck, what is this?" she said, holding up an orange-and-green print skirt. "This looks like an old curtain. I'm throwing it out." She tossed a pink toiletry bag on the bed, along with some spreadsheets that Rose had brought in case she had some free time.

Finally, Vanessa smiled. "This is more like it," she said, holding up a crimson tank dress that Rose had packed in case she magically lost ten pounds at the spa and got the nerve to wear it. "This dress is perfect. Sexy. Very you. Go put it on."

"I can't wear that," Rose protested. "I need to lose weight first. A lot of weight."

"Put it on," Vanessa insisted in a scary voice, and Rose knew when she was beat. A few moments later, she slipped the dress over her head. It hugged every curve. Far too well.

"See," she said, holding her arms out. "I look like the Michelin man in a cocktail dress."

Vanessa shook her head. "You look amazing, Rose. That hot, hunky chef isn't going to know what hit him. I'd be surprised if you got any cooking done this weekend. Now go. And I'm going to want all the details when you get back tonight."

Rose slipped on her sandals and grabbed her purse, more than a little embarrassed about going out in public in such a revealing outfit. But while Vanessa might have been able to get her to change her clothes, Rose still hadn't changed her mind about the cooking lessons. Food was the last thing she needed right now, and she was going to turn the prize down.

No matter how hot Jack Gerard was.

JACK TOOK OFF HIS APRON and hung it up on the rack in the small office to the right of the kitchen. He looked at the clock, grimacing as he realized his cooking student would be here any moment.

He'd much rather spend the weekend creating culinary perfection in his hot, busy kitchen with the rest of his staff, but Tracy, his publicist, had said it would be good for the restaurant, good for his image, to give some stranger cooking lessons. The local newspaper was going to do a feature on him and his student, and Tracy thought it would get picked up by the wire. And so he'd reluctantly allowed himself to be pressured into giving up a whole weekend for a Visitors Bureau tourist promotion.

Unfortunately, he already knew the kind of woman that would be walking into his restaurant to claim her prize. She'd be skinny, well manicured, perfectly coiffed and dressed. She'd gasp in horror at the calories in his dishes and proceed to do nothing but nibble on rice cakes all weekend.

And he'd have to act like he was having a good time in her company, because the last thing he needed was for her to complain to the press about his bad attitude. No matter how successful Gerard's was, Jack knew that in this business everything could change in an instant. Hot as he was now, two years in, he was still too new. Sure, Gerard's was booked four months out and his upcoming cable show looked to be on a fine course, considering the fact that the network had already rented and stocked a studio space in town. But he hadn't been around long enough to prove that his restaurant could stand the test of time.

In another decade things would be different. He'd have more leeway to do what he wanted and say screw it to the things he didn't. At this stage in his career, when he was quickly building a name for himself as one of the best in the business, his reputation was everything. And Jack wanted every person who ate in his restaurant to go home with a taste of heaven on her lips. He wanted every person he shook hands with, talked with, to think, "Jack Gerard fed me the best meal I've ever had."

"Hey, Boss." His sous-chef, Larry, poked his head in the door to the small, crowded office. "I think your lady is here. In the bar."

"Great," Jack said, running his hands through his hair, getting ready to plaster a fake smile on his face for the next two days.

Larry grinned. "Hey, if you don't want to give her some lessons"—his fingers made lecherous quotes around the word "lessons"—"I'll take your place. It would be my pleasure, Boss."

"Thanks for the backup."

Now he was curious. Larry had as much disdain for the anorexic type as he did. All chefs wanted the people around them to truly love food. Constant dieters never did. What were the odds that his student was a hot, curvy babe?

Jack stepped out of the kitchen and into the restaurant. Several regulars were dining, and he took a moment to say hello. Everyone was rapturous over what they'd ordered. Content that they were going to serve a very large, very satisfied crowd at Gerard's, Jack felt some of his tension fade. He scanned the bar for his pupil.

But before he could locate his student, his gaze caught and stuck on a woman who had come straight from his triple-X dreams. Glossy, wavy black hair framed her heart-shaped face. Big, heavily lashed blue eyes blinked nervously as she scanned the restaurant for her party. Best of all was the figure that she was showcasing to perfection in her clingy red dress. Jack found himself salivating over her large breasts, big enough that he'd need two hands for each one as he laved them with his tongue.

An image of her on his bed, her wrists tied together behind her back, her tits jutting out at him, into his mouth, flashed through his brain, sending his cock surging against his fly.

As though they felt the heat of his gaze, her nipples beaded beneath the thin fabric of her dress. He grinned and made his way over to her, cooking lessons forgotten. For a woman like this, he'd find the time to squeeze her into his schedule.

And into his bed.

She crossed her arms across her chest, unaware that the movement made her breasts spill up and out the top. Every man in the room was eating her up and asking for seconds, but Jack was determined to get there first. It was, after all, his restaurant.

The first taste of honey should be his.

"Hello," he said, and the woman spun to face him, an O of surprise on her red lips. Up close, she was a buxom Snow White, so much hotter than any Disney character had a right to be.

"Hi," she said, giving him a small smile.

"Are you looking for someone?"

She looked around the restaurant uncertainly. "I'm supposed to be meeting Jack Gerard here, but it's so busy maybe I'll just leave him a note with the bartender."

Jack grinned. He couldn't help it. This incredible woman was his tourist. And here he'd been cursing his luck for agreeing to a weekend of cooking lessons. Things were looking up. Even the way his name poured out of her porn-star lips gave him a raging hard-on. He couldn't wait to get started.

He held out his hand, pleased by the jolt of awareness that shot through him as their palms met. "It's nice to meet you. I'm Jack." The woman's eyes grew bigger, and he could see small flecks of green in the deep, rich blue. "And you are?"

"Rose. Rose Morgan."

"You and I are going to have a lot of fun this weekend, Rose," he said as he leaned down closer to her sweet-smelling hair. "I hope you're hungry."

2

ROSE GAPED AT JACK GERARD. She was hungry all right, starving even. But not for food.

All she could think about was sex.

Hot, wild sex.

Jack was broad shouldered, tanned, and utterly gorgeous. His square jaw made her heart pound like a snare drum, as did the fact that he was six feet of pure muscle, delivered straight from her fantasies into real life.

Vivid images of this dark-haired man, whose green eyes glowed against his tan, plunging in and out of her while she screamed for more assaulted her. What would it be like to run her fingers through his thick, dark hair? Would she have to stand on her tippy-toes to press her lips to his? Would his dark green eyes fade to black when he was braced on his forearms over her in bed, coming in her, so thick she could barely stretch to fit him?

Oh, God, what was wrong with her?

She forced herself to pull her hand back from his warm, sensual grasp, to take a step back to distance herself from his potent maleness, but she got stuck against a wall of humanity at the bar. Her words caught in her throat, but she pushed them out anyway.

"I'm afraid I can't accept the cooking lessons."

He raised an eyebrow, and she got the sense that he was laughing at her. But in a nice way. "You can't?"

She shook her head, trying to be more emphatic, more firm. Something she was terrible at. Especially when all she wanted to do was stare at Jack for two straight days. Oh, yeah, and have acrobatic sex with him while she was at it.

"I promised my friends I'd spend the weekend with them," she said, feeling like a prim schoolmarm. She had a vision of Vanessa telling her not to mess this up and quickly forced it away. "I'm afraid you'll have to find someone else to give the prize to."

Someone who'd probably spend more time in Jack's bed than his kitchen. Someone skinny and confident and all the things Rose knew she was never going to be, no matter how many spa diets she went on.

But instead of nodding and telling her that he understood her predicament, Jack's hand made its way around to the small of her back and he was guiding her through the throng of people to an empty table at the end of the bar.

"Why don't we have a drink?"

Okay, so she'd have one drink with Jack. And then she'd leave. Since they were in the heart of the wine country, she racked her brain for a beverage that wouldn't offend but was still low calorie.

"I'd love a white wine spritzer," she said just before Jack set down two martini glasses filled with cocoa brown liquid.

"How about a chocolate martini instead?"

It sounded like heaven, but that was beside the point. Rose was starting to shake her head when Jack grinned and she forgot what she'd been about to say.

"I know we're in Napa," he said with a grin, "but sometimes a martini is the right way to get things started."

Rose looked up from the martini. What did he mean by "getting things started"? Everything out of his mouth so far had sounded like an invitation to join him in bed. Which was ridiculous in the extreme.

A man like him—sex in a chef suit—would never, ever want to be with a woman like her. The minute she'd walked into the restaurant she'd felt like an utter fool for wearing her formfitting tank dress in front of a man who was no doubt used to ultrafashionable, perfect women. Everyone in the restaurant was probably wondering what he was doing with her.

All at once, Rose was overwhelmed by sudden fury at everyone and everything. At Elliot for being an asshole. At her parents for buying her that gym membership in high school in a passive-aggressive maneuver to let her know that she needed to tone up and lose weight. At Vanessa for not knowing for one second what it was like to be less than perfect, less than desirable. At Carrie for turning down the kind of marriage proposal that Rose could only dream of.

Before she knew what she was doing, she picked up her martini and took a sip. As the smooth, rich flavor ran across her tongue and slid down her throat, she groaned, "Oh, God, that's amazing."

Jack's eyes turned hot as he stared at her across the small, candlelit table. "I agree, Rose. Absolutely amazing."

He hadn't tasted his drink yet, and for a moment Rose got the sense that he was talking about her, not the drink. She shivered under his gaze. He looked like he wanted to eat her, not his own scrumptious cooking, for dinner.

She took a deep breath. Talk about setting herself up for disappointment. Hadn't she learned her lesson yet? How many men would have to dump her, before she finally accepted the fact that earthly gods like Jack Gerard did not go for round, boring accountants?

She tried to put the drink down, but she couldn't help herself. She needed another sip. One more orgasmic taste. *Okay,* she thought, savoring the rich chocolate flavor, *that's enough pleasure for one night.* She needed to get back to the virtuous plan. Low-calorie food, a hundred laps in the pool, and no wild sex with a stranger.

"I'm sorry," she said in her no-nonsense accountant voice, the one that let her clients know that they'd better pay their bills ASAP or face dire consequences. "I really need to be going now. And I can see how busy you are tonight. Thank you for the drink, and good luck with everything."

She stood up to leave, but Jack was faster than she was.

"One lesson," he said, blocking her with his body.

Rose couldn't breathe with him standing so close, his hard chest pressed up against her breasts. She felt her own chest rise and fall quickly, saw his eyes flicker to her breasts. He was so persistent, and she was so bad at saying no.

"I can't," she said.

"I insist," he said, his hand on the small of her back again, sending electric shocks straight through her.

"Just one," she finally said, feeling certain that he wouldn't let her loose until she agreed.

She was desperate for some air. For some space from the most arousing man she'd ever set eyes on. The most intoxicating man that had ever touched her. Even if it was only a couple of square inches on her back through her dress, it was still the most deeply sensual thing that had ever happened to her.

No wonder why she'd never really understood the allure of the Kama Sutra. *You've got to work to keep your man happy,* her mother had always said, and because Rose was an overachiever at heart she'd memorized the ancient sex manual. But what no one bothered to mention was the fact that sex was a hell of a lot more than where you positioned your arms and legs. It was all about chemistry.

And Lord knew she'd never gone up in flames like this with any of the men she'd been with. Especially not Elliot.

Jack brushed a lock of hair away from her eyes, and a shiver of awareness nearly made her cry out in pleasure. "One lesson," he repeated, "but if you enjoy it, I hope you'll want more."

Rose licked her suddenly dry lips. Unfortunately, what she wanted couldn't possibly be what he was offering—even though he seemed to be staring at her like a starved man at a gourmet buffet.

Why, she wondered, was he so insistent that she take his cooking classes? Could it be an ego thing?

The curl he'd tucked back behind her ear fell across her forehead again. "You have beautiful hair."

"It's too unruly," she said automatically, but his surprising compliment made her feel bad about jumping to conclusions about his motives.

That was the problem with getting dumped one too many times for a thinner, younger model. It was making her cynical. Not as cynical as Vanessa, certainly—she still held out hope that there really was such a thing as true love—but enough that she needed to keep her distance, from here on out, from any and all gorgeous men. Especially ones like Jack Gerard, men that made her breath catch and the vee between her thighs feel heavy and warm. If she was smart, she was only going to go after pasty, boring accountant types like herself. Men who were afraid of being dumped by her, instead of the other way around.

Besides, Jack couldn't possibly need her to fall for him to boost his ego. She saw the way everyone in the restaurant had fawned all over him when he'd emerged from the kitchen.

She was going to enjoy his one lesson tonight, keep her distance (although she would certainly admire him from across the kitchen, how could she not?), and then she'd enjoy the rest of her weekend in Napa with her friends.

That was her new plan, and she was sticking to it.

JACK KNEW HE WAS MAKING AN ASS OF HIMSELF by drooling all over Rose, but he couldn't help it. She was a goddess. He wanted to rip her red dress off and take her on the polished bar top, crowded restaurant be damned.

He had been planning to conduct his cooking lessons in a corner of Gerard's kitchen. But now that he'd met his student, he scrapped that plan. He needed to be alone with her, so that he could convince her to . . . he was getting ahead of himself. Maybe he should gauge whether or not she was interested in him first. For all he knew, she might be more into the manicured, pin-striped-suit type. Which he most definitely was not. Or worse, maybe she had a boyfriend.

Fortunately, Jack had a good backup plan for where to take Rose so that he could have her all to himself to uncover her secrets. And if she was in fact single, hopefully she would be interested in exploring a whole lot more than the proper way to beat an egg with him.

"Are you ready to go back to school?"

Her smile lit up the dimly lit bar. "If you say the word 'school' one more time I might have to back out on our lesson after all. After I got my master's, I pretty much vowed that I'd never set foot again in a classroom."

A master's. And that lush, round, soft body.

Brains and ass. She was his dream woman come to life.

"Trust me," he said, matching her grin with his own, "these lessons will be unlike any classroom experience you've ever had." Unless, of course, she'd let someone eat lemon meringue off her stomach in college.

He pulled her out onto the sidewalk, holding her hand a little too hard. He needed to get a grip. She was nervous about their cooking lessons. So why did he have to keep coming on to her like a teenager that couldn't wait to get inside his first pussy?

He let off his grip the slightest bit and she asked, "Where are we going?"

He liked that breathless tone. Evidently, so did his cock. "We're filming my cooking show pilot in a building down the street. I've got everything set up for the cooking lessons," he lied. The chateaubriand that he'd been planning on working with was sitting in his restaurant's walk-in refrigerator.

Rose licked her lips in that sinfully nervous way of hers, and Jack itched to taste them for himself. Somehow, though, he had a feeling that Frenching her on the sidewalk within five minutes of saying hello might not be a good way to convince her to stick around for more lessons.

Not that French kisses weren't on his menu. Because they definitely were.

They veered half a block off Main Street, and Jack wanted her so badly that he practically kicked open the door to a small warehouse. He admired the round curve of Rose's hips as she walked inside, then he flipped a switch on the wall. The room lit up, illuminating an enormous kitchen set, surrounded by lights and cameras.

"Wow. Your studio is amazing," she said, turning back to smile at him over her shoulder.

"Thanks," he said, even though he didn't care about his cooking show, or his restaurant, or anything but how long it would take to get Rose out of that red dress. Somehow, he needed to lo-cate the suave restaurateur with a knack for putting people at ease. Otherwise, he was bound to scare her off.

He put some distance between them, hoping that sticking his head into the freezer would be the kitchen version of a cold shower. "Have a seat," he said, gesturing to one of the red wood stools at the island. "Tell me about yourself, Rose."

She perched on the edge of the chair. "I'm an accountant," she said, and something in her voice made him look up from the freezer.

"You don't like it?"

She frowned. "No. I mean, yes, I like it. It's sort of boring, I guess."

"Says who?" She bit her lip, and he felt like a jerk for brow-beating her. So much for witty banter. "You know, lots of people hate to cook. And my job would be their private version of hell. But I love it and couldn't do anything else. I wouldn't want to. You know what I mean?"

That smile he loved so much found its way back. "I do," she said, and he was glad when she let the rigid lines of her body re-lax on the bar stool. "I might as well admit it, then. I like num-bers. Always have. They're the one thing I can always count on."

Abruptly, she closed her mouth, and he could see that she thought she'd said too much. She hadn't and he wanted to know more about her, but she was already changing the subject, saying, "So, what are we going to make tonight?"

"The best meal you've ever tasted," was his reply as he opened the pantry door and scanned the shelves, quickly assessing his options.

"Just as long as it's low carb and low fat," she muttered under her breath.

He started laughing before he could stop himself.

"You don't have to laugh at me," she said, her voice giving away her hurt feelings.

Jack's smile fell away as he turned to face her. "I'm not laughing at you. I thought you were kidding."

"I'm on a diet," she said, and he hated the way her face turned red in embarrassment.

"Now you're really kidding, right?"

She looked at him with surprise. "Of course not. I've been on a diet since I was ten. I've tried them all. And one day," she added in a voice that wavered enough to break his heart, "one of them is going to work."

The whole idea of this goddess depriving herself of food—what he considered to be God's gift to mankind—really pissed him off.

"Why would a gorgeous woman like you do that to herself?" His voice was rough and hard.

Rose hopped off the bar stool and took a step away from him, back toward the door. She opened her mouth to respond, and he saw the wheels turning in her head. She pressed her lips together without saying anything, and Jack had to force the vision of her lips closing over his cock to the far recesses of his mind. *Patience, Jack.* His dick throbbed in his pants as he watched Rose war with herself over what she was about to say.

"Because I'm fat."

Jack slammed the pantry door shut. "I don't ever want to hear you say that again. Ever. Do you hear me?"

Rose's pink cheeks turned white beneath the force of his words. But even though he knew he was digging his own grave, even though the Visitors Bureau was going to get an earful, he couldn't shut up.

He grabbed her shoulders. "I can't believe you actually have the nerve to think you're fat. You are an incredibly beautiful woman. A goddess."

"No," she protested, but he wouldn't let her talk, wouldn't let her deny what he knew to be true with every fiber of his being. Not until he'd made his point. And somehow he knew that words alone would not make Rose a believer. He'd have to show her how amazing her body was by making it come alive beneath his hands.

"You are a lush, curvy woman. The kind of woman every man dreams of being with," he said, then leaned down and took what he wanted more than anything else.

A taste of sweet, delectable Rose.

3

$\mathcal{J}$ACK'S LIPS TASTED LIKE CHOCOLATE and cream. Rose could hardly believe he was kissing her, that his tongue was sweeping into her mouth, claiming her, forcing her to allow the onslaught. One look at his big, hard muscles, the breadth of his shoulders, the calluses on his hands, and she'd known that he wouldn't be gentle. But oh, God. She shuddered as he sucked on her lower lip and one of his hands slid down her spine.

Rose had had her share of masturbation fantasies over the years, but for all her knowledge of the Kama Sutra, they'd been pretty tame scenarios with movie stars and candlelight and roses. Suddenly, she could see the allure of the kinkier stuff. Jack lightly bit her lip, and she found herself hoping that he'd rip her dress from her and take her right there on the countertop. Just slide his hot, hard length into her with no thought for her needs. She'd be ready for him. Her lace panties were soaked after only thirty seconds of the most incredible kiss she'd ever experienced.

But when he pulled away from her, when she saw that he was deciding between continuing to ravage her mouth and regretting taking advantage of her, Rose knew she had to make a choice. She could let him go and they could cook dinner like two strangers.

Or she could take matters into her own hands. Ding, ding, ding.

"Don't stop," she said as she pulled his face back down to hers and kissed him passionately. She pressed her full breasts up against his chest, loving how hard and hot he felt against her.

He pulled back again, damn him, and Rose got that familiar sick feeling in the pit of her stomach. The one that said, *He doesn't want you, you idiot. His kiss didn't mean anything and look how you've read so much into it. When will you learn?*

"I'm sorry," she said as she tried to push away from the hard wall of his chest. But he held her firmly against him, his strong fingers wrapped around her wrists. "I shouldn't have done that. This isn't going to work. I can't take the cooking lesson with you."

She was so embarrassed, so horrified by the way she'd thrown herself at him because of one little pity kiss he'd given her that she barely heard him growl, "Don't you ever apologize again for kissing me." She looked up at him in surprise, pathetic hope flaring within her, and he added, "Not unless you want me to bend you over my knee and spank that ass of yours."

Rose knew that she should be shocked by how forward they were being with each other. From hello to dirty sex talk in mere minutes. But she was too aroused to care about propriety, about what was right, and taking it slow.

Her sex throbbed at the image he evoked. Bent over his lap, his huge, callused hand coming down over the bare, tender skin of her bottom. The thought of it made her so wet her inner thighs grew slick.

Elliot had tried to get her into S&M, into spankings and bondage games. When he'd finally given up she'd been more relieved than anything. But tonight, everything looked different. Naughty looked nice. Bad looked good.

Rose looked the sexy chef in the eye, knowing that she was playing with fire. Hoping she was, in fact.

"I'm sorry," she said, daring him to make good on his offer.

He looked at her for a long moment, as if he was trying to assess her response. Her heart was beating nearly out of her chest in anticipation. Somewhere in the back of her head she could hear a faint voice of reason telling her to run the other way, to not give in to her heretofore undiscovered kinky side. But for the first time in Rose's life, she refused to heed that cautious voice. She wanted to have naughty, passionate, raunchy sex with a stranger.

A stranger who wanted her. Who thought she was a beautiful, lush woman.

"Didn't you hear me?" she taunted. "I'm sorry. Very, very sorry."

This time, he couldn't mistake her intent. Jack swept her up into his arms and carried her over to a long suede couch in the back corner of the room.

"Be careful," she said without thinking. "Don't hurt your back."

Jack's eyes burned with desire. "Now you're really going to get it."

Rose shivered under his gaze. Strangely, the thought of being at his mercy made her wetter, hungrier for his touch.

But she didn't have time to dissect that crazy thought, because the next thing she knew, she was lying facedown across his lap and her dress was up around her waist.

Surely he expected some kind of protest from her, didn't he? Rose tried to think of something provocative. What would Vanessa say in a situation like this? But all she could summon was a moan of ecstasy.

Because Jack was running his finger slowly up the inside of her thigh.

She felt the huge bulge of his penis beneath her stomach. She ached to touch it, but she could barely remember how to use her hands.

"My God, Rose," he said, his voice husky and deep, "you're more beautiful than I could have imagined."

He slipped a finger into her panties, and Rose stopped breathing. He was less than an inch from her pussy lips and she was aching for him to touch her, to slide one of his thick fingers into her.

"Touch me, Jack," she begged, not recognizing the desperate voice that rang out in the studio.

But instead of caressing her between her legs, Jack remembered his original intent.

Of the promise he'd made to punish her.

"I've got to discipline you first," he said as he pulled his fingers out from her panties.

Rose's body answered his warning with another flood of arousal. Slowly, so slowly she wanted to scream, he pulled her panties off. She felt the cool air on her naked butt cheeks, and it was nearly enough to break the spell, for her to ask herself what she was doing lying half naked on a stranger's lap. But then Jack's palm came down on her skin, softly, so softly that she could barely feel it.

She found herself raising her hips, pressing herself back into his hand.

"You like that, don't you, Rose?" he said, and as she whispered, "Yes," she felt him grow bigger against her stomach.

"Harder," she begged.

His hand came down again, with slightly greater force this time, and Rose gasped with pleasure. And then again and again, never hard enough to hurt, never as hard as she so desperately wanted it. But she wasn't disappointed, because with each stroke of his hand on her flesh, his fingers slid closer to the place she so desperately needed him to touch.

All thoughts of modesty, decency completely gone, Rose wriggled her bottom up, trying to get him to take his spanking further.

"Have you learned your lesson, Rose?" Jack asked, and she thought his voice sounded tight, desperate even.

Her soul had been possessed by lust, and so she said, "Not yet," knowing that his hand would come down on her again, harder this time, prolonging the delicious torture. "Touch me, Jack," she cried. "Touch me now."

His fingers slipped in and out of her, first one, then two. And then he found the hard nub of her arousal and the best orgasm of her life hit her like a tidal wave, pulling her under, making her gasp for air. She couldn't think, she could only feel. And everything she was feeling was so good, so pure, so real.

Sex had never been like this. It had never been so elemental. The naughty girl inside of her that had just come alive—exploded into a million pieces, was more like it—made a silent prayer to Jack to continue to sweep her up in his spell. She didn't want to have to think. She didn't want to wake up from this moment and be afraid. Of everything that she'd learned to be afraid of when it came to men. And sex.

Fortunately Jack seemed to have ESP, because without pause he repositioned them both so that Rose's back was pressed against the softness of the cushions on the suede couch. Her skirt was bunched up around her waist and one of her nipples had popped out of the bodice of her dress.

Somewhere in the back of her brain she knew that under any other circumstances she would have been horrified by her behavior. But nothing since the moment she'd laid eyes on Jack could be considered normal. "Magical" was the only word for it.

Suddenly Rose believed in all the wonderful, mysterious things the accountant in her had been trained to deny.

ॐ ॐ ॐ

JACK HAD NEVER BELIEVED IN LOVE at first sight. Or, rather, at first orgasm. But when Rose fell apart across his lap, her sweet, juicy ass red from his handprint, her cunt so wet from her arousal, he could have sworn that something inside him had been about to burst too. Something more than just his cock.

The thought of entering her was enough to send a huge spurt of pre-come into his boxer shorts. Still, the new emotion he was feeling toward this breathtaking woman he'd known less than thirty minutes colored everything in a new light.

Right now lust took precedence, and he thrust aside all thoughts of tender emotions. He wanted to watch Rose come all over again, on his fingers, on his tongue, as he slipped inside her wet heat. But first, he wanted to taste her.

Over the years he'd developed his palate to the point where he could detect the slightest nuance of flavor. A hint of rosemary. A touch of virgin olive oil. A dusting of lemon.

Jack knew without a doubt that Rose would be sweet. So sweet.

Jack wanted to stare at Rose, lying so provocatively on the couch gazing up at him, forever. But he couldn't resist leaning down and kissing her forehead, her cheek, her chin. He dipped into her mouth. His tongue mated with hers, and he couldn't keep from pressing against her. She groaned as his hard-on pressed between her legs.

"I'm too heavy for you," he said, trying to force himself to leave her softness. It would kill him, but he was man enough to do it.

"No. God no," she said as her fingers dug into his hips. She pulled him against her, and even though he hadn't so much as taken off his belt, his cock settled deeply against her. "You feel perfect." Something flashed in her eyes, and then she placed his hand on the perfect rosy nipple that had escaped her dress during her much-deserved spanking. "This feels perfect."

Jack ran his thumb over the tightly budding point, and her eyes fluttered closed.

She hadn't seen perfect yet.

Jack nibbled on her earlobe, and she pressed her breast into his palm, her cunt into his cotton-covered cock. His words were barely a whisper. "I want you to keep your eyes closed," he said. Rose bit her bottom lip as if she was trying to decide whether to agree with him or not.

"No matter what happens, no matter what I do to you, do not open your eyes."

As if to emphasize his words—and the threat of sweet punishment that lay behind them—he bent his head down and gently raked his teeth over her nipple at the exact moment that he slid two fingers deep within her.

She cried out and bucked into his hand, into his mouth. Jack sucked at her, his tongue swirling hard, tight circles around her areola. Her muscles tightened around his fingers. She was so responsive, so ready for every touch, every kiss.

His thumb found her clit and it was hard again, ready for the slightest pressure to send her over the edge. But this time, he had to have her in his mouth. With the quick movements that he had honed after so many years of multitasking in the kitchen, he slid down until he was looking at the most gorgeous pussy in creation. But there would be time to admire the work of art lying beneath him later.

Jack would have liked to have been the kind of man who could put off his own pleasure for hours.

But he wasn't.

He'd always been a fan of quick and dirty—in and out of the kitchen. He specialized in recipes that made it seem as if he'd spent hours in the kitchen while in reality he'd only been working on the dish for ten minutes. Sex was no different. Why waste time with slow caresses and softness when hard, fast, down-and-dirty sex would feel so much better?

Later there'd be time for lengthy explorations, for drawn-out caresses.

Right now he needed to take the simple and direct approach. Screw Rose's brains out, plunge heavy and hard into her wetness, stretch her wide with his cock.

His mouth covered her clit and he groaned as her essence filled him. She was even sweeter than he'd imagined. He lightly flicked his tongue over her clit while his fingers moved up and down her plump lips, into her tight, perfect vagina.

On a scream she threaded her hands through his hair and pushed him into her as she rocked in a rhythm of pleasure.

Rose's eyes were still closed—good girl—and in an instant his pants were off and he'd rolled on a condom. He entered her, and she was so tight he only got in an inch before he had to pull out. He had all the staying power of a horny fourteen-year-old.

Her eyes shot open, and she opened her mouth to say something.

She was a very bad girl. And since he needed a moment to cool off, he put a note of sensual warning in his voice. "What did I say about opening your eyes?"

She quickly shut them and tried to pull him into her again, but much to his surprise, Jack found that he was having too much fun with their game. And he knew that she was having as good a time. Through sheer strength of will he forced himself to delay his own orgasm for a few more minutes.

"I have no choice," he said. "I'm going to have to punish you, Rose. Again."

A flush moved up her chest, across her cheeks. He wondered if he was pushing her too far. If she'd grown tired of their game and thought that he'd crossed the line from kink to freak. But then the corner of her mouth quirked up, the tiniest bit. It was enough to let him know that she wanted the punishment as much as he wanted to give it.

"Turn over," he instructed, and she slowly obeyed his request. He put his hands on her hip bones and pulled her ass up toward him. "I want you on your hands and knees," he said as her full breasts pressed into the arm of the couch.

Her pretty red dress had fallen back down over her hips, and he slowly, deliberately pushed the silky material up her thighs. She shivered as his fingertips ran sensual patterns over her skin.

"Are your eyes closed?" he said in a low voice.

"Yes," she whispered, and he loved the anticipation in her voice as she wondered what he was going to do to her.

Her dress up around her waist again, Jack stared at her pink, slick perfection. She was so beautiful. So perfect.

He reared up behind her, the tip of his cock no more than an inch from her opening.

"Do you want to feel me inside you?" he asked.

"Yes," she said, the word shaky with need.

"I'm right here, Rose. You just need to find me."

It took every ounce of control he possessed to keep from ramming into her, to hold himself back from taking what she was offering him.

Unsure of what he was asking, she said, "I don't know what you—" but he wouldn't let her finish.

"My cock. It's right where you want it."

Her movements uncertain, she wiggled her rear end backward. He couldn't help it: He pressed the tip of his cock up against her vulva.

She gasped and pressed herself into him, as if she wanted to swallow him whole. He forced himself to pull away. He was punishing her, wasn't he? He couldn't make it that easy for her. But as his cock strained toward her, he wondered who he was really punishing.

"Go slow, Rose," he instructed her. "Take me in one inch at a time."

She was panting now as she moved her sweet pussy, framed by her rosy butt cheeks, toward his throbbing cock one slow centimeter at a time.

And then she found him.

"Rose," he groaned, unable to keep her name in his throat as she swallowed his head. "You're so tight."

He could hear the smile in her voice, the satisfaction as she said, "I know."

She waited there, squeezing his cock with strong muscles, and his hands found her large breasts, squeezing, kneading them in the same rhythm that she milked him.

Sweat coated his chest beneath his shirt as he forced himself not to plunge into her as far, as fast, as he possibly could. What the hell was she waiting for?

And then he realized what was going on. She had turned the game around on him. She wasn't going to do one more thing, make one more movement, unless he told her to. Even though she knew damn well that he was dying to ram into her. Dying to come.

Sweet Lord, Rose was going to be the death of him.

"Another inch," he ground out.

Rose complied, thank God, but as he slid into her, everything in him rejected his initial plan to go one slow inch at a time. He wasn't strong enough to hold out another second.

He gripped her hips with his hands and pushed all the way into her sweet pussy. She gasped and bucked into him, and everything Jack ever thought he knew about sex became irrelevant.

Rose was the teacher and he was the student.

She took everything he gave and milked him in firm strokes. He curled his body over hers and found the back of her neck, where her curls had fallen away, with his teeth. Branding her with his mouth, he exploded in an orgasm stronger than any he'd ever experienced. Her breasts filled his hands again, and he gave himself up to the woman he'd been waiting for all his life.

Rose.

4

*S*HOCKED" WAS THE ONLY WORD to describe her state of mind.

Actually, if Rose could have managed to pull her brain out of its orgasmic fog, she could probably have come up with a few others. Like "ecstatic." Or "euphoric."

Both of which brought her right back to "shocked."

Had she really done all of those spectacularly dirty things with a man she'd just met? A gorgeous, Napa Valley chef, no less?

Rose waited to wake up. Usually, she woke from her hot dreams before the kiss, definitely before the orgasm. This had to be a first: Her subconscious had let her go all the way.

"Hungry?" Jack said as he kissed the back of her neck one more time, then slid out of her and sat back on the couch.

Funny, her dreams had never been quite so lifelike before.

She readjusted from her spread-eagle-on-her-knees position on the couch so that she was sitting in the opposite corner from Jack. She popped both of her breasts back into the built-in cups in the bodice of her dress and pulled her skirt back down to cover her thighs.

Rose knew she should have been embarrassed by what had just happened. She should have slapped Jack's face. Told him she wasn't that kind of girl. Instead, to her continuing surprise, she grinned and said, "Starved."

When Jack smiled back at her, his eyes holding hers several moments too long, she knew that her wild, sex-crazed romp must be messing with her head in a big way. Especially if she was imagining that Jack wanted anything more than a quick roll.

So, even though she was certain that she'd enjoy tonight's cooking lesson—and that she'd be happy to take whatever else Jack offered her by way of cooking lessons and, hopefully, hot sex for the next two days—she needed to tread cautiously.

Because if she wasn't careful, if she let great sex delude her into thinking that Jack felt anything real for her, she'd end up with something much worse than five chocolate-chip-cookie pounds on her hips.

She'd end up with a broken heart. And getting dumped twice in one week was a record she didn't care to make.

Jack didn't remind her of anyone in her past who'd hurt her. Quite the opposite, in fact, given that he was far better looking, far more successful, far better at giving her pleasure than any ex-boyfriend ever had. Which almost made her situation scarier. Because if so many losers had dumped her, what would a man like this do if she gave in and let herself fall for him beyond a one-night stand?

Trying to focus on food, rather than Jack's mouthwateringly sexy features, she asked, "What are we making?"

Jack looked worried. "I should probably be honest with you. . . ." He paused way too long for Rose's comfort.

Oh no, she was thirty seconds too late in preserving her dignity. Here it came: *You're really great and I'd love to teach you to cook, but now that we're done having raunchy sex I need to get back to work.*

Rose took a deep breath. Why couldn't the fairy tale ever work out for her? Would it kill the man upstairs to give her one full night with Jack? Five or six hours of blissful sex, food, and time spent with someone wonderful?

But no. All she got was a quick spanking and sex on the couch. Not that she was complaining about the sex, of course. It had been wonderful. And the spontaneous spanking had been amazing. Too bad it had felt like an appetizer. And she was being sent home before the main course.

She swallowed back angry tears. She was sick to death of being patted on the head like a little girl, of being told she was second, third, fourth best. Channeling her inner Vanessa, she raised her hand, not allowing him to finish his sentence.

"I already know what you're going to say," she said, trying to keep her stupid voice from trembling, "so you can save your breath. It was a pleasure meeting you, Jack. And I'm sure your food is wonderful, but I've really got to get back to my friends now."

She stood up with as much dignity as she possessed, hoping she didn't look too wrinkled and messy from all the wild sex. She took a step toward the door, only to stop dead in her tracks at Jack's loud curse.

"Don't let me screw this up, Rose." He looked up at her, his green eyes full of something that made Rose's stomach flutter. "I had planned to do the lessons at the restaurant. But then the tourist ended up being you and I forgot all about food. I don't have anything prepared here and we're gonna have to wing it."

Rose gaped at Jack. She didn't want him to stop talking. Every word out of his mouth was better than chocolate. Especially the part where he said she made him forget all about food. That had to be a pretty big statement for a chef, didn't it?

"I'd really like to make it up to you," he said, and Rose brushed her hair away from her eyes to get a better look at the miracle that was taking place right in front of her.

"You want to make it up to me?" she said in disbelief.

Hope flared in Jack's eyes, along with more than a little unsated lust. "If you'll let me."

The corner of her mouth quirked up. He wasn't kicking her out. He wanted to make this evening really special after all. She made a silent apology to you-know-who. Next Sunday she'd go to church and grovel in person. Rose had never before been in the position of power with a man. Some devilish imp she'd never known to exist inside her prodded her to take advantage of it.

"Okay," she said, trying to act as if she wasn't quite convinced. "I suppose I can give you another chance." Was that really her saying those words in that teasing, sexy tone? Who knew it could be so fun having the upper hand with a man? No wonder Vanessa was always jerking her dates around. The power was heady, sensual.

A surefire aphrodisiac.

Pitching her voice low and sexy, she put one hand on her hip and said, "So, what's on the new menu, Chef?" forcing him to think fast. Or else.

"We're going to spend the weekend on a menu of . . ." He let his words fall away and came to stand before her. His lips a breath away from hers, he finished his sentence. ". . . aphrodisiacs."

Hot damn, Rose thought as he took her lips in a passionate kiss. He really does have that ESP thing down.

JACK HANDED ROSE a red-and-white striped apron. "I hate to cover all that gorgeous skin up," he said, "but cooking can be dirty business."

"What," she said, as she pulled the apron over her head and began to tighten the ties at the waist, "you aren't just going to lick the food off me?"

Jack threw his head back and laughed. The confident Rose seemed to be back to stay. So many times since that first moment he'd seen her standing in the bar, he'd felt her uncertainty and had wanted to kiss it out of her. Yes, she'd had wild, fantastically dirty sex with him, but that didn't change who she was at her core. His instincts told him that Rose was special and he needed to treat her with great care. Or else she'd bolt before they could explore the massive sparks that exploded between them.

His instincts also told him that beneath her quiet exterior was a sexpot just dying to emerge. And he was the man who was going to show her the woman she really was.

He undid the ties on her apron and pulled her against him. "Good idea."

Her stomach growled, and she laughed as she smacked his hands away. "Seriously, you need to feed me and quick."

Jack reluctantly let go of her and turned back to his cupboards, opening up each door, one by one. Finally, he pulled out a bar of bittersweet Scharffen Berger chocolate.

Rose leaned her elbows on the counter and sighed dramatically. "Even I know that chocolate is an aphrodisiac. I thought you were going to surprise me with something like chestnuts. Or watercress."

"Chocolate's an oldie but a goodie. Bet you didn't know that chocolate contains more antioxidants than red wine, did you?"

Rose choked on a laugh. "Can't sentiments like that get you lynched in the wine country? Last I heard, red wine was curing cancer and creating world peace."

Jack held a finger up to his lips. "I'll be safe, just as long as you keep that little tidbit strictly between you and me."

"Okay, but on one condition."

Jack raised an eyebrow. "You're quite bossy for a student, you know."

Rose's smile could have lit up the entire studio without any electricity. "You really think I'm bossy?"

"In a good way," he clarified, but she was already waving away his answer.

"How exciting," she said softly, and then she added, "I'll keep your secret for a glass of red wine."

"Bossy and easy too," Jack teased as he grabbed a bottle of excellent Pinot Noir from the wine refrigerator beneath the marble island. He deftly uncorked it and poured a glass for Rose, sliding it across the island without spilling a drop.

"Much as I love chocolate," Rose said, tapping the bittersweet chocolate bar with her index finger, "I hope we're not skipping the meal and going straight to dessert. I'm going to need real sustenance to keep up my energy."

Jack dearly wanted to keep her "energy" up, so he dumped his plan for a sensual chocolate dessert and scanned the recipe archive in his brain.

"We're making bittersweet chocolate ravioli."

Rose took a sip of Pinot and licked a drop off her lower lip. Jack couldn't take his eyes off that beautiful patch of skin, couldn't stop remembering how good her mouth had tasted.

"I'm sensing a theme here," she said. "Chocolate martinis, chocolate ravioli. If I didn't know better, I'd think you were either trying to fatten me up or make me h—" She blushed and took a large gulp of wine.

"What was that last word?" he asked in as offhand way as he could manage, even though he was about three seconds from taking her again, rough and fast, on the cold cement floor.

Her whispered word, "Horny," might as well have been a

mouth wrapped around his penis, considering the way his cock grew in his pants.

Okay, he was never going to make it through this meal if he didn't focus. So instead of responding in the way he wanted to—ripping off her apron and dress and driving into her again and again until they both exploded all over again—Jack opened the refrigerator and stuck his head in.

The cool air didn't come close to bringing his temperature down. Somehow, he didn't think anything could when Rose was in the same room.

Willing his synapses to fire, he reached for Grade A organic ground beef and a couple of eggs. Shoving his raging libido down as best he could, he pulled sugar, cocoa powder, baking soda, salt, and flour out of his pantry.

"I hope this doesn't come across as insulting," Rose said after a few moments had passed, "but is this actually going to taste good?"

Jack turned around and looked at the ingredients spread across the island. He had to admit, from a layman's perspective the idea of mixing bittersweet chocolate with ground beef and the onion he'd grabbed from the drawer to his left was fairly odd. Not quite disgusting, but definitely on the verge.

Fortunately, Jack had a little magic up his sleeve, in the form of twenty years of culinary experiments. Some bad, some good, some amazing, some vomit-worthy. At the Cordon Bleu they'd thrown worse situations than this at him. Fish and orange marmalade. Soy sauce and cake batter.

Fortunately, he had a feeling that tonight's off-the-cuff recipe was going to be a good one. Who knew, maybe he'd add it to the menu at Gerard's. In honor of Rose, of course. He already knew what he'd call it.

"Rose's Chocolate Ravioli," he said, thinking out loud.

Rose sucked in a breath, loud enough that he could hear her. "Is that what this recipe is really called?"

He smiled into her blue eyes. "It is now."

She looked shy and unsure and overwhelmed, so he said, "Get off that gorgeous bottom of yours. It's time for my student to get to work." He threw her a chef's hat, which she caught with a rather bemused expression.

One sip of wine later, she stuffed her hair into the silly hat, got up from the stool she'd been sitting on, and soaped up her hands beneath a chrome faucet.

"Lay it on me, Chef."

TWO HOURS LATER ROSE LOOKED UP from her empty plate into Jack's eyes. It had been a truly perfect night. One she didn't want to end. He'd patiently shown her not only how to make pasta—chocolate pasta, no less!—but also how to look beyond the numbers and details in a recipe to what her senses were telling her. For Rose, listening to his lesson on the art of tasting was like looking inside his soul. And it was a glimpse of beauty. She'd never dreamed of meeting a man like this. One who not only encouraged her to eat but who was also teaching her how. One who was aware of all the little things, of the small pleasures.

Food had always been the enemy. The one time she'd actually let herself enjoy a meal in front of Elliot, he'd made a barely veiled comment about the size of her butt. Scratch that. He'd come right out and said, "I don't think your ass really needs all that pasta, do you?" Rose was so used to hearing comments like that from both boyfriends and family (especially her painfully svelte mother) that she hadn't considered dumping him. Instead she'd forgone pasta to try to keep him by her side.

But after Jack had taught her how to hand-roll ravioli, after they'd sat with a glass of wine while it had boiled and Jack had kept her laughing with hilarious stories about working in a restaurant kitchen, after he'd so lovingly fed her succulent bites of pasta from his own fork, Rose found herself looking at food in a new light. She'd never enjoyed a meal more, and yet she had a sense that one of her frozen Weight Watchers meals would have done more damage.

Jack looked at their empty plates, their empty glasses. "Did you enjoy your lesson?"

"So much, Jack. It was wonderful. My friends will be amazed when I make this for them."

"Have I convinced you to stick around for another lesson or two?"

His question was teasing, but underneath she sensed the slightest bit of anxiety. That small hint of worry was more endearing than any smooth line could be.

Of course she wanted to spend the weekend with him. When was the last time he'd looked in the mirror? But it was more than his fantastic, dark good looks that made her want to be with him. He was charming, funny, warm, interesting.

Wonderful.

He was also fun to tease, however, so she made a big show of putting her hand on her chin and staring up at the planks of pickled pine on the ceiling of the warehouse. "That depends," she finally said, expecting Jack to know she was just playing around, "on what we make for dessert. I don't think I'll be able to really make up my mind until then."

She looked up at him, lapping up his gorgeous smile, which told her he was going to play along as he cleared their plates over to the sink, which was surrounded with dirty bowls and baking sheets.

"You're right," he said, and she let the warmth of his voice fill her to the brim. "Everything hinges on dessert. And the only way I can truly do the dessert lesson justice is at my house. In my kitchen."

She had a vision of waking up in Jack's bed after a night of ravenous lovemaking and had to remind herself that he was only taking her to his house to make dessert. Not because he was planning on doing her in every room. After all, he hadn't so much as kissed her since they began dinner preparations. The quickie on the couch might have been an accident, right?

But damn it, she thought, hadn't she already spent thirty years being prudent? And for what? She wasn't married. She didn't have the children she longed for. Or the love she'd dreamed of for so long. She'd been given this night with Jack. And she was going to squeeze every last ounce of life—and pleasure—out of it.

Choosing her words carefully, she said, "I'd love to see your kitchen, Jack," all the while hoping that it was only a short walk to the bedroom.

5

ACK HELD ROSE'S HAND as they walked the three blocks
through Napa vineyards to his charming shingled house, complete with a porch swing out front and a view of the vines from
nearly every room. The night was dark, the moon barely peeking
out from behind the clouds, but even if she'd been blind she
would have known she was in the wine country. Her senses had
come alive in Jack's studio kitchen, and now she took in the
heady scent of the growing grapes cooling after a hot summer
day, the fragrant dirt beneath them.

It was as if wine was being pumped into the air all around
them. And she was getting drunk without taking a sip.

Jack held open his front door. He flipped the lights on as she
walked into the foyer. As she rounded the corner into his living
room, Rose finally knew what home felt like.

It was full of soft, comfortable chairs and sofas, the kind you
could flop down on after a hard day. The myriad piles of cooking
magazines and hardcover cookbooks made her fingers itch to
settle in for the night and flip through the glossy pictures.

"Your house is beautiful," she said, taking in the paintings and the colorful walls. His hand warmed the small of her back as he steered her into the kitchen. She stopped in surprise.

"I hope you're not disappointed," he said.

"No, of course not. I was just expecting—"

"Stainless steel and granite and butcher block and the latest of everything? Sub-Zero refrigerators and a Cuisinart on every counter?"

She laughed. "You caught me. I thought I had you all figured out."

"I learned to cook in my grandmother's kitchen. It was barely as big as my foyer. But everything I loved was in there. My grandmother. My mother, when she wasn't busy with one of my younger brothers or sisters. And all those meals that made me who I am. I remember when the Realtor showed me this house. She didn't want me to see the kitchen. She said I could rip everything out, modernize it. But as soon as I laid eyes on it, I saw my grandmother holding me up at the sink, helping me wash my hands. It was already perfect. Red Formica, faux-wood-paneled cupboard doors, and linoleum floors may not be everyone's cup of tea. But they work for me."

Standing in Jack's kitchen, listening to him talk about his grandmother, pushed Rose over the edge of reason. She was falling for him. How could she not?

"They work for me too," she said in a husky voice, and the next thing she knew she was in his arms and he was carrying her out of the kitchen, down a dimly lit hallway.

Straight to his bed.

His mouth was on hers and she was devouring him like she'd devoured the chocolate ravioli. His kiss was sweeter than any dessert, and she nearly laughed out loud. If she could patent the sex-with-Jack-Gerard diet, she'd make a killing. But she'd rather be dirt poor than share this man with any other woman.

Just the thought of Jack kissing someone else like he was kissing her, running his hand down another woman's stomach until his fingertips found the band of her panties, made her so angry that she growled her jealousy into his throat.

For thirty years she'd followed a safe, timid, quiet path. But something about Jack—everything about him—brought out a side to her that she never knew existed. A savage, reckless, sensual woman that was dying to do naughty, wicked things to a beautiful man.

And if there was one thing she'd already learned tonight, it was that timid was overrated.

Naughty wasn't.

A new self-confidence surged through her, and she flipped them over so Jack was lying beneath her. Before she could think, before she could stop and realize that she wasn't behaving like herself at all, she grabbed both his wrists tightly between her hands and pulled them above his head.

"You're mine tonight," she said, her voice raw and unsteady, full of the need to show him all the reasons why she was the only woman he'd ever want, ever again.

"Take my dress off," she ordered, briefly moving her hands from his wrists. Smart man that he was, he quickly complied, pulling the soft red cotton up past her hips, past her breasts. She wiggled her shoulders as he pulled the dress up, then over her head. Shaking her hair free, she reveled in being completely naked as she straddled Jack's shirt-clad chest. Taking the dress from him, she quickly bound his wrists to the iron bed frame.

She'd never been so blatantly kinky with any man, but Rose knew that every move she was making was perfectly right.

♔ ♔ ♔

JESUS, HE COULDN'T BELIEVE ROSE had tied his wrists to his bed with her dress. He'd always had to hold back his insatiable sexual appetite when he was with a women, but tonight, with Rose, he was being given free reign to every fantasy.

First, spanking. Now, bondage.

What made it even better was the fact that this little game was Rose's idea. Not his. Then again, now that he thought about it, maybe the spanking had been her idea too. She had goaded him into making good on his threat, hadn't she?

He was amazed by Rose. Because even though they hadn't talked about their pasts, he had a feeling that relationships, and men, had been hard on her.

For the first time since his first real girlfriend, Jack felt completely at ease during sex. She'd broken up with him for some wonder-bread rich boy after telling Jack that he was too rough, too dirty, that he didn't know how to treat a real woman.

Tonight, he was finally able to let the down-and-dirty Jack emerge. All because Rose, beautiful, lush, Rose, was having her naughty way with him.

Her teeth nipped at the corner where his upper and lower lips met. He groaned his pleasure, knowing he could give in to his every carnal, uncivilized urge.

Her teeth worked their way down his body, grazing the sensitive skin on his neck. Deftly, she unbuttoned his shirt, running her smooth fingertips over his tanned skin, her teeth stopping at his taut nipples, her tongue dipping into the concave lines on his abdomen.

She pulled his shirt from the waistband of his pants, made quick work of his belt, the button on his slacks, his zipper. She spread open the fly on his pants and then her lush, wet mouth was on the cotton of his boxers and she was sucking his cock into her mouth through the soft fabric.

Too soon, her mouth was gone, but her fingers were back, reaching into the flap in his boxers, setting his shaft free.

With every bite, with every lash of her tongue on his skin, Jack felt his cock grow bigger. He was so ready, on the verge of begging Rose to take him in her mouth again.

But she was one step ahead of him, running a finger down the hard length of his penis. "You're so big," she said, and he grew at least another inch. She dipped her head down to lightly flick the small hole at the tip of his head with her tongue.

"So hard," she said, gripping his shaft with her hand, running it up and down him so slowly that he practically shot in her fist.

"So hot," she breathed right before her mouth came down on him, soft and silky. He bucked into her, not caring about anything but his fierce need to come in her sweet mouth.

Her fingers reached around to cup his balls, and she gently squeezed them in time to the circular movements of her tongue on him.

One more suck, one more squeeze, one more lick, and he was gone.

"Rose," he groaned, and in that moment everything went black. The pleasure of being blown by this woman was more intense than anything he'd ever experienced. No chocolate cake, no apple pie had ever been this sweet.

Again and again his cock convulsed in her mouth. His hips pounded into her, into the bed, then back into those plump, rosy lips. He'd never come like this before, like it wouldn't stop, like every second in Rose's mouth made him harder, not softer. And then her hands were on his balls again, and one of her fingers found that sensitive spot behind his penis, and her teeth were raking his skin just enough that he grew harder still. She stopped sucking, but her tongue continued to sweep up and down his length, cleaning him off, readying him to explode all over again.

"Rose, I—" he started to say, wanting to tell her that he'd never, not once in the thirty-six years he'd been alive, had two orgasms so close together. Even in the best of circumstances he'd needed ten minutes to recover. Considering it was Rose, he'd cut it to five, but ten seconds was ridiculous. It was impossible. It was—

His brain shut down completely as the volcano started at the base of his cock and rose all the way up, slowly taking him over in a way that he hadn't known existed. He pulsed into her mouth, hardly able to believe how intense this second orgasm was, so close on the heels of the first in Rose's tight, wet, sucking mouth.

"Please," he said as he tugged at the bindings at his wrists, "I need to touch you."

He'd never thought to hear the sound of his own voice begging, in his own bed, but there it was, desperate and rough. Rose let one of his hands slip free, and he found the wetness between her legs, the hard nub of her arousal, her pussy lips so wet and plump. She shifted her body so that his hand had better access to her cunt, and he slipped one finger into her, then two. Her muscles tightened on him and she groaned, her sweat-slicked body rubbing against him.

Just when he thought she was going to come, just as he was waiting for the glorious pressure of her pussy coming down on his fingers, she moved off of him. He laid back, secure in the knowledge that Rose had a plan. And he couldn't wait to find out what it was. Especially when it took every ounce of control to keep from pulling his second wrist loose and rolling her beneath him.

She rummaged in his bedside table and he smiled, knowing, hoping, praying that she'd found a condom and was going to roll it onto him. A soft rip and her fingers were on him again, rolling the latex down. She settled her knees on either side of his hips and he was inside her and it was even better this time. Even tighter. Even hotter.

He tried to think about something other than his own throbbing cock. He tried to think about finding her clit with his finger. He tried to remember to suck her nipples into his mouth.

Somehow he managed to hold off from coming again until Rose's gasp filled the air, followed by a small scream of pleasure.

Her sweet cunt clamped down on him and he was lost to everything but the primal, elemental need to thrust in and out of her wetness. Roaring from the eruption that seemed to be starting at the tips of his fingers, his toes, Jack pulled her face down and kissed her hard. As hard as he'd ever kissed a woman. And still, as he pushed inside her, he wasn't close enough.

Moments later, he was gathering her in his arms, her warm, soft, exhausted body curling into his chest, her hair brushing his earlobe. He pulled the duvet over them and they slept.

6

*W*ARM. HAPPY. SEXY.

Lying in the crook of Jack's arm, her thigh over his, Rose didn't want to open her eyes. Last night had been so magical, so perfect. She wanted nothing more than a thousand more nights just like it. But light streamed in Jack's white-paned window. A mockingbird ran through its playlist of songs, each sounding more desperate than the next, mirroring the worries in Rose's heart.

She didn't want to open her eyes to a man who, in the harsh light of morning, might look at her and realize that last night had been nothing but smoke and mirrors.

Nothing more than a sexual fantasy that they had played out with each other.

Holding her breath, she slid out from under Jack's tanned, muscular arm. He stirred in his sleep and pulled her tightly against the hard planes of his body.

Rose went perfectly still. Jack's chest rose and fell in an even pattern, and his face was relaxed, with none of the animation it had when he was demonstrating how to sauté onions in white wine but all of the beauty.

Okay, she needed to try to sneak out of bed again. Only this time, she needed to move quicker. On three, she'd slip out and be dressed and gone before Jack noticed.

One. Two. Thr—

A large hand cupped her bottom. "Bread."

Rose gasped in surprise at Jack's quick movements, as well as the fact that he had woken up from a deep sleep to talk about dreaded carbs.

His eyelids opened, and his vivid green eyes smiled down at Rose's gaping mouth. "Let's make bread," he said, and it was all she could do to nod.

Especially when he added, "I've just got one thing to take care of first," then proceeded to disappear beneath the covers and show her that he was, indeed, a master when it came to tasting things slowly, deliberately, and thoroughly.

FEELING MORE THAN A LITTLE NAUGHTY, Rose put on one of the aprons hanging on a hook beside Jack's fridge. She didn't have any clean clothes with her, so she was wearing one of Jack's T-shirts. It covered her from her neck to her knees, but with the worn cotton sliding against her naked breasts and thighs, she felt sexier than if she'd been wearing the most seductive lingerie.

She couldn't remember the last time she hadn't strapped herself into one of her chest compressors the minute she'd gotten out of bed. Jack, who was shooting her chest lusty glances from inside the pantry, where they were gathering ingredients, liked her free-swinging boobs quite a bit.

Underwear was overrated. Rather than waste all that time searching for the perfect undergarment in Victoria's Secret, she could be spending her time having sex. Naughty, perfect sex.

Her nipples hardened beneath Jack's T-shirt and apron, and when she looked up from her musings, the look on his face snatched her breath. His gaze locked on her tight, aching, cotton-covered nipples.

Giggling, Rose marveled at how perfect and sexy Jack made her feel. Like she was at least as capable of turning a guy on as a size two was. She pointed to the top shelf of the walk-in pantry and said, "I think I need some help reaching the honey."

She'd never played the helpless female card in all her thirty years. As a top-earning accountant who could take care of her own bills with her paycheck and could take care of her own orgasms with an array of mail-order dildos, she'd never needed to.

Then again, she'd never had wild and raunchy sex with a gorgeous stranger minutes after saying hello, either.

Jack narrowed his eyes, but he didn't argue. Instead he pressed himself up against her, his front to her back, his hard, thick cock pressing against her soft, round ass. As he reached up for the bottle of honey, his breath tickled her ear as he said, "In medieval times, seducers would ply their lovers with a fermented drink made with honey."

Instinctively, Rose shifted her bottom into Jack's hard-on. His hand slipped under the hem of her T-shirt, and she held her breath as she waited for his wonderfully calloused finger to find her clitoris. He was close, so close, and she was soaked and ready for his touch. Ready to come again even though he'd just thoroughly laved her with his tongue beneath the sheets.

When his finger finally found her, it was sticky.

With honey. Another aphrodisiac.

She moaned as she pressed her face into a bag of lemons, her behind into his huge penis, barely covered by boxers. She opened her legs wider, and he settled his thick shaft between her butt cheeks, while his fingers pressed soft, sticky circles against her clitoris.

"I can't wait, Rose." His voice was rough as he pressed his hips into her.

Moments later he was kneeling on the floor of the pantry, his face on her pussy, his lips on her clit, sucking and licking and devouring. Within seconds she was coming again. Hard. So hard she was screaming with pleasure.

Somewhere in the back of her consciousness she heard paper tear, and then he was pulling her down onto his lap and she was taking him in again. His shaft pressed deep into her cunt as she straddled his hips. She drove herself up and down, down and up on his glorious penis, taking him deeper than she'd ever thought possible, and yet it wasn't deep enough.

She couldn't get enough of this man.

This wonderful lover who gave her more than any woman had a right to expect.

Everything exploded, reds to blues to greens to blacks, as one orgasm morphed into the next. Jack was sucking her hard nipples through the soft cotton of his T-shirt, his hands playing with her oh-so-sensitive flesh beneath the fabric, and the friction of tongue on cotton on skin was delicious.

"Rose," Jack said in a husky voice that Rose could have sworn was filled with wonder, "you're incredible."

Exhausted from her three orgasms that morning—so far, anyway—she couldn't so much as manage a thank-you. Her stomach rumbled loudly and broke the spell. Pulling her head off Jack's broad shoulder, she took a page from Jack's book and said, in a repeat of his performance that morning in bed, "Bread."

He grinned, and she marveled yet again at how one minute she was mating with Jack like their bodies had been created for one another, and the next they were smiling and laughing, like she would with her girlfriends.

Only Carrie and Vanessa had never made jokes with a nine-inch cock buried in her. That crazy thought gave Rose a fit of giggles.

"What's so funny?" Jack said, but Rose was laughing too hard to tell him, and soon he joined in. Together they laughed at nothing on the floor of his pantry, their bodies still entwined, the erotic art of bread-making forgotten.

"GOOD THING I DIDN'T MEET YOU in cooking school," Jack mused fifteen minutes later as he watched Rose sprinkle yeast and sugar over warm water in a small bowl before stirring them together. They were finally getting started with today's buttermilk-honey bread recipe.

"If you'd been around to tempt me, I wouldn't have made it past Introduction to Dishwashing."

Following his directions, Rose moved slightly to her right to combine buttermilk, butter, honey, and the yeast mixture in a large bowl. "Are there any female instructors at the Cordon Bleu?" she asked, her voice all innocence as she added salt and flour and concentrated on whisking.

Jack raised an eyebrow, wondering where she was going with her question. "Of course."

She shrugged, and in that straightforward manner that never failed to turn him on, said, "In that case you could have slept your way to an A."

He grinned as she added the remaining flour a half cup at a time. When she reached for the wooden spoon to beat the dough with, he reached for her. "You're the only one who's ever figured out my secret to a diploma with honors."

He bent his head down to capture her sweet, naturally red lips. He licked at the spot of flour in the corner of her lower lip, then moved in, his tongue slipping against hers, sliding into her mouth, his lips hard, then soft, on hers.

"You taste like honey," he said, "everywhere." He could feel her blush without having to see it. Rose, perfect, lush Rose, was a continual contradiction. Capable of whipping him into a sexual frenzy one moment, skewering him with her smart mouth the next. Looking so uncertain and self-conscious in her sexy red dress, only to tie him to the bed with it hours later.

But much as he wanted to sweep everything off the kitchen counter and make love to Rose, they needed to get the bread in the oven before the next millennium. Reluctantly, he pulled back from her beautiful, flushed face.

"Five more minutes of work to do, and then we let it rise for an hour."

Turning back to the island in perfect understanding, Rose reached for the dough. He covered her hands with his own, his body cupping hers just as they had in the pantry, on the couch the previous night. He tried to ignore his raging hard-on. "Kneading dough is an art." His hands pressed into her fingers, her knuckles. The dough responded beneath their combined touch, becoming smooth and satiny.

"I think I'm a natural." Rose's voice filled with surprise and what he hoped was a large dose of happiness.

"You are."

She was a natural at everything. He'd been amazed by how quickly she'd caught on during both cooking lessons. She had a great sense for proportion, an instinct for what flavors would meld well. And a great appreciation for the finished product.

He couldn't get away from the emotions coming on stronger and stronger with every passing moment. Even more amazing was the fact that he didn't want to.

Over the years he'd gone to bed with many women. Women

he'd picked up in a bar. Women who had happily followed him home after a late night at Gerard's. But Rose was different. Quick to laugh, incredibly bright and capable, yet so soft and welcoming.

Why would any man in his right mind try to resist a woman who was this quick to laugh? Who was so much softer, warmer, than any other woman he'd ever been with.

Rose was utterly irresistible.

She placed the dough in a greased bowl, carefully oiled the top, and covered it with plastic wrap. She carried the bowl to the window to rise and placed it on the sill. Jack stopped breathing as a ray of light illuminated her.

He couldn't deny what he knew with a bone-deep certainty: He'd found the woman he was supposed to spend the rest of his life with.

It was strange. He'd always been an impulsive guy, but never when it had come to love. The truth was, he'd never been in love before. He hadn't been looking for a wife, and he knew he should have been reeling at the thought of giving up life as a bachelor. Sure, he knew he should be thinking about details like jobs in two different cities, how being married would affect his work hours.

But he wasn't worried or anxious. And the reason was simple: Everything seemed right with Rose.

Now the only thing left was to make sure she felt the same way. Which meant it was time for seduction. Baking bread be damned.

7

Rose stood at the window, entranced by the vineyard outside. "Are these grapes yours?" He didn't answer and she turned to repeat her question, but the look on his face—a powerful mix of hope and desire—stopped the words in her throat.

Finally he spoke. "Yes, I own the land and the vines. Twenty acres are mine."

Rose wrapped her arms around herself. Jack's life—his restaurant, his vineyard, his perfect, cozy house—was like a dream that he was allowing her to share for the weekend. But since she knew she would wake up soon enough, she wanted to make the most of every second.

"Do we have time for a quick walk around your property?"

He grinned. "We sure do, gorgeous," he said, then disappeared down the hall.

Gorgeous. He'd called her gorgeous. She hugged herself tightly, hardly able to take it all in. No one had ever said such nice things about her before. When she added the emotion in his eyes into the equation, her stomach did a funny dance.

Saying good-bye to Jack on Sunday was going to be the hardest thing she'd ever have to do. But no matter how wonderful this weekend was, facts were facts. Come Monday morning, Jack would forget all about her. After all, he had a glamorous, celebrity life to go back to. She'd be nothing more to him than the memory of a round accountant who'd come like a desperate, sex-starved woman beneath him a dozen times.

Moments later he reappeared wearing a pair of worn blue jeans that hugged him in all the right places. Rose tried desperately to pull her eyes away from his six-pack. Sure, they'd had a boatload of sex, but until now she hadn't really gotten the chance to see Jack in all his glory.

One thing was for sure. If he hadn't been a supremely talented chef, he could have made his living modeling for *Playgirl*.

His words shook her ever so slightly out of her lust-filled haze. "I hope you don't mind wearing this."

He handed her a blue tank dress with a Hawaiian print on it. "My sister's bigger than you, but a couple of dresses that she left are all I've got."

Rose held the dress up by its straps. "I'm sure it will fit great," she said, praying it was true. *If the dress is too small I'm going to die,* she thought.

"I'll go change in the bathroom." She scurried off to a pretty yellow powder room behind the kitchen. Jack hadn't really seen her naked yet—just snippets of skin and body parts here and there—and Rose decided she'd rather keep it that way.

Fortunately, the blue tank dress fit. When she returned to the kitchen, Jack was gone, so she picked up the mud boots he'd left for her and carried them out to the porch. Slipping them on, she covered her eyes against the bright morning sun and scanned the property.

He stood silhouetted against the vine-covered hills, utterly a part of the land around him. Her heart stopped beating in her chest, growing too big, too full for her to handle. She was already in too deep, and she had to fight the urge to turn tail and run.

Away from Jack, away from his perfect house and his perfect grapevines.

Away from the sensuality that she couldn't resist.

Away from his chocolate brown eyes that seemed to see all the way into her heart.

But she was too slow, too indecisive. He turned, smiling broadly when he saw her. "I've got a surprise for you," he said, and she couldn't help but go to him. His pull over her was too strong to fight.

"You look good on my land," he said as he grabbed her hand. Rose swallowed the thrill that shot straight to the pit of her stomach.

She didn't know how to respond. "Okay then, can I move in?" would come off sounding desperate, rather than flirty. "I know," held a confidence she definitely didn't feel. "Thank you," wasn't the least bit witty. So she said nothing, silently lacing her fingers through his.

"These are Viognier grapes," he said, picking a small, green grape from the vines and popping it into her mouth. "What is your mouth telling you?"

"Sour," she said at first, but then she swallowed and was left with the opposite sensation. "And sweet," she said, surprised by the contradiction of the grape.

"Exactly," he said, looking pleased by her response. "I should have planted Cabernet Sauvignon and Chardonnay like everyone else, but I couldn't resist the challenge of the Viognier. It was my grandmother's favorite varietal. She used to say that drinking a young Viognier made her feel young again."

"That's wonderful that you're so close to your family," she said, wishing she had the same kind of memories, the same wonderful associations between the love she'd been given and the world around her. But her father had always worked late at his accounting firm, and her mother had watched TV to fill the void.

"How does your grandmother like your Viognier?" she asked, wanting to hear more about the wonderful woman who'd made such an impact on her grandson.

Jack bowed his head, as if he were studying the burned edges of the leaves that had fallen to the ground. "I wish I knew. She died the year of my first bottling."

"I'm so sorry," Rose said, squeezing his hand, cursing herself for bringing up a painful subject.

He looked up into her eyes, a small smile on his lips. "I named the wine after her. Viviana." He looked up at the blue, clear sky and said, "I'll bet she's looking down at us, delighted that the grapes are as much of a pain in the butt as she sometimes was. It's her fault that I've been fighting for these grapes, year after year."

She couldn't help but laugh at the wonderful, all-encompassing love in Jack's voice. Even when he was insulting his grandmother, the love shone through.

"You're laughing, but it's true," he insisted. "Viognier grapes aren't resistant to disease. They can't be picked too early or too late. I had to throw out every case of wine my second year because it was such god-awful swill. Unfortunately, I didn't figure that out until I served it to one of the top food critics in the country and she spit it out all over the rug in my living room."

Barely stifling a giggle, Rose said, "I take it you got good press out of that?"

Jack groaned. "Don't remind me," he said. And then, as if they weren't smack-dab in the middle of a conversation, he did the strangest thing. He stripped out of his jeans, and, naked save his mud boots, he went running through the vines.

Could her life get any weirder? Still, she couldn't resist following his gorgeous, streaking path up a small hill, straight to the most glorious swimming pool she'd ever seen.

With the most glorious naked man in all creation standing on the edge, waiting to dive in.

JACK WOULD HAVE NEVER THOUGHT of coming to the pool without Rose's help. But as soon as she'd said she wanted to go for a walk through his vineyard, he'd begun to visualize water sliding between them, caressing Rose's curves.

He'd been so caught up in this vision of their next erotic adventure that it had taken everything in him to speak coherently about his grapes. Fifty feet from the huge pool surrounded by grapevines, he'd torn his clothes off like a madman and jogged up to the water, then waited impatiently on the edge for Rose to join him.

Worst case, Rose would think he was a nutcase. Best case, she'd find his actions spontaneous and romantic.

He prayed for spontaneous as she came into view at the top of the pond. "Come here," he said, as he watched her take in his nakedness. Her eyes were wide, and he hoped she liked what she saw, because he was as erect as he was ever going to be.

Rose, sweet, delectable Rose, continued to be full of surprises. He barely had time to blink before she ripped off her dress and jumped into the water. A hand reached out for his ankle, and he was falling in. He sucked in a breath just before his head went under, and instead of coming up for air right away, he opened his eyes and reached out for Rose as she tried to swim away.

The sight of her spectacular breasts swaying so provocatively underwater, of the sweet curve of her ass wiggling side to side as she flutter-kicked undid him.

Jack had spent thirty-six years without Rose in his life. But he knew with every fiber of his being that he could not go another day without her.

Swimming naked in his pond with Rose wasn't the time or place to make declarations. He knew that. And yet, waiting another moment would have been too long.

They came up for air, and he stared across the blue water at her. Rose belonged to this place, to his home, to the vines and the kitchen and his bedroom. The bottom edge of her dark, shiny hair, barely straight even with the heavy weight of water on it, brushed against that spot on her collarbone she loved to have kissed. She was a goddess of the vines. A queen of the mountains that sheltered them, mountains that he wanted to explore with her, making love in the caves, beneath a pine tree, in a cool, clear stream.

He walked through the water to her, swimming when it grew too deep. And then she was in his arms, her legs wrapped around his waist.

He bent his head to kiss her, but before he did, he said, "Stay with me, Rose. For more than this weekend."

She pulled away. "What?"

"You belong here. In Napa. With me."

He would have taken her mouth right then, but she unwrapped her legs too quickly. "It hasn't even been twenty-four hours," she said, panic underlying her words.

But Jack was sure of his feelings. "Let me convince you, Rose," he whispered.

Like magic, she floated back into his arms.

"You barely know me," she said.

"Oh, but I do," he said in the instant before his lips found hers.

Soft, he wanted everything to be soft, gentle. He wanted to tell her he loved her, that he'd always love her, but he knew it was too soon, that those words might scare her away. Instead, he'd take his time loving her. He'd show Rose that she was the most special, most incredible woman he'd ever met. That he'd ever meet. That she was the beginning and the end for him.

But all his intentions could not overcome his desire to possess her.

His lips went from soft to hard, his tongue swept possessively into her mouth. He bit down on her bottom lip and she cried out, but the sound was passion, not pain, and his teeth continued their path of delicious destruction down her neck. Her pulse leaped beneath his tongue, racing in time to his own heart, but he wasn't done nipping his way down her soft skin. His lips sucked at her collarbone, his tongue dipped into the hollow, and then he cupped her breasts with his hands.

His mouth followed, roaming every silky inch of her skin. First one breast and then the next. Her nipples hardened beneath his thumbs, tempting him to lave the hard, tight nubs with his tongue. Again and again, until Rose was writhing, crying beneath him, wrapping her legs around his hips.

He felt her warm, wet heat as she sank onto his cock, and he thanked God that he'd put on a condom as he'd waited for her by the edge of the pool. She threaded her fingers behind his neck and tossed her head back, leaving her tits open to his mouth, his hands. She rode him faster and faster, and he had to touch her. Had to feel her soft curls, her plump pussy lips, the swollen core of her desire.

His hand slipped down her belly. He got no further than her pubic bone before he lost control. With firm strokes he pressed his fingers into her clitoris. Pumping into her with his cock, pressing into her with his hand, Jack roared his pleasure into the quiet Napa valley sky.

8

Rose unwrapped her arms from behind Jack's neck. Turning away from him, she swam to the edge of the pond. Hoisting herself out of the water, she pulled on her borrowed dress as quickly as she could, shoving her feet into the mud boots before hightailing it back to his house.

She knew better than to believe that Jack truly cared for her. Whatever he was feeling was nothing more than great sex.

It would have been so easy, so wonderful to go along with him, but it wouldn't have been fair. Not to Jack. And not to herself. Because once the lust wore off and he woke up next to her thinking "What is she doing here?" the hurt would be unbearable. She needed to get away from Jack, go back to the hotel, convince her friends to take her home.

Too bad she already knew that San Francisco wasn't her home anymore. Jack's linoleum floors, soft cotton sheets, and wide front porch were home.

She ran through the vines, her tears blinding her as she pushed into his front door, through his kitchen, wanting to get her dress and heels and leave.

But she'd forgotten about the bread.

The unmade loaf sat in the window, illuminated by the sun. While they'd been making love in his pool, the honey bread had been rising.

She couldn't leave. She wasn't strong enough to fight against the one thing she'd been searching for her whole life.

Love.

She heard his footsteps behind her. She knew what he'd say.

"You're special, Rose." Her heart flip-flopped within her chest. "I'll keep telling you until you believe me."

Still looking at the risen dough, she didn't turn around.

His voice was closer now. "I'll keep showing you until you can't deny it anymore. Ever again." His words were rough, full of emotion.

She didn't go to him. She couldn't, not with her fear so plain on her face. Wiping her eyes with the back of her hand, she walked to the windowsill and picked up the bowl of dough.

"I believe you," she said quietly, even though she didn't. Even though she couldn't.

Why would this man, Jack Gerard, ever think a woman like her was special? She wasn't exciting. She wasn't famous. She wasn't glamorous. She wasn't a size four sexpot with Barbie doll breasts and legs up to her armpits.

But since she wasn't strong enough to leave, there was no other option but to grab this time with Jack with both hands, to let herself keep falling, no matter how much it would hurt when she went back to her empty life on Sunday evening.

Taking a deep breath, she forced a smile to her lips. It was a small one, but it was all she could manage. She turned around, grateful for the heavy weight of the bowl, because it kept her shaking hands from betraying her shaky heart.

"Let's bake bread," was her peace offering. Thankfully, he took it. In silence, they gently deflated the dough and turned it out onto a floured board. Dividing it into two equal portions, Jack showed her how to form the dough into round loaves, which they placed on parchment-lined baking sheets.

"The dough will rise again for thirty minutes, and then we bake it."

Rose nodded, and because his face looked so serious, too serious, she leaned over and kissed him. "How about a quick shower?"

His grin put the sunlight to shame as it effortlessly lit up the room. Grabbing his hand, Rose got ready to make the most of her remaining time in heaven.

JACK DIDN'T REGRET WHAT HE'D SAID. He didn't regret anything he'd done. But still, he wondered what was going on behind Rose's deep blue eyes. He'd seen the shock, the disbelief, and something else he hadn't been able to name in the pool. She'd run from him and he'd wanted to chase after her, to hold her tightly against him. But he'd understood that at that moment, flight had been her only option.

And then again in the kitchen, when she'd been standing in front of the window, he'd felt her loneliness and he'd wanted to knead it out of her. But it hadn't been what she'd needed, so he'd reined in his need to try and make everything better.

Finally she'd turned to him, smiling, and he'd wanted nothing more than to tell her all the reasons why she was the woman he'd been looking for his whole life.

Instead he'd let her take him into the shower, let her mouth tease and taste him everywhere, let her soap him up, until he'd

been gripping the walls, coming into her mouth. Then he'd
shown her that he was as good a student as she, drinking in her
passionate responses to his touching, his kisses, his fingers as
they'd stroked inside her.

After he dried her off with a fluffy, sage green towel, she
wrapped it tightly around her and stood in the middle of his
bedroom.

"I really don't want to put that dress back on."

"It's fine with me if you want to do the rest of your lessons in
the nude," he said, deliberately misunderstanding her.

She let go of the towel with one hand to playfully smack his
chest. "You know that's not what I mean. I've got to go back to the
hotel to change." The towel slipped down just enough that he
could almost see the tip of her nipple.

"Smack me again," he said, pressing a gentle kiss to her mouth,
hoping she'd drop the towel.

But she was a woman on a mission, and she pulled it up
higher. "Clothes," she said, breathlessly. "I need clothes."

"No, you don't. I like you naked best," he said, but he knew
when he was beat, so he headed for the dresser in the guest room
and pulled out another sundress.

Rose looked at the brown-and-purple frock and groaned.
"This is the best you can do?"

"I never said my sister had good taste in fashion, did I?"

"No," she muttered as she dropped the towel, "you certainly
didn't. Although I can't help but wonder if you're using this horrible dress to try to convince me to stay nude."

Before he could shout "Please," she slipped the ugly dress over
her shoulders, hiding her luscious curves from view.

She turned and looked at herself in the mirror. And grimaced.
"Oh, God, I look hideous. There isn't an underground tunnel I
can take to get back to the hotel, is there?"

Jack still thought she looked amazing, unflattering sack of a dress or not.

"Clothing aside," she continued, "I've got to head back to the hotel to change and find my friends to let them know that I haven't been killed by an axe murderer. Should I meet you later?"

"I'll go with you," he offered quickly, hating the idea of letting Rose out of his sight for even an hour.

ROSE PRACTICALLY RAN THE FOUR BLOCKS back to the spa. Or she would have, if everybody and their dog hadn't approached Jack to say hello, or tell him how great his food was, or how they couldn't wait for his cooking show to debut, or was he going to be signing his new cookbook at the farmer's market on Sunday?

On the one hand, she felt incredibly proud to be the woman next to Jack. On the other hand, she knew everyone was thinking, *What is Jack Gerard doing with that oversized fashion victim?*

To Jack's credit, he proudly introduced her to everyone and didn't seem the least bit embarrassed to be seen with her. It was too bad loving Jack could only lead to heartbreak. Because he was the most incredibly lovable man she'd ever met.

Finally, she opened the door to her room at the spa. "This is a really nice hotel, isn't it?" she babbled, her brain scrambled from everything that had happened in the past twenty-four hours. "Have you ever been here before?"

Rose immediately wanted to take the words back. Of course he'd been to the hotel before. And the way he nodded, with his head bowed so she couldn't see his eyes, only testified to the number of weekend flings he must have had here. This very room, possibly.

Rose took a step back from the bed, where she was rummaging through her bag for a semicute outfit. She would never be able to sleep in the bed now, with visions of Jack and all his lovers going at it.

The message light on the phone on the bedside table was blinking—she hadn't thought to check her cell in between all the hot sex—and she was glad for the excuse not to have to make more small talk with Jack.

Especially when she couldn't get the image of his string of sexy lady friends out of her head.

"My girlfriends are probably wondering where the heck I am," she said as she sat down on the edge of the bed and dialed in the retrieval code, surprised to find out she had three messages.

"Hey, it's me," Vanessa said, sounding slightly put out. Rose felt immediately guilty for having skipped out on their girls' weekend together. If only Jack weren't so wonderful, so talented with his hands and mouth. Vanessa's voice cut into Rose's Top 10 Sexy Things About Jack list. "I just tried your room but you weren't there, so I'm hoping that means you're getting lucky with the chef hottie. Too bad I can't say the same for myself. I'm posing for a painter and he's got this stupid rule about . . . I'm too wound up to talk about it. Don't worry about me, I'll be back Sunday afternoon. And I'll have gotten exactly what I want by then. Let Carrie know that I'm AWOL, would you?"

Rose was confused by Vanessa's message. She was posing for a painter? Was this something she'd set up ahead of time and forgotten to mention?

But Rose had two more messages to listen to. Carrie was next and immediately launched into apologies about meeting a man named Tyson, and needing to speak with James. Rose smiled. She was glad that Carrie had found someone already, although Rose had to admit that she was worried about how fast it had happened. Rebound relationships were perfectly normal. Not that she had any personal experience with getting a guy on rebound until this weekend, of course.

She hit the pound key to play the final message. "Hi, Rose! This is Hilary Jones from the Napa Valley Visitor's Bureau, and I wanted to check in with you to find out how your cooking lessons with our very own fabulously talented Jack Gerard are going. I was hoping we could take some pictures of one of the lessons for our newsletter and website. Could you please give me a call?" She left her number, and Rose quickly grabbed the pen and pad next to the bed lamp and wrote it down.

She hung up the phone, and Jack, who'd been staring out the window, turned to her. "Is everything all right with your friends?"

"They're fine. At least I think they are. Neither of them have spent much time here since last night. I guess we're all off on adventures this weekend." She gave him a bold smile. He said he liked saucy, didn't he? Before this weekend she hadn't known she'd had a saucy side, but she was having a lot of fun exploring it. In bed and out. "I want to leave them a quick message," she said, wondering how she was going to mention Jack without gushing while he was in the room.

Of course he read her mind. "I'll wait for you in the lobby."

After the door clicked shut, she pulled off the ugly borrowed dress and slipped on a matching set of red lace bra and panties. She'd have to remember to thank Vanessa for insisting she bring them. She grabbed a red scoop-neck T-shirt that flattered her full bust and a jean skirt that she hoped made her waist and butt look smaller than they actually were.

She dialed Carrie's room. "Carrie, it's Rose. I just got your message and I'm so happy for you! Don't worry about having fun, I haven't been spending much time at the hotel either. I won cooking lessons with a local chef, and, Carrie, he's incredible. I'll tell you all about it on Sunday. Only, is it horrible if I don't want to leave?"

She hung up, feeling like she'd revealed too much, even to her best friend. She dialed Vanessa's room. "Vanessa, it's Rose. Sorry I wasn't here last night. You aren't going to believe the weekend I'm having. Although maybe you would. Because Jack Gerard is incredible. We've hardly done any cooking, because, well . . ." She was sounding like a lovesick idiot, and she cut the message short. "Can't wait to see you on Sunday," she said. "Try and be nice to your painter," she added. "I'm sure he's already in love with you."

Hanging up the phone, she ran a brush through her hair and put on a quick application of mascara and lip gloss before going to find Jack. He was at the reception counter, chatting with the gorgeous brunette clerk. All of her insecurities welled up again, and she hung back behind a potted plant.

The woman looked up and spotted her. "There she is!"

Jack spun around and smiled. "I was starting to worry that you'd ditched me," he joked, not knowing how close he was to the truth.

Rose forced a smile. "I forgot to tell you. Hilary from the visitor's center called. She wants to know how the lessons are going."

"What are you going to tell her?" he asked as he waved goodbye to the clerk.

Forcing a light, sassy tone into her voice—she was going to enjoy the next twenty-four hours, she had the rest of her life to be an insecure mess—she said, "I might have to tell her the truth."

"Which is?"

She felt more than a little wicked, and frankly, wicked felt so much better than insecure. "That we haven't left the bedroom long enough to make it to the kitchen."

Jack threw his head back and laughed. "I'd love to see the look on her face if you really said that."

Rose giggled. It was one thing to be saucy and crazy with Jack. But she could never say something like that to a stranger.

"She also wants to take our picture. During a cooking lesson."

"Think we can keep our hands off each other long enough?"

he asked as they turned the corner and arrived at the door to his restaurant. Her face grew hot. She'd been thinking the very same thing.

A few seconds later he ushered Rose into Gerard's. "I want to introduce you to the guys at the restaurant." She was inordinately flattered that he wanted her to meet his friends and coworkers.

"Larry, come meet Rose," Jack said to an enormous, but very handsome, man with a crew cut and about a dozen tattoos. Larry took his time looking Rose up and down. She felt herself blush under his scrutiny but quickly realized that Larry not only wasn't repulsed by her ample curves but was fairly salivating over her.

Larry kissed the back of her hand like she was royalty. "It is a pleasure to meet you," he said, and she felt her blush burn hotter. She was about to thank him when he said, "But you're with the wrong guy. I'll give you everything you want. Diamonds. Rubies. Crazy good sex. Just dump this loser."

She expected Jack to laugh at the joke. But he didn't. She took in Larry's earnest expression again and realized he might be serious.

"I've never fired anyone over a woman," Jack said. "But if I had to . . ." He let his words fall away, but the threat was obvious.

Rose's mouth fell open. Were they actually fighting over her? God knew she didn't want to come between two men who were close friends as well as coworkers. But she'd be lying if she didn't admit to a slight thrill at the fact that two very sexy men were about to come to blows. Over her.

Fortunately, Larry heeded Jack's warning. He put his hands up in surrender—the effect of which was a little lost given the ten-inch chef's knife in his left hand—and said, "As long as she's happy with you, Boss, I'm happy." Turning back to Rose, he added with a wink, "But you know where to go if he ever treats you wrong." With that he headed back over to the large tri-tip he was slicing into thin slivers.

Several other people in the kitchen waved their hellos, but Jack's possessive behavior had made them wary. He'd threatened to fire his sous-chef over her. Who knew what crazy stunt he'd pull next in the name of lust?

Because Rose knew that's what was driving him. As Vanessa always said, most guys thought a hard dick meant true love.

Jack's words broke into her cynical musings. "I'll give Hilary a call. She and the photographer can watch us make lunch." He leaned over and whispered the rest in her ear. "And then you're mine until tomorrow afternoon. No interruptions." His seductive tone left no question in Rose's mind as to what he had planned.

Frankly, she was already painfully aroused and couldn't wait to be alone with Jack to have her very naughty way with him. Again. She was perfectly happy keeping the safe, quiet Rose locked up for another day.

The real world would intrude soon enough.

9

ILARY AND HER CREW arrived ten minutes later, and the kitchen grew loud and bright as they set up the lights.

"Maybe I should change?" Rose said, but Jack shook his head.

"You're dressed perfectly," he said, and he meant it. But at the same time, he had other reasons for wanting her to remain in her adorably laid-back outfit. He wanted to get this cooking lesson and photo shoot done with as quickly as possible. His time with Rose was running out, and every minute counted.

Plus, he couldn't wait to slide his palms up her T-shirt later tonight. His gut told him there was something lacy beneath the denim. Just thinking about her panties—slipping them off her thighs, past her calves, over her perfect feet—made him ridiculously hard.

Food. He needed to concentrate on food.

And then he could focus exclusively on Rose.

"Spaghetti in red wine," he said. "A classic wine country dish."

The cameras were already flashing as he handed Rose an apron and donned one himself. She wasn't looking him in the eye any-more—he guessed it was because she was afraid that the camera would see the emotions they couldn't hide—but Jack refused to stand for it.

"Stand here, next to me," he instructed Rose in a business-only voice. She moved closer and he said, "I'm going to teach you how to chop parsley."

He put his hand on hers and she pulled away. "I know how to chop," she said.

Instead of arguing with her, he placed his hand on hers again, more firmly this time, and after laying several parsley leaves on the clean cutting board, he forced their hands to become one, deftly chopping the herb into minuscule pieces. He'd never thought the aroma of parsley was a turn-on before, but then again, he'd never done it with Rose before either.

Even surrounded by a dozen people, as they worked chopping herbs, grating farm-fresh Parmesan, adding garlic, prosciutto and pepper flakes to the heating olive oil, it was as if there was no one else in the room.

Fifteen minutes later their meal was prepared, and Jack could have sworn that Rose had forgotten all about the cameras, all about Hilary. It was one of the many things he loved about her: She gave her all, all of the time.

Hilary took a bite of the dish and gasped with pleasure. "Oh my gosh, this is wonderful, Rose!" She fanned herself. "I don't know if it's the pepper flakes or the heat from the stoves, but I am burning up."

Rose smiled at Jack, a secret, wicked smile. They both knew why the kitchen was so hot. And it had nothing to do with peppers or hot ovens. Sparks flew when they were together.

"I think we've got enough shots," Hilary said as she nodded to her photographer to pack up his lights and equipment. Shaking

Rose's hand, she said, "Enjoy the rest of your lessons with Jack. He's a very talented teacher." Rose's face flamed and, again, Jack knew what she was thinking. Little did she know that she'd taught him a few things and not the other way around. "If you don't mind, I'd like to give you a call on Monday to do a little interview about the experience."

"Sure. Great," Rose said.

Jack waited until Hilary and her crew had left before asking Larry, "You guys got it covered here without me tonight?"

He filled the sink to wash the pots and pans he and Rose had used for the cooking demonstration. Larry grunted without looking up from the veal he was beating with a wooden mallet into thin, tender cutlets. Not that Jack would have hung around if they had needed him. For once, his restaurant was going to have to run—and run well—without him.

The thought stilled his hands. Never had he thought to value anything more than his food, his restaurant. When he'd imagined himself with a wife and kids, they'd always been fuzzy, existing somewhere in the background of his hectic life.

Meeting Rose had changed everything. To his utter surprise he found that he wasn't upset by this profound shift of priorities. If he was lucky enough to have her in his life, she would always come first, far above his restaurant, his cooking show, his book tours, and everything else that made up the daily life of a famous chef. And yet, at the same time, he knew Rose would be his greatest supporter and that his best ideas would be inspired by her.

He stopped his runaway thoughts to acknowledge the fact that neither of them had spoken of the future, of love. Yet. But that didn't change how he felt. And he was confident that everything would work out, even if they'd only met twenty-four hours ago.

"Leave the rest," he said. When she ignored him and continued to scrub at a spatula, saying, "I got 'em dirty, so I'm cleaning them up," he couldn't help but grin. Ah, yes, she was most certainly the woman for him.

He dug into the dirty dishes with renewed gusto. He'd have to remember to send Hilary a very expensive bouquet of flowers for bringing Rose Morgan into his life.

SATURDAY AFTERNOON WENT FROM PERFECT TO GLORIOUS and back again. The sun was shining, the sky was a bright, piercing blue, and Rose was falling harder and harder for her private Napa tour guide. Hopping on the bicycles in his garage, they rode to wineries—owned by his friends, of course—and were plied with the best Pinots and Chardonnays and Cabernets she'd ever tasted. As soon as the vintners saw Jack walking in the door, they opened their private label bottles, wines that would have sold for hundreds of dollars in San Francisco restaurants. Just when she began to feel overly tipsy, they headed to a gorgeous red barn in the middle of a field of cows and goats, laid out a blanket and feasted on mouthwatering goat cheese, pepper sausage, and French bread.

"Is this really how people live around here?" she asked. "Or are you just showing me a fairy-tale day in Napa?"

Jack grinned and swallowed his final bite of a crisp cracker loaded with a sun-dried tomato spread. "A little of both, I guess," he admitted. "Everyone you've met today works incredibly hard. But since making cheese and wine and olive oil is their passion, I've found that more often than not, everyone really enjoys their job. And their life. People are forever making up reasons to get together. The harvest, the crush, the first new buds of spring." He refilled her glass with cool, bubbly lemonade. "I don't know if people who live in Napa are so happy because we're surrounded by so much beauty—the vines, the hills, the oak trees—or if we're so happy that we help to create and preserve the land around us." He cut a ripe, juicy, yellow-and-green zebra tomato into fourths.

"I've never seen a tomato that big." She took a bite, the juice dripping down her chin. Jack caught the brightly colored liquid with the tip of his finger before it dripped onto her skirt. "Or had one this good," she added, although one touch from Jack made her forget all about the sweet, tangy tomato.

"Organic farms do well here in the country." Rose wasn't sure that Napa, a bustling town with world-renowned restaurants, wineries, and artists qualified as "the country," but it sure sounded fun. "Even some of the wineries are going organic. Like Green Vineyards, for instance. Tyson Green is a great guy who's really a pioneer in the industry. Anyone who's willing to forgo big profits for a few years to get his techniques down is a hero in my eyes."

The name Tyson rang a bell in Rose's head. Wasn't that the name of the vineyard owner that Carrie had mentioned in her voice mail?

Thinking about Carrie's weekend fling brought Rose full circle to her own. "I've had such a wonderful time with you today," she said quietly.

"Move here, Rose."

Rose knocked her glass over and the lemonade seeped in between her toes in her sandals.

"I want to be with you. Napa. San Francisco. I don't care where. I want to learn everything about you."

She got up so abruptly that she knocked over a platter of cheese and crackers. "Stop asking me to stay."

"Why should I? I want you with me."

"I can't, Jack. I can't." She turned to look for the exit, for her bike, so that she could pedal away from him and his hot eyes, his insistence that he wanted to be with her. She knew better than him what he needed, couldn't he see that?

But he was quicker than she was, and he blocked the door before she could get to it. "Tell me why you refuse to believe me when I say how much I care about you."

Frustrated at everything, at her whole life, at the lesson she'd been forced to learn so many goddamn times, she yelled, "Because you won't want me forever, Jack. Okay, so you think you want me now. Fine. It won't last. It never does. And if I'm stupid enough to quit my job and move here to be with you, how are you going to feel when you want to dump me in six months for someone younger? Prettier. Thinner. Someone who fits into your life better than I ever will?" She didn't give him time to answer. "No one will ever understand why we're together. I don't understand it," she said, trying to keep the stupid sob that was rising in her throat from coming out and washing over both of them.

Jack stared at her with eyes as dark as the dead of night. She didn't want to hurt him, didn't want him to think she didn't appreciate this glimpse of paradise, no matter how brief. Because she did. "I'll always remember this weekend with you, Jack, as one of the most special times in my life. But it won't last. It can't. I'm not going to let you make a mistake you'll regret. And blame me for later."

Out of breath, out of energy, Rose got to the end of her soliloquy. She stood silent, wishing Jack would let her go back to the hotel, back to her life, without making things any harder on her.

But he didn't move, didn't speak. He simply stared until she grew horribly uncomfortable beneath his heated, all-seeing gaze. "Say something!" she demanded, unable to stand his ongoing silence.

"You're so unbelievably sexy, Rose. And you don't even realize it. I know you've been hurt before. I don't know anything about your ex-lovers, but I do know that they didn't deserve you."

Rose looked up into eyes that she knew would never lie. That would never look at her to say, "Why don't you go on a diet this week?" She felt herself crumple and reached out to steady herself, but Jack was already there.

"I won't let you fall, Rose," he said. "I'll never let you down." She felt so safe in his arms, and loved, as he cradled her like a baby. She was finally ready to knock down the last of the walls that she'd constructed around her heart.

The sun was starting to set as they rode their bikes back to his house. Rose felt freer than she'd ever been. Lighter. More joyful. Jack was better than Disneyland and Christmas all rolled into one.

They put the bikes away, and Jack gave her that look that made her stomach turn to jelly. "What do you say to a long, hot bath?"

He'd been so kind, so understanding about her insecure "moment" earlier, and she was able to let the playful Rose emerge again. "Now how'd you know I've always preferred baths over showers?"

He rubbed his chin as if he were giving her question deep thought. "Must be that I've been picturing your skin, damp and pink, all day long."

Her grin faded, replaced by desire, and she boldly led the way back into his house, through the kitchen, down the hall to the master bedroom, straight for the enormous tub in the corner by the oversized windows. The moon lit up the black sky and streamed into the room. Jack lit a match, and a second later, vanilla perfumed the room as a dozen candles shone from every counter and corner.

Rose had never felt so good. And she wanted nothing more than to share her happiness with Jack. In every way. And so she decided to thank him for his beautiful words to her in the barn by giving him a show that she hoped he'd never forget.

He'd already taken off his shirt, and she was made momentarily speechless by his hard, muscular chest. She wanted to throw herself into his arms, tackle him to the ground, make him hers again and again. Instead she said, "Have you ever watched a woman bathe before?"

His hands stilled on the button at the top of his jeans. His Adam's apple moved in his throat as he swallowed before he said, "No."

His reply was hoarse, and Rose smiled a purely feminine smile, the one she seemed to have permanently on her face since he'd slipped his hand inside her panties on Friday night.

"Good," she said as she pointed to the upholstered chair in the corner of the room. "Why don't you go sit over there and we'll both pretend that you're not here. I've always wondered what it would be like to be secretly watched while I was . . ."

She let her words fall away, but the word "masturbating" hung heavy in the air between them. For a long moment he didn't move, and she wondered if he was going to obey her command, knowing that even if he didn't, they would have the time of their lives in the hot, soapy water. But when he slowly made his way over to the chair, she was glad, so glad that he trusted her. That he had faith in her to take them to the moon and back. She'd never had that kind of faith in herself before. Not until Jack.

Accessing an inner coquette that she hadn't known she possessed, she forced herself to block Jack's darkly arousing figure from her mind. The more he felt like a voyeur, the more she felt the tingles of being watched by something unknown, the hotter their night would be. Turning to the mirror, she gathered her hair in her hands and lifted it up, twisting it into a knot on top of her head. Several tendrils curled around her neck, framing her face.

Already she was so wet, so ready for Jack. Self-confidence, she was quickly learning, was a powerful aphrodisiac.

She unzipped her jean skirt and let it fall to the floor in front of the pedestal sink. As she stepped out from the circle of denim, she pulled her top off and dropped it there as well. Clad in her sexy red lace bra and panties, she bent over the faucet at the end of the huge, whirlpool bathtub and turned the knobs. For the very first time, she wasn't afraid of her near nakedness. Hot water filled the porcelain, and steam rose from the tub, making the tendrils tighten and dampen against her skin. She wanted so desperately to turn to Jack, to see his expression, but she knew the payoff would be greater if she played her part. Humming softly, she undid the front clasp on her bra and shrugged it off her shoulders. It fell silently to the floor. Her panties quickly followed, and as she bent over to pick up the lingerie, her ass, her pussy flared and opened to Jack's gaze. She heard him growl, and a shudder of arousal shot through her, from the inside out. Her nipples beaded though the air was moist and the mirrors were fogged with condensation.

Gingerly, she tested the water with her toe. It was hot, but wonderfully so. Stepping into the tub, she turned until she was facing Jack, then closed her eyes and slid into the water. She moaned with pleasure as warmth enveloped her muscles. She was a little sore—not from the bike ride but from so much wild, wonderful sex. Without opening her eyes, she felt Jack's gaze burning through her, and she wanted his mouth on her. His hands.

Pretending he was with her in the tub, pretending her small hands were his big, rough ones, she ran them across her collarbone, then up and over her breasts. Again and again she cupped and caressed her tits. She'd never really appreciated them, always thought they were too big, too heavy, until now. She was thankful, so thankful, that she could turn herself on this way. That she could turn Jack on so much. She was utterly certain that he was seconds away from diving into the water with her and thrusting his perfect cock into her wet, ready pussy.

The vision of Jack filling her, harder, fuller, forced one hand from her breasts, down her belly, straight to her clit. On a moan she spread her legs wider and rubbed her fingers against the aroused nub. She thought about Jack sitting in the corner watching her, about the show she was giving him, about the way his lips would feel closing over her clit, and she broke apart. Her head went back against the tiled rim of the tub and she cried out in ecstasy.

JACK HAD DONE EVERYTHING he could to play along with Rose's game. He relished her boldness, and so he'd let her strip and massage her breasts without any interference. He'd been on the verge of taking her on the cold, tiled floor nearly every second of her tantalizing show, but when she'd started coming, well, there were some things a guy simply couldn't resist. And this was at the top of the list.

He dropped his jeans, rolled on a condom, then stepped into the water and pulled her on top of him. Her wet heat enveloped him, and he forgot to worry that it was too soon to come, that he needed to hold back to increase her pleasure. He thrust high and deep inside her and then his mouth was on hers and he was sucking at her lower lip and coming as hard as he ever had as her muscles danced and clenched at his shaft.

Their kisses were frantic, and the pleasure was so intense that he felt as if he was drowning beneath the water. Her breasts slapped and slid against the hairs on his chest and he wanted to stay here, like this, in his bathtub with Rose forever.

Afterward, they lay panting, but when she shivered in the rapidly cooling water, he pulled them both up and wrapped a thick towel around her. "Get dressed," he said. "There's something I want to show you." He shoved on his jeans and T-shirt and walked quickly to the kitchen, gathering up everything he needed and putting it in a basket.

Ten minutes later, they were driving up the valley into Calistoga, a town at the northern tip of the county. Turning onto First Street, he pulled the truck over in front of an old, dilapidated barn. Helping Rose with the steep step out of his truck, he grabbed a couple of thick blankets from the truck bed. Her hand safe and warm in his, together they walked up a short flight of rock stairs.

Rose had been quiet since their bath, but it was a good kind of quiet, so Jack wasn't worried about the lack of conversation. He pushed open the splitting barn door and said, "I'm thinking about turning this into my next restaurant. You're the first person too see it. I want to know what you think."

"I think," she said, giving him a dazzling smile, "that it's going to be absolutely wonderful."

"A lot of hard work," he said, loving it when she cut him off to say, "But what could be better than turning a rustic barn into a gourmet restaurant?"

He grinned. Bringing Rose here had been a good move. The right move. More glad than he could say that she shared his vision for what this big, open, hay-filled space could become, he shook out the blankets and spread them on the floor.

"Would you do me the honor of the first meal?"

He held out his hand, and as she took it and they sat cross-legged on the blankets, Jack's heart had never been so full. And when she reached for the hem of his T-shirt and pulled it out of the waistband of his jeans, saying, "I hope dinner can wait another hour," he pushed the basket of food aside. Damn, she was brilliant.

Christening his soon-to-be restaurant with a picnic meal had merely been a good idea. Making love on the floor of it was a great one.

10

EVERYTHING WAS PERFECT. The gourmet picnic was so delicious that she couldn't believe Jack hadn't planned it well in advance. Thick, crusty French bread, nutty cheeses, roast chicken in garlic and rosemary that made her mouth water all over again just thinking about it, and an off-the-cuff crème brûleé that was quite possibly the best dessert she'd ever had. When they finally drove back to his house and slipped beneath the sheets, the moon was falling in the sky and they gave in to an exhausted slumber, wrapped around each other.

Rose woke as sunlight streamed over her face. Despite having slept for only a few hours, energy coursed through her veins. She was too happy to feel tired. Too filled to the brim with the most wonderful man she'd ever met.

She'd never had the nerve to dream this big. Or this good. But Lordy, she must have done something right during her thirty years to deserve this one weekend in heaven. Maybe, if she was really lucky, a little longer than that. He wanted her to move in with him. What if she did?

As if he felt her admiring gaze, Jack's eyes popped open. "Good morning, gorgeous." A muscled arm looped around her neck and pulled her down for a kiss. "I wish we could spend all day in bed together, but my fans await."

He was such a ham and she giggled, loving how he didn't take himself, or his success, too seriously. "I don't know if there's room for you, me, and your ego in the bed," she teased. But she knew he had a life to live, and a business to run. And now that she'd accepted his feelings for her, she wasn't going to be all clingy and get in the way. "I know you've got to get back to your restaurant."

She sat up in bed, and as the covers fell from her body, his eyes shot to her breasts. "Nope. I'm supposed to sign cookbooks at the Napa farmer's market. I'd love it if you'd keep me company. Not to mention that I have a feeling a gorgeous brunette is going to attract more people over to my table than I could ever hope to do myself."

Rose basked in his compliments, feeling more beautiful than ever. "Sure, that'll be fun. When do we need to be there?" she asked, dreaming of another long, hot bath with Jack.

He looked at the clock and threw the sheet off, giving her the wonderful opportunity to feast her eyes on naked male perfection. "Ten minutes."

Fortunately, she'd thought to pack an extra dress and panties in her oversized purse. So while Jack pulled on boxers, jeans, and a Hawaiian shirt, she slipped on a strappy pink sundress that Vanessa had assured her made her waist look minuscule. She made a feeble attempt to tame her hair and was brushing her teeth with the spare travel toothbrush she kept in her purse when Jack came in and said, "You're a wonder, prepared for anything."

She shot him a white, foamy grin and shoved him back out into the bedroom before she spat.

Five minutes later, they were on their way. Already the two blocks to Main Street were familiar, a fact that warmed her heart and made her feel like a budding local. Jack, of course, was already attracting attention. Could she help it if she had a gorgeous, talented boyfriend?

Rose savored the word "boyfriend" in her head. Nothing could go wrong this time. She was sure of it.

JACK ENJOYED COMING OUT to the farmer's market every Sunday. Even if he wasn't signing cookbooks, he liked to check out the best local produce and chat with the locals. But he'd never enjoyed himself quite as much as he did today.

With Rose by his side.

As expected, she drew people over to them with her friendly smile and warm glow. There was rarely a break as he signed cookbooks, took pictures with fans, gave culinary tips to budding chefs. Rose was quick with a joke, ready with a smile, and made the most nervous person feel comfortable.

He was stroking Rose's back and whispering mischievous suggestions about what he'd like to do to her in his hot tub later that night when a vaguely familiar woman stormed up to them.

"Hello, Jack, remember me?" she said, her lipstick a little too bright, her eyes slightly wild.

Oh, no. He did remember her. He'd met her about six months ago, after a night that had made him wonder why he'd ever decided to open a restaurant. The main stove top had been on the fritz, his dishwasher had called in sick, and the customers had been pickier than three-year-olds, incapable of ordering anything straight off the menu. With so many substitutions, he might as well have tossed his menu down the disposal.

By the end of the night he'd been exhausted, irritated, and desperate to unwind and put the evening behind him. He'd had his bartender pour him a stiff drink. The woman seated next to him had been round and soft and all the things he should have liked, but even before he'd gotten to her hotel room he'd realized she was too brash, too desperate. He'd tried to back out, but he'd been so beaten down by the day that it'd been easier to just do her and leave.

Now, here she was, glaring down at him with a slightly crazy gleam in her eyes. His brain did a frantic scramble for her name.

"Would you like a cookbook?" he asked, trying to figure out a way to get her to leave before Rose figured things out. It wasn't that he wanted to hide anything from her, just that their pasts were better dealt with in a less awkward, less public forum.

"You don't even remember my name, do you?" the woman accused. She shot a venomous glance at Rose and hissed, "We're all the same to you, aren't we?"

Rose's eyes grew big, but she stayed rooted in her seat.

"Look—" he began, but the woman cut him off.

"I've got you figured out. All you're interested in is taking an innocent tourist back to her hotel room so that you can screw her and forget her." The woman's eyes narrowed. "No wonder why you didn't return any of my phone calls." She turned to Rose. "Don't let him suck you in too. I thought we'd shared a perfect night together, but it was all just lies."

WATCHING THE ANGRY WOMAN was like looking in the mirror. All of Rose's fears, everything she knew to be true about herself, about her life and what it could be, came back in a rush. She found her limbs moving, making her stand up. She bent to pick up her purse from the patch of dirt next to her chair, but she was hardly cognizant of what she was doing. Her blood felt like slick sludge as it continued to circulate through her, her movements robotic and off.

"Rose," Jack said, turning away from the next person in line, shielding her face from their prying stares. "I'm sorry that happened."

Jack's face swam before her eyes, transforming into the face of every ex-boyfriend who'd ever told her to lose weight, who'd enjoyed what she'd done to him in the sack but not enough to forgo a twig of a woman at the altar. She'd believed he was different. Oh, God, she'd been so stupid. He was probably one of those guys who jacked off over dirty magazines with pictures of big girls. She was exactly like that woman. The one whose name he'd forgotten after one perfect night. Another overweight nobody from San Francisco for him to get his rocks off with.

"It's not you," she said in a dull voice. "It's me."

She was desperate to leave him before she let herself cry in front of him. She picked up her bag, holding it close against her chest, but she couldn't bring herself to leave. Not when a small, pathetic voice in her head was whispering, "Maybe he'll beg you to stay. Then everything will be all right."

She waited there, her purse guarding her heart like armor, for him to say something. She was unable to look into his eyes until she heard him softly say her name.

"Rose, I know I have some explaining to do about that woman. About my past. I'm not going to lie to you. I've been with women. A lot of women. But you're special. None of them have even come close to you. Your beauty. Your smile. Your brains. Your guts."

Rose swallowed hard, and her trembling legs made her step back into the booth of the person behind them.

"When I say you're gorgeous, I mean it. When I tell you I want to spend the rest of my life with you, I mean it. I love you, Rose. And I've only ever loved one woman in thirty-six years, Rose. You. Since you came into my life on Friday, I see everything differently. My whole world has changed. For the better."

Everything inside of her melted at Jack's passionate words. She would stop jumping to conclusions. She would listen calmly to his explanations. She would be bigger than her insecurities. She opened her mouth to say, "I forgive you," but the sudden sadness in his eyes stopped her as surely as being run over by a bus would have.

"I'll always love you, Rose," he said, "but how can you say that it's not about me? About us? I want to be there for you. I want you to be there for me. But if you don't think what we have— what we could have—is worth fighting your own demons for, it'll never work between us."

"*It will never work between us*" was all she could hear. Like a chant in her head, she couldn't get past it, she couldn't get the words to stop repeating.

The bottom fell out of her world, and Rose couldn't see past the tears streaming down her face. She ran as fast as she could, leaving Jack behind in a cloud of dust and sorrow. She had thought that he was everything she'd ever wanted. But now she knew the truth.

Straight from his mouth, to her heart. Like a butcher's knife.

1 1

Rose had made her choice. She didn't want to fight for a life with him. He knew he should start trying to figure out how to go on living without her. But damn it, that wasn't what he wanted. He wanted to fight for her. Somehow, someway, he'd have to find a way to get through to her.

Sunday morning went from bright and limitless to dark gray. Nothing seemed to matter anymore. But he still had his cooking, his career, so he turned back to the crowd of people waiting for him to sign his cookbook.

He wished he could ignore the pity in their eyes as he woodenly scrawled his name inside the front cover. Everything Jack had ever touched had turned to gold.

But not Rose. She'd run from him. Just as he'd been afraid that she would.

As soon as he signed his last book, he sought refuge in the only place where he hoped he could learn to feel whole again. The kitchen in Gerard's. He slipped in the back door and barely looked up as his employees greeted him. He picked up a knife and began to dice carrots. Onions. Anything to take his mind off Rose.

But she'd been in here. They'd chopped parsley together. And it had been one of the most erotic, fulfilling experiences of his life, showing her how to dice herbs.

He dropped the knife onto the cutting board and went to his office. He began to shut the door behind him—something he never, ever did—but Larry's huge form was blocking the doorway.

"Hey, Boss, trouble in paradise?"

Jack covered his face with his hands. He was going to cry, for God's sake.

"Everything's covered here," was all Larry said as he backed up out of the office and closed the door behind him with a soft click, leaving Jack completely, utterly alone.

ROSE NOW KNEW NAPA WELL ENOUGH to find her way back to the hotel, even in her anguished haze. She tripped over a large stick and fell to the ground. Lying on the sidewalk, she'd never felt sorrier for herself than she did right at that moment.

Why couldn't Jack have been her Prince Charming? Was it so much to ask that she find a man to love her, to want to be with her when they were old, surrounded by grandchildren?

She sniffled loudly and shifted her weight to get up. She grasped the windowpane of a nearby store, her eye catching on a real estate flyer's headline.

"Fall in Love with the Wine Country."

She couldn't take her eyes away from it.

Fall in Love with the Wine Country.

He'd said he loved her, hadn't he?

Fall in Love with the Wine Country.

But she'd been busy being self-righteous about some one-night fling from six months ago that he'd had every right to; she'd been busy wallowing in decades-old self-hatred; she'd been busy vilifying all the men who'd come before Jack, making him the scapegoat for everyone who'd ever told her she wasn't good enough.

And so she hadn't really listened to what Jack had said. But he'd been right. She needed to let him be there for her. Just as she would be for him. Because if he loved her more than she loved herself, their relationship could never work.

She pressed her hand against the windowpane, staring at nothing. Someone from the realty office came out to ask her if she needed help with something, but she didn't hear them, didn't respond. In two days with Jack, he'd made her feel sexier, more confident than ever before.

She'd wasted her first thirty years falling for the wrong men. She wasn't going to waste the next thirty by letting the one good one get away.

But she already knew "sorry" wasn't good enough. She needed to prove it to Jack, had to show him how much she loved him. That she was going to do everything in her power to trust him. And herself.

Rose was too practical to think that it'd be easy. She knew it was going to be a long, hard road to self-acceptance, to liking her curves. But if Jack was willing to stick by her side, through thick and thin, she knew they'd come out the other end.

Together.

In love.

Forever.

ROSE TOOK A LONG SHOWER, hoping for inspiration. She wished Vanessa or Carrie were around to help her think up a grand gesture of love, but they weren't in their rooms, at the pool, or in the restaurant.

She'd dug her own grave; it was up to her to dig herself out.

There was only one really good way to show Jack how much she loved him: food. She'd have to speak his language, but apart from what he'd taught her this weekend, she didn't know how to make anything other than ramen noodles and instant coffee. No, that wasn't completely true. Didn't everyone say that she made the best Betty Crocker chocolate cake they'd ever tasted?

Throwing on jeans and a tank top, Rose was out at the corner grocery store in a flash. Her heart pounded as she prayed they'd have what she needed.

They did.

She grabbed a box of cake mix and a can of frosting and somehow managed to sweet-talk the hotel's chef into letting her use his kitchen to bake it.

An hour later, she emerged with a lopsided cake. On shaky legs, she headed down the street to Jack's restaurant.

Please, God, let him be there, she prayed. But really, she was mostly praying that he'd still love her.

IT TOOK LESS THAN FIVE MINUTES for Jack to decide he wasn't good at feeling sorry for himself. Yes, his world had crumbled when Rose had left. Yes, he had a hole in his heart the size of a fist. But he was going to get on with life, because he had no other choice. More important, he was going to figure out a way to win Rose back. Until then, he'd have to suck it up and deal.

"Anyone want a soda from the bar?" he asked as he stepped through the swinging door into the restaurant.

And nearly collided with a chocolate cake.

Held by the woman he loved.

Hope flared so suddenly in his chest that he lost his breath. But Rose had had that effect on him the first moment he'd set eyes on her. She'd simply taken his breath away. For now and always.

Her eyes were bright with unshed tears, and her mouth was wobbly around the corners. She held the lopsided cake out to him and said, in that whispery little voice that did all sorts of crazy things to his insides, "I made this. For you."

Jack dipped one finger into the frosting, then sucked it off. "I love it," he said, but they both knew what he was really saying.

"I love you," Rose said, beating him to it. "And I'm sorry."

He could tell she wanted to say more, but he couldn't let her. She was his now, and they'd work everything out slowly, over the next sixty years or so.

"What did I say about apologizing to me?" he said, grinning at her like a lovesick fool, taking the cake from her, and putting it on a nearby table.

"That you're going to have to bend me over your knee for a spanking."

Jack pulled her against him, and just as he felt her breath on his lips, he said, "I love you, Rose." They kissed like long-lost lovers, unable to get enough of each other. "Now," he said, as he picked up the cake with one hand and grabbed her hand with the other, pulling her out the door and down the road to his house, "get ready for that spanking."

Touch Me

1

VANESSA COLLINS UNFOLDED HER TANNED LIMBS and stretched out on the chaise lounge by the sparkling blue pool at the Napa Valley Hotel & Spa. She sipped from a half-full glass of champagne, then set it down on the round table beside her chair. Sliding her Chanel sunglasses off, she closed her eyes and leaned her head back against the mesh fabric.

The Friday afternoon sun was warm as it caressed her skin, she looked hot in her tiny white bikini, and a young, muscular waiter had just refilled her glass. She was going to hang with her two best friends, Carrie and Rose, tomorrow. Everything was perfect.

So, then, why did she feel so disgruntled?

Not to mention bored out of her mind.

Vanessa sat up and blinked open her eyes, inadvertently catching every male within a fifty-foot radius devouring her before they could avert their eyes. She waited for the rush to come, the heady power of knowing she could have any one of these men—married or not—in her bed inside of five minutes.

Ten seconds later, she was sick of waiting. There was no rush anymore. It was too damn easy. What was the fun of luring a man into her web when there wasn't any luring that needed to be done?

She lifted the slim champagne glass to her lips and chugged the rest, but for some reason, even a bubbly buzz wasn't making a difference in her mood. It wasn't mellowing her out, and it certainly wasn't making any of the men by the pool look more appetizing.

What was wrong with her?

Maybe, she mused, it had something to do with Carrie being such a huge downer on the ride from San Francisco to Napa. A pang of guilt hit her right beneath her ribs. It wasn't Carrie's fault that she'd been dating such a prissy, rich jerk for two years. And that she hadn't had the sense to dump him until he was shoving a four-carat diamond onto her ring finger.

Vanessa and Carrie hadn't always seen eye to eye, but they'd always been there for each other. This time was no exception, even if Carrie was walking around with a big fat diamond in her pocket.

Vanessa had never been the jealous type. Frankly, she'd had no reason for envy. At thirty-two, she'd built up a wildly successful PR firm in the city, she was gorgeous, and she'd always gotten whatever she wanted—be it a man or the biggest contract in town. She'd always thought herself immune from jealousy and could hardly believe it.

She was jealous of her two best friends.

First, Carrie with that ring (even if she was giving it back) and then Rose winning a date with that gorgeous chef, Jack Gerard. Vanessa still couldn't believe that Rose had almost turned down the opportunity to take cooking lessons from a hot, hunky chef on the rise. Especially since Vanessa knew exactly what she would have done with those "lessons," and it wouldn't have had anything to do with a kitchen.

Something stirred deep in her gut. That guilt thing again. Why couldn't she let Rose have some good luck for once? She loved Rose dearly, but she'd always thought that she was far too insecure, far too afraid to take a risk. Which was why Rose was such a bang-up accountant, of course. No risk there.

Feeling more bitchy than usual, Vanessa forced her mind away from the naughty image of Jack Gerard naked and tanned beneath crisp white sheets, away from huge, sparkling jewels.

She needed to do something to get her energy back on track. Something other than lounging by the pool, fending off admirers. If she wasn't mistaken (and she never was), mister forty-and-newly-divorced was making his way over to her chaise lounge. It was all the push she needed, and ten minutes later, wearing a tiny pair of white running shorts and a white jog bra, Vanessa sauntered through the lobby and out into the soon-to-be-setting sun. Every eye was on her. Even the women whose husbands were ogling her couldn't help but admire her slim, toned muscles, her tanned thighs and calves, her tight stomach, her lush red hair pulled back into a loose ponytail. Still, Vanessa wasn't happy.

Something was wrong. Seriously wrong. She hoped a long run through the grapevines would clear her head and bring her some answers. Vanessa knew she was successful because she made plans and she stuck to them. This weekend, the plan was to hang with the girls and to have a weekend fling with a hot piece of ass that she never planned to see again. Vanessa had no intention of letting anything throw her off course.

Especially not something that felt like unmanaged emotions. She didn't do unmanaged emotions. Carrie and Rose rode the roller coaster enough for all three of them.

She ran harder, her breaths coming closer together, a fine sheen of sweat appearing across the top of her chest. Vanessa didn't want any part of that whole girly, weepy thing. She never had, and she didn't plan to start now.

Forty-five minutes of hard running later, she slowed down to a jog on Main Street, already looking forward to a hot shower and a cool drink at the nearest local hot spot. Her eyes glossed over the storefronts as she passed restaurants and boutiques, tasting rooms and art galleries.

And then she saw it. The most incredible nude she'd ever set eyes on. The dark-haired, dark-eyed, pale-skinned woman was sex on canvas.

Vanessa could already see it hanging behind her desk, the second thing visitors would see upon entering her domain. The first, of course, being Vanessa herself. The painting was gorgeous, but she knew that she, herself, in the flesh, was even better.

Anyone else would have gone back to the hotel, cleaned up, and come by the gallery the next morning. But Vanessa wasn't anyone else. She wanted the painting now. Even though she didn't have any money with her. Even though a Closed sign was up on the pane glass door.

As far as she was concerned, the painting was already hers. All that remained was for her to arrange the details.

She knocked on the glass door, and a man got up from behind the cash register in the corner. Six feet of muscles and sinew and gorgeous sun-blond hair pulled back into a ponytail. She could already feel the stubble on his square chin and rugged cheekbones burning her between her thighs.

All traces of ennui fled as her heart raced faster than it had in years. Anyone else would have tried to chalk up her sweaty palms to her hard run, but Vanessa knew better.

She was coming apart on a sidewalk in Napa Valley because

she'd just seen something that she wanted more than the painting in the window: a magnificent man in paint-stained jeans.

SAM MARSHALL LOOKED UP from tallying up the day's sales and nearly dropped the stack of credit card receipts to the floor. His hands started tingling from the tips of his fingernails to the base of his wrists. He had to take a deep breath.

He hadn't had that sensation—of needing a brush in his hands, a canvas before him, paints of every color so that he could create in an endless rush of inspiration—since Marissa. In his mind he was already painting the woman knocking on the glass door to his gallery, and the lines between what was and what would be on canvas were blurred.

The metal feet on his chair were shrill against the cement floor as he scooted out. He got up to let her in and knew that he was going to paint her. Nude. Surrounded by grapevines. The closer he got to her, the further the prickling sensation spread. All the way up his arm, past his elbow, into the joint of his shoulder.

Conveying on canvas this woman's unique combination of razor-sharp edginess and passion was going to demand every ounce of his artistic ability. But he couldn't wait. Sam would do anything to end his six-month slump. Everything he'd painted since Marissa had left had ended up in a Dumpster.

Standing before him was so much more than a beautiful woman. She was the chance for his artistic redemption.

Sam turned the lock to open and spun the knob.

"I want the painting in the window."

"Come in," he said, the calm words at odds with the pounding of blood through his veins.

"I don't have my wallet with me, but I couldn't go another moment without knowing that she was mine."

Something hit Sam low in his gut, in the place you didn't

punch a guy, even when he deserved it. He knew what it was like to want Marissa. He had wanted her. And he'd had her, all right. Until she'd destroyed him.

The crazy thing was, thinking of how his ex-muse had left him cold for an older, wealthier lover didn't hurt quite as much as it normally did. As it had for six months. Even five minutes ago, his memory of Marissa had been bigger, harsher, more erotic.

"She isn't for sale," he finally said, pleased by the fire in the redhead's eyes.

"She is now," she said, her long, taut legs moving out into a wide stance. "I'll double your asking price."

He didn't respond. He couldn't. Because the truth was, he hadn't really heard what she'd said. He'd been too busy studying the flecks of blue and black in her gray eyes.

"Okay," she said, "you win. I'll triple it."

He shook his head, her words finally getting through. "This isn't about money."

Something else flashed in her eyes. It wasn't fire. Lust, maybe? Anger?

The buzzing moved across Sam's shoulders, down past his ribs. His fingers twitched with the urge to capture those eyes on canvas.

Her tongue flicked out to her bottom lip. Sam knew women, and he knew what this one was trying to do. She was using her potent sensuality to convince him to let her have the painting.

"If it isn't about the money, then why don't you tell me"—her voice was throaty, enticing—"what you would like in exchange for the painting."

Her nipples grew hard beneath her thin, white, tummy-baring tank as if she were giving him a free sample of what she had to offer. He ached to pull the fabric from her skin. He could only guess at the color of her breasts. For a painter, guessing was never acceptable.

Fortunately, he wasn't so far gone that he couldn't play her game. "How bad do you want it?"

She took a step closer, and the prickling moved all the way down his chest, past his waist.

"Bad," she whispered. "Real bad."

The words went straight to his cock, which grew hard as it pressed against the zipper of his jeans.

Hell yeah, bad was the word for it. Sam knew a dangerous situation when he saw one. Because the last thing he was ever going to do was sleep with one of his models. Especially one that made him feel this artistically alive.

Somehow he had to figure out a way to paint her without stepping over the line. Especially when it was a line that he already wanted to cross.

"Will you do whatever I ask you to?"

Any other woman would have slapped his face for what he was insinuating. But not this one. She smiled, and her lips curved up with such mystery that she put the Mona Lisa to shame.

"Anything."

He couldn't hold back the note of surprise as he repeated the word. "Anything?"

She raised an eyebrow. "You heard me the first time."

What a woman she was. "Three days," he said, and for the first time something other than utter confidence swam in the depths of her gray eyes.

"Three days," she finally repeated. "Of what?"

He reached around her and pulled out the band that held back her hair. The buzzing moved up his neck, into his skull as his fingers found the perfect curve of her cranium.

She stood perfectly still, letting his fingers linger a little too long on the nape of her neck, allowing him to rearrange her hair around her shoulders. He brushed the overly long bangs away from her eyes and took her in.

Everything in the room but her face and those lips and the slant of her cheekbones was lost to him. "I'm going to paint you."

Her tongue came out again, licking at the corner of her mouth, but this time Sam knew it wasn't practiced. It wasn't planned. It was instinct.

"I'm all yours."

"In the nude," he added, upping the ante, making sure they were clear, that everything was on the table.

"I wouldn't have it any other way," she replied, and he found that his breath had been taken away.

He turned his back on her and grabbed his brushes. "We'll start now." It wasn't a question. He couldn't let her leave.

"Of course," she said, and he didn't have to look at her to see her satisfaction.

Too bad he couldn't take her up on her offer. Already he could imagine how good it would feel to slip inside her pussy, slick against his heat, tight against his thick shaft.

But there would be other sexy women to share his bed. He wasn't willing to lose the creative spark that had hit him the moment she'd knocked on his gallery door.

2

⟡⟐⟡⟐

$\mathcal{V}$ANESSA FOLLOWED SAM OUT the back door, already wet, ready to take whatever he was giving. From what she could tell, even in baggy jeans he looked to pack quite a punch. God, was she glad that she'd gone on that spontaneous run. There was nothing she'd rather do than pose naked for this sexy painter.

Except screw his brains out, of course.

She was absolutely positive that the woman in the painting she was going to buy—or barter for, she supposed—had been his lover. He was good. She already knew that from the quick glance she'd given the paintings on the surrounding walls of his gallery as she'd followed him out the back door. But nobody was *that* good.

The sensuality that dripped from the canvas came from a deep and personal knowledge of his model's body.

Of her heart.

Vanessa simply couldn't wait for him to start familiarizing himself with her own dips and curves. Particularly the hollow between her thighs. She'd been with plenty of suits, a rock singer or two, but never a painter. And he looked to be about as yummy as they came. Hard and rough and artsy.

No wonder so many society women were patrons of the arts. The bigger the check, the hotter the sex.

Making a mental note to ask Carrie about the ins and outs of the art world on Saturday, she followed her painter down a short alley. She was surprised to find that it opened up into a small, private vineyard. At the end of August, it was only a month or two from the crush, and the purple grapes hung heavy on the vines. She could smell their sweetness as they caught the final rays of sunlight.

A small red barn stood in the middle of the vines, and she watched as he slid open a large wooden door and disappeared inside. Moments later he reappeared with a pad of paper, a green plastic chair, and a thick white painter's tarp. He put the chair down outside the barn door, the pad of paper and pencil on top of it, then walked back to where she was standing. He threw the tarp down beneath a row of vines and stood back to check his setup.

"Is that where you want me?" she asked, deliberately choosing her words to let him know that he could definitely have her. Right now, please.

He'd been devouring her with his eyes from the moment she'd set foot inside his gallery. It was clear what he felt went far beyond mere artistic inspiration.

He shifted his glance from the tarp to her face. She found herself blushing beneath the heat of his gaze. Would wonders never cease? She never blushed. As a teenager she'd possessed an inner poise, a self-confidence that had set her apart from her peers. But this man, this painter with his burning green gaze, had the power to make her blush.

Hot damn. What else could he do? She couldn't wait to find out.

"I'm Sam Marshall," he said, not answering her question, knowing as well as she did that the answer was obvious. Of course he wanted her to pose on the tarp, why else would he have laid it there?

Two could play that game, she thought. "I'm Vanessa," she said as she kicked off her running shoes, then slipped her thumbs into the top edge of her white running shorts. She held his gaze as she slowly slid the shorts past her tiny white lace panties, down her thighs. She bent over slightly at the waist and lifted one leg off the ground, slipping a foot out, then the next. Her shorts dangled from one French-tipped nail. "Vanessa Collins."

His lip twitched and she thought he was going to grin. Instead he strolled over to the plastic chair and sat down, looking far too relaxed for Vanessa's liking. Bored, even.

"If you'd be more comfortable posing in your bra and panties, that's fine." He opened up his sketch pad, then his eyes returned to her. "For now."

Everything in Vanessa ached to prove to Sam that she was going to be the best nude model he'd ever had. Better than the bitch hanging in the window, that was for sure. (Vanessa was still going to hang the painting in her office, of course.)

She was going to be his every fantasy come to life.

And then he was going to make all her fantasies come true.

SAM KNEW HE LOOKED LOOSE and relaxed sitting in the chair, waiting for Vanessa to take off her clothes. It was something every painter learned early on in art school. At eighteen, when faced with his first hot nude model, it had been difficult to keep his hard-on a secret. But that was nearly twenty years ago, and he'd painted his fair share of hot babes since then.

Today, however, he should have been an actor, not a painter. Because Vanessa was driving him crazy. He wanted to toss his sketch pad into the bushes and drive into her without so much as a kiss. She'd be ready, he already knew that. He knew it with every word that came out of her sexy, dirty mouth. He knew it with every flash of her gray eyes as they raked up and down his body, always pausing at his rapidly growing cock.

Where the hell had his self-control gone?

She stood before him in white, wispy panties and a jog bra, and Sam's fingers itched to do a hell of a lot more than capture her image in black and white. He wanted to explore her slim hips with the palms of his hands, to run his tongue into the indentation behind her knees, to taste the salt of her tanned skin.

Oh, shit, while he'd been salivating over her, she'd gone and crossed her hands across her chest and was pulling her jog bra up her rib cage. Past the soft mounds of flesh at the base of her breasts. Past the perfect circles of her areolas, a shade all her own, not a dusty rose after all. More like the color her cheeks had turned when she'd blushed earlier, standing in the late afternoon sun in his small Cabernet Sauvignon vineyard. She pulled her top past the hollow of her collarbones, over her head, and when it was gone, her hair fell in waves around her shoulders, the wispy ends brushing the tips of her nipples.

His mouth went dry as he stared at her breasts. Did he actually think he could paint this woman? Already, he knew his hands would be shaking with lust when he tried to start drawing.

Why couldn't he have been a landscape painter? Why had he always been so drawn to the human form? He'd have to ask her to close her eyes while she posed so that he didn't embarrass himself. He needed time to get a grip.

And she hadn't even taken her panties off yet.

He was on the verge of telling her to leave them on. He wasn't sure he could paint with her sweet pussy right there for the taking, especially when he could tell how bad she wanted to be taken. That she *expected* to be taken. He'd always been able to read people: It was an artist's gift. And he knew without a doubt that Vanessa Collins always got what she wanted.

Only this time, no matter how much control he had to exert over himself, she was only going to get the painting she desired.

Not the painter.

Unfortunately, by the time he got the words "leave your panties on" gathered together in his brain, she'd slipped them off. He'd never had a chance.

Her pussy lips were full. And perfect. They were slick and wet. For him. His cock pounded against his zipper again, begging to get out, to find out what it would be like to slide into her cunt.

She stood before him, naked and glorious and so incredibly beautiful that bits of poetry sprang to mind. She was the perfect muse, not the least bit uncomfortable with her nudity.

Or his obvious sexual desperation.

"Don't be shy about arranging my legs. Or arms. Or anything you need to touch and move. I'm up for anything."

Every word out of her mouth was better than a porn flick.

"Yes," he wanted to shout. The answer was yes. And that's what he would have said if his entire life hadn't been on the line. If his future as a painter didn't depend on getting his groove back. Even with Marissa he'd eventually been able to think about painting, about something other than getting off.

With infinite grace, Vanessa lowered herself down onto the thick, soft, white canvas. She shifted her weight until she was on her side, her cheek resting on the palm of her right hand, her left thigh up over her right.

Even her ankles were perfect. Slim and strong and tanned. For the first time, Sam understood why women had covered their ankles for centuries lest they tempt men beyond control.

Good Lord, he wanted to touch her. He wanted to wrap his hands around her ankles, prop them on his shoulders, spread her wide, and drive in between her wet, sweet lips.

The sun had gone behind the roof of his barn, the light was rapidly fading, the heat of the day had dissipated, but Sam was sweating. He needed her to stop looking at him like that. Like she wanted to devour him. Like she was waiting for him to pounce on her.

"Lie on your back," he said, knowing he was being curt but unable to help himself.

She turned her hips from him, until her round, yet firm, ass was resting on the tarp. She put her arms up above her head, arching her rib cage the slightest bit. Her legs were stretched before her, bent ever so slightly at the knee.

It was as if she had tied herself to an invisible bedpost.

She was perfect.

Her head was turned to him, her eyes burning a hole through him as he gripped the pencil and began to feverishly draw her, starting at the dip of her belly button, her concave stomach.

His fingers stilled. He couldn't draw her pussy. Not with her taking him apart with her eyes like that.

"Look up at the sky," he said, surprised he could speak for the raging lust, the violent need to scrap his sketches and move straight to raw color that was ripping through him.

In her eyes, he saw that she knew why he wanted her to reposition. She knew he couldn't handle it. That he couldn't handle her. That he wanted to screw her any and every way he could and then come back for more.

He knew she liked that he was completely in her power. The

small Mona Lisa smile resurfaced on her lips and she turned her face away from him, up toward the rapidly darkening sky. The way she tilted her chin up, elongating her neck so beautifully for him, made him wonder if she'd posed before.

Jealousy burned through him at the thought of other men, other women, taking her beauty in. He wanted to capture her perfection on canvas for the world to see, and yet, he wanted her to remain his alone.

It was just as he'd thought when they'd been standing in his gallery, sizing each other up. His salvation might be his very damnation.

POSING NAKED FOR SAM, Vanessa had never felt so ripe, so sensual before. Maybe, she wondered wickedly, she should have auditioned for the *Playboy* college centerfold at Berkeley. One of their scouts had given her his card when she'd been serving beer at the campus bar, but being a bunny hadn't been in her plan at the time. Not to mention how much fun Rose and Carrie had made of her for taking his card. Of course, that had been before she'd known how utterly glorious it was to lie exposed like this beneath an artist's eyes.

Then again, Vanessa knew that she was dripping like a bitch in heat because they were Sam's eyes, not those of some creepy photographer hoping to cop a feel.

Endless visions of what would come *later* drove through her mind.

Sam's big hands fondling her.

Sam's chiseled mouth tasting her.

Sam's big, hard cock plunging into her.

Five minutes. That's how long she'd give him to forget all about his sketchbook.

The heady scent of the vines surrounded them, and Vanessa

felt drunk with desire. She'd been to Napa before, but it had never seemed so sensual, so filled with promise. Who knew, if Sam turned out to be as good in the sack as she was guessing he'd be, she might make a weekend in Napa a regular thing. A nice little hot-sex break from her usual city grind.

Extremely pleased with herself for stumbling straight into a sexual fantasy, Vanessa stretched like a sleepy cat on the tarp. She heard Sam shift in his chair and the knowledge of how badly he wanted her made her grow wetter, even more aroused. Just thinking about him watching her and getting more and more excited got her, well, even more excited.

Her hints couldn't have been any more blatant. The only way to be clearer was to rip his pants off and start sucking his dick. She grinned at the mental picture that conjured up, quite enjoying the thought of shocking Sam more than she already must have.

She shivered as the breeze kicked up. Sam's voice cut through her thoughts. "It's getting dark. You can get dressed."

She blinked open her eyes and shifted to her side, her head propped up on her palm again. "Now why would I want to do that?" she said, infusing every word with undeniable sensual promise.

He stared at her, hard, but he didn't say anything. A muscle in his jaw jumped out, then back.

She gestured to the vines, the nearly black sky. "It's perfect out here."

Still, he didn't say anything, but that muscle jumped faster in his cheek. She knew she was getting to him, and she couldn't resist pushing him further. "I love how it feels to be naked like this, outside, in your vineyard. And I've only just met you. I feel so naughty."

She forced a throaty, sexy laugh, but the fact that he wasn't on his knees beside her, having his way with her, had really started to grate. She felt a prick of something that might have been insecurity if such an emotion had been within her realm of feeling.

She did what she should have done an hour ago and took matters into her own hands. If he wasn't going to make the first move, she certainly wasn't going to be shy. "Why don't you take your clothes off and join me, Sam?"

Sam stood up so quickly that the plastic chair shot out from under him and crashed against the barn wall. "I don't sleep with my models."

He was good, she had to give him that. Talk about making her beg for it. No one had ever had the nerve to make her do that. He was even playing it like he was serious. Like he actually wanted her to put her clothes on and get the heck out of there.

"Is this a new policy?" she purred, slowly standing up, advancing on him, her bare feet crunching through the brown grape leaves that had fallen to the ground.

She could have sworn he was fighting with himself on whether to stand his ground. But she sensed he'd be man enough to face her, to face his own need.

He stood perfectly still as she closed the distance between them. "I can't sleep with you," he said again, and she smiled an all-knowing smile that intensified the uncomfortable, hunted look in his eyes.

Not to mention the raw desire he couldn't hide. Couldn't shake.

"How was she, Sam?" she asked, less than a foot from the hard planes of his body, knowing he would know exactly whom she was referring to.

His jaw tightened. There it was. The woman in the painting

had something to do with his reluctance to screw Vanessa's brains out. She'd always been smart about people. It was nice to be proved right again.

"She was rounder than me, wasn't she?" she whispered. "Softer." She closed her eyes, letting herself sway into him until her breasts were a breath away from brushing against the fabric of his T-shirt. "I've never been with a woman before. She makes me wonder what I've missed." She was pretty certain he forgot to breathe for a moment. "The first time you kissed her, what did she taste like?"

She waited with her eyes closed, taking in the sweet smell of the dirt, of the night. His breath was ragged now, and he didn't answer her question. She hadn't thought he would.

"Did she taste like honey? Or was she more like powdered sugar? So sweet, so soft that you couldn't help but dip your tongue in for more. Even though you know you shouldn't. Even though she was bad for you. So bad."

She opened her eyes enough that she could see his mouth, the pulse beating rapidly in his neck. She moved her hand to touch him, to run her fingers over his lips, but a breath away, she stopped.

"Did you run your brushes over the canvas and imagine that you were running them over her? Did she beg you to touch her? Did you have to close your eyes to get away from her heat? Her wetness?"

Vanessa felt her own breath go as she fell into her own game. The air went still as she spoke; even the birds stopped singing as if they, too, were hanging on her every word.

"As you painted her, did you ache to be inside her?" The light was so faint that she nearly missed his exhale, as if someone had punched him hard in the gut. "I can only imagine how long, how hard your nights were. How hard you were from dusk till dawn. Wanting her. Because touching yourself, thinking of her was never enough, was it? And all that time, she knew how you wanted her. How you watched her. How you came again and again thinking of her.

"Did you ask her to touch herself? Did you tell her you wanted to paint her with her hands between her legs? Her hands cupping her breasts? Did she arch her back and scream her pleasure for you?"

The light had gone completely as she'd spoken and Vanessa had never been so aware of another human being in her whole life. She knew Sam's penis would be hard, that one touch, one stroke, one kiss would send him over the edge. But still, she wouldn't let herself touch him, not until he begged her.

Which didn't mean, however, that she couldn't touch herself.

"I can see the two of you together, Sam," she said, "and it makes me hot. So hot. And if you won't touch me, I have to take matters into my own hands." She slid her fingers down the flat plane of her belly, over her slick, waxed mons, finally finding the hard nub of her clitoris. "Do you know how good I feel right now, imagining you taking her clit into your mouth, sucking it, pulling at it as you plunged your long, thick fingers into her?" She slid a finger into herself as she whispered, "That's what I'm doing right now, Sam. I'm touching myself like I imagine you touched her." Her free hand caressed her breasts.

"I'm going to come, Sam," she said as her breath grew heavy, "and I want you to imagine yourself coming as her muscles gripped and pulled at your cock, milking every last drop from you."

The force of her orgasm hit, and it was so much better, so much stronger than she'd expected, than she'd hoped it would be, that it nearly knocked her feet out from under her.

Without a single word, without so much as brushing against her with his fingers, he'd brought her to one of the best orgasms of her life. She felt shaken by the force of her response.

No doubt about it, her painter was good. Very good.

And he hadn't even touched her yet.

3

SAM HAD NEVER EXPERIENCED ANYTHING like Vanessa in his life. She was the most unabashedly sensual woman he'd ever met. His fingers ached to touch her. His cock was nearly tearing through his zipper to get at her wetness. He deserved a medal of artistic honor for this.

Picasso had never written about this, about starving himself of his muse for the sake of art. But then, Sam knew Picasso had freely slept with whomever he'd wanted. Especially his muses. Sam didn't think any nude model in her right mind had ever dumped Picasso. He'd been too successful. Larger than life.

Which was exactly why Sam had to hold out on his god-damned libido. Even if he ached to be inside Vanessa. Even if the sound of her panting, post-orgasm, was making his dick throb painfully in his jeans.

Sure, he was doing well professionally, but he wasn't larger than life. He wasn't an icon. He wasn't the painter everyone was trying to emulate. There weren't books written about him. There weren't courses taught on his methods at art school. He made a great living, but he hadn't achieved all his dreams.

And that's what it all came down to: He needed Vanessa to jump-start his drive to paint again, to juice him up. If he could only channel his sexual frustration into his art, he could jump over the line from great to astounding.

There was a good chance that intense sexual frustration was a gold mine, because right now the only thing stronger than his urge to make love to her was his compulsion to capture her on canvas. He wasn't going to forget this longing, this desperation. Which meant that every minute with her, every moment he didn't run his fingers down the crevasse between her breasts might very well be the inspiration he needed to lead him to the creative promised land. So he said, "Have dinner with me," certain that torturing himself with several more hours in Vanessa's presence was far better than not having a muse at all.

He could feel her surprise in the dark at his invitation. He could practically see her smile. "I'd love to," she said.

It took everything in him to move away from the heat of her body, to pick up her clothes, barely illuminated by the moon that was rising over the barn roof, to hand them to her, to say, "I need to clean out my brushes before they dry out," to leave her standing there, naked and perfect and sexier than any woman had a right to be.

He worked on autopilot, forcing his hands through the motions, knowing the exact moment she walked inside, even though she barely made a sound. He felt as if he were being stalked, knew that he was, in fact, and found that it was yet another thing he liked about her.

She left him to his task as she walked around his gallery, studying the paintings and the sculptures. From the start, Sam had been confident enough in his talent that he'd paid little attention to what the critics said. They'd mostly loved him, but still, he was surprised to find himself anxious for Vanessa's opinion.

Finally done with his brushes, he wiped his hands off on a clean rag and moved to join her in front of a small sculpture.

It was Marissa, of course. Everything for those two years had been about Marissa. She'd been a sickness, a compulsion, and he'd been slave to it. To her. She was his best work. Until Vanessa walked in just hours before, all he had left.

Was he about to repeat history with Vanessa?

Even if he was, it didn't matter. He needed to ride the wave of inspiration she'd provided. On Monday, he'd take stock and find out if his will to paint again, if his talent, his focus was back. Or if Vanessa was simply a blip in the screen of his fading career.

Her sultry voice broke into his overly angst-ridden thoughts. "You have a way with your hands," she said.

Gently, she ran her hands over Marissa's hips, then up to the small of her waist, one finger sliding into the valley of her spine, then up to cover her breasts.

Sam held his breath. Everywhere that Vanessa's hands went, he remembered touching Marissa. She'd been soft and warm and wet. Everything Vanessa had thought she was. And yet, somehow, his vision was turning around in his head, and Marissa was no longer lying beneath him.

Now, it was Vanessa who was so supple and soft and beautiful and perfect.

Her hands moved to Marissa's throat, her thumbs pressing into the hollow, as if she were trying to cut off the statue's breath.

At that moment, she looked at him, and it was no longer about Marissa.

It was about Vanessa.

ღ ღ ღ

HE WAS CLOSE. SO CLOSE. She had him in her back pocket. She'd
been with guys who'd been hung up on their exes. And frankly, it
had gotten old real fast. But this time, she sensed something different. It didn't take a rocket scientist to figure out the difference:
His ex had been his muse. And when they'd broken up, she hadn't
merely left him with a broken heart.

She'd stolen his art too.

Vanessa didn't believe in lying, either to her friends or herself.
And the truth was that she'd never thought of herself as a particularly giving person. She gave to the Red Cross and The Leu-
kemia Fund every year, but writing a check was easy. It had been
just as easy to remain emotionally detached from men. To sleep
with them, then walk away, with no regrets, no doubts or questions about the future.

But with Sam, she couldn't hold herself aloof. Maybe it was because she was drawn to what he'd created on paper, in clay.
Maybe it was because she loved sex and knew that Sam would be
at the top of her list of hot lays. But she couldn't deny the unmis-
takable urge she had to erase his ex-muse, his ex-girlfriend from
his memory. And she was certain she could do it, no matter how
lush, how exotic, how sexy the other woman had been. An uncomfortable sensation of possessiveness crept up Vanessa's spine,
almost as if she were jealous of Sam's ex-muse. Quickly, she
shook it away.

She wasn't jealous of what Marissa had had with Sam. No, the
reason she wanted to wipe Sam's slate clean was simply because
Marissa had been a bitch. A selfish, man-eating bitch. In every
painting that hung on Sam's gallery wall, Vanessa could see it in
her eyes, the curve of her mouth, the expression that said, "You
can have me. Until I leave you for someone better."

Vanessa had always had a healthy respect for bitchy women.

She was one herself and knew the power in it. But this time, there was a score to be settled. And she was the woman to do it.

The last hour had been all about a seduction of the obvious kind. Naked. Wet. Willing. It was the kind of seduction that went straight to a man's cock.

Now she would try a different kind of seduction altogether. One that would involve Sam's heart. She would make him realize that he liked her, that he was having fun. He would learn that she was intelligent, that she challenged him to think with his brain, not just with his penis.

Most men were easy. You went straight for their penis and didn't have to worry about the rest. But getting into bed with Sam would require her to be more tactical that that. It was going to require a combination of desire and affection.

Vanessa had never had to go there before and had to admit that she was looking forward to the challenge. It was time to shake things up.

It was time for slutty to become smart *and* slutty.

THIRTY MINUTES LATER, she was freshly showered and wearing white slacks and a white scoop-neck top. No bra, of course. It was an outfit that showed a whole lot less skin than she normally did on a Friday night. Incredibly alluring, yet classy. And given the way Sam's eyes heated up when he saw her, she was dead on.

Utterly gorgeous as he waited for her on the sidewalk in front of Gerard's, Sam had on clean jeans and a long-sleeved black Metallica T-shirt from their St. Anger tour. Somehow she knew this was as dressed up as he got. She'd always gone for men in tuxes, but suddenly, she could see the appeal of a dressed-down man. Plus, she liked his taste in bands, having always had a soft spot for the local San Francisco heavy metal band.

He didn't kiss her cheek, didn't reach for her hand, simply gestured for her to enter the restaurant. She was a woman used to being wooed, used to being fawned over, and his reserve was oddly alluring.

She sensed that if they never so much as touched palms, when they finally connected it would be *so* much better.

Her breath caught at the thought of that first touch. When would it happen? Where? How? His mouth on her lips? His hands on the small of her back? Would she reach for him, desperate to finally feel his heat pressed against her? Would he brush her hair away from her shoulders and bite her softly below her earlobe? Would he throw caution aside and slide his hand into her panties, into her wetness?

Her silent erotic questions made her nipples grow taut beneath the thin sheath of her top, and Sam's eyes locked on them as though guided by the heat of her skin. She took a deep breath as he turned to the maître d', reminding herself that tonight during dinner she'd have to put more than her body to work: She'd have to bring into play her brain and her wit too. Sure, he was aroused, it was obvious that he wanted her. By the time she was done with him, Sam would be begging her to have sex with him.

"They've got a table ready for us," he said, then stepped aside to let her move in front of him. A gentleman, that's what he was.

When was the last time she'd gone to dinner with a man who hadn't been trying to feel her up beneath the tablecloth, who hadn't been inviting her for a quickie in the bathroom between the salad and main course? She nearly sighed at what a surprisingly nice change Sam was from all those other men, then immediately gave herself a silent smack upside the head for being so sappy.

She was on operation get-in-Sam's-pants, not on mission fall-in-love-with-him.

As Sam held out her chair for her, careful not to brush her skin with his hand in the process, Vanessa grinned at the utterly ridiculous thought of falling in love. A part of her, the wicked part that usually had free rein, was tempted to mess with him, to purposefully lean back against his arm as he moved away. But the sensual anticipation building between them was too enticing for her to mess everything up on a whim.

He sat across from her, and she was mesmerized by his hands as he shook open his napkin and laid it across his lap. Again, she reminded herself what this dinner was all about. She was going to help Sam forget his ex-muse and lover while also getting what she wanted—namely him and his undoubtedly gifted cock—in the process.

Two glasses of Pinot Noir magically appeared on their table, "courtesy of Jack, who isn't here tonight, but is always glad to have you at Gerard's," and Vanessa lifted her glass in a toast.

Sam's eyes narrowed slightly as he followed her lead. She knew he didn't trust her, which she liked. It meant he was a smart man.

"To the wonderful weekend we're going to have," she said, lightly clinking her glass against his.

The Pinot was deliciously smooth as it ran down her throat into her empty belly. She was counting down the seconds, certain that he was going to say something serious, something to set her straight about his intentions.

"Posing is hard work," he said right on cue, and she had to fight back her grin. Men were so predictable, it killed her. Even this one, who had managed to surprise her several times during the past couple of hours. "Your muscles will ache, you'll be dying to change positions, you'll be bored and wish you'd never agreed to it."

She put her glass down, leaned her elbows on the table, and

placed her head in her palms. "I'll tell you what's really hard," she said, "Statistics 101. I was a senior at Berkeley and I needed the class to graduate. It was boring and difficult." She saw his eyebrows raise, taking in the new knowledge that she wasn't merely a hot piece of ass. She had a brain too. Which meant that it was time to bring his head back around to her ass by saying, "I nearly had to do my professor to get an A."

His mouth moved, ever so slightly, and she could see he was fighting with himself about whether to give in to a grin at her audacity. So she added, "Oh, wait, I did sleep with him. He was young and hot and I ran into him at a bar on Telegraph right before finals. But I would have gotten an A anyway. Guess I had a knack for stats after all."

She knew he couldn't hold it in anymore, she'd played her cards just right, and she let herself soak up the sound of his laughter. "I could never get my head around numbers," he said when the glorious sound of his amusement stopped washing over Vanessa. "That's why I became a painter."

"No," she said, shaking her head, taking another sip of wine. "You became a painter because you're a painter."

His glass was halfway to his lips when he put it down. "You're right," he said. "I never had a choice. Never wanted one either. I suppose there were a lot of things I could have been, but this was the only life I wanted."

She nodded, because she completely understood what it was like to be born into something. It had always been her calling to tell people what to do, what to like, what to keep an eye on.

"So you're a statistician?" he asked, and she liked that he was interested in her, that he was comfortable teasing her.

"Nope, PR. But if I'd been born into royalty I would have gone that route instead."

His grin was sudden this time. "You like to control the world?"

She raised an eyebrow. "I can't believe you have to ask."

He laughed again, and she was shocked by how much she liked the sound of it. By how much she liked him. She hadn't seen him smile before now, and she realized how much she'd been missing in his studio. Yes, he'd been mysterious and gorgeous and sort of wounded, and she'd wanted to have sex with him in every way imaginable.

But was it possible that he was even sexier when he smiled?

Now that was a first.

A young female waiter came up to their table, and the adoration she heaped on Sam was embarrassing. "Sam, we haven't seen you here in a while. I've missed you." She blushed and stammered, "I mean, we've all missed you. You've probably been really busy painting, huh?" She was smart enough to press her lips shut and cut off her lovesick babbling, but her throat bobbled nervously and Vanessa actually felt sorry for the girl.

Sam took it in stride, probably used to women blabbering all over themselves when he was in the room. No wonder, she thought, staring at him over the rim of her wineglass. He was some seriously hot piece of ass.

"Yeah, I've been really busy, but it's nice to see you too, Julie." His smile was genuine, and Vanessa found herself liking the way he didn't preen his feathers at the hero worship. Working to make the waitress more comfortable, he asked, "What are the specials tonight?"

Yet again, in the sweet way that he dealt with a young girl in puppy love, he had put all of Vanessa's other lovers to shame. She couldn't imagine how nasty, how snide her latest CEO would have been to a young girl who thought he was cute.

As Julie rattled off dishes, Vanessa continued her slow perusal of her artist "lova" for the weekend. Throughout, she couldn't tear her eyes from Sam's hands.

She hadn't been kidding when she'd said he had a way with them. They were beautiful. Large and hard, as if he spent more time with a hammer than a paintbrush. Tanned with a light dusting of hair on his knuckles. His nails were short and surprisingly clean for someone who spent hours working with color and clay every day. She could only imagine how they'd feel caressing her skin, slipping into her and . . .

The waitress interrupted her lusty thoughts, and it took Vanessa a moment to surface. She wanted Sam, not sautéed leeks on a bed of polenta. But she knew she needed to bide her time, so she put a smile on and said, "Whatever special is the best. That's what I want." She felt Sam's eyes on her, knew he liked how she'd ordered.

"PR has always seemed like a bunch of smoke and mirrors to me," he said after the waitress moved away.

"You don't like to be told what to do, do you?"

"Nope."

"Me either," she said as she bit into a Parmesan tuille *amuse bouche* and closed her eyes in rapture. "Good. Very good." He nodded in agreement, and she got around to his question. "I like what I do because it's a constant challenge to take something great and get people to talk about it, think about it, want to own it, or read it, or sing it in their cars. And it's even more of a challenge to get a buzz going when something really isn't worth it."

"Most people are afraid of things that challenge them," he said.

"A challenge makes me hungrier," she said, staring at the gorgeous man who was her biggest challenge to date. "Makes me want it more."

He stared at her mouth while she spoke, as if he were trying to memorize the shape of her lips. Before she was aware enough of what she was doing to stop it, she found her lower lip between her teeth.

Biting her lip was something she never did. It would have meant that she was uncertain about something, and Vanessa was always certain. But now, with Sam, it was natural. It wasn't that he made her uncertain. Or nervous.

Sam made her feel. Something deep and strong. As odd a sensation as either of the others would have been.

The sheer novelty momentarily threw her off. "I don't think you're afraid of challenges either, are you?" she said, trying to get herself back on track. He shook his head, so she continued, "I'm going to paint you this weekend. You're going to pose for me."

Again that light flickered in his eyes, some combination of admiration and disbelief. "And you have what artistic training exactly?"

She shrugged as she forked a bit of beets and Gorgonzola into her mouth. "None. So what?"

"So then you wouldn't mind if I got behind your desk and did your job on Monday?"

"You'd be great at it," she said simply, and he stared at her for a long moment before he picked up a clam in wine and garlic and held it out, across the table, to her.

"Taste this," he said, and she slowly placed her mouth around the clam, her lips a breath from his fingers. Her heart raced as she sucked the sweet, soft meat into her mouth and swallowed.

"Like it?" he asked. She took a sip of her wine, hoping the alcohol would momentarily temper her lust. It was either drink Pinot or leap across the table and ride him in front of a bunch of strangers.

Not that riding him wasn't a fabulous idea, just not in the plan for tonight. Not his plan, and suddenly, not hers. She couldn't remember the last time she'd exercised patience, actually waited for anything. She'd always taken exactly what she'd wanted when she'd wanted it, but with Sam anticipation was proving to be a potent aphrodisiac.

"You're going to be nude for me," she said, and he didn't look surprised by her words.

"I wouldn't have it any other way," he said, echoing her earlier words, and she nearly came in her seat. Sam Marshall was a rare breed indeed.

4

*I*T HAD BEEN ONE OF THE BEST NIGHTS he could remember in a very long time. Certainly post Marissa, but even, if he was being completely honest with himself, better than the nights he'd spent painting Marissa, then taking her to bed.

He'd never met anyone like Vanessa, woman or man. She lived for now, not the future, not the past. In all the time he'd spent with Marissa, he'd never been able to get comfortable. Instead, he'd worried constantly about the future, never sure what her mood, her happiness level would be one minute to the next. Always doubting her commitment, knowing deep down that someday she'd leave him. That he was nothing but a stepping-stone for her.

Vanessa walked back toward him from the bathroom, with every eye in the restaurant on her unabashedly confident sexiness. There was an awful lot to appreciate about the woman.

Not for the first time, he wondered if he wasn't the stupidest bastard this side of San Francisco for not jumping into bed with her.

He scooted back in his chair and followed her out of the restaurant, eyes glued to her tight ass as it swung slightly from side to side. He'd lived in Napa for many years, but the night had never seemed quite so full of promise.

And that's when he decided: He was going to take her home and make love to her all night, into the morning. Despite his Herculean efforts to deny how much he wanted her, there was no other choice, really. He wasn't a big enough man to turn down a woman like this, no matter if it meant bidding his creative muse a permanent farewell.

Her head tilted back as she stared up at the moon. He was mesmerized by her long neck. He wanted to press his lips against the pulse there, so steady, so firm. "Vanessa," he said, and when she turned her eyes to him, she knew that he'd changed his mind, that he was ready for her.

He reached out to pull her against him, to finally surrender to his need for her, but before he could touch her, she whispered "Good night" and was gone.

VANESSA LAY IN A SCALDING HOT BATH, her heart pounding. Had she actually turned down an offer to have wild sex with a gorgeous stranger? She'd never, not once in her life, played hard to get. She didn't see the point. But tonight, she knew with a certainty that frightened her that Sam wasn't ready yet. And, somehow, neither was she.

She'd charmed him tonight, and he'd charmed her right back. She'd known she'd won the moment he'd said her name. Yet she'd found herself unwilling to give in quite yet. Instead she wanted to savor the anticipation a little bit longer.

So instead of lying in a naked sweaty tangle with Sam, here she was, soaking in bubbles. Alone. More impatient, more frustrated than she could ever remember being in her life.

She'd pounded on Rose's door and Carrie's too, but neither of them had been in their rooms. She left a quick message for Rose while the water filled the tub. "Hey, it's me. I just tried your room but you weren't there, so I'm hoping that means you're getting lucky with the chef hottie. Too bad I can't say the same for myself. I'm posing for a painter and he's got this stupid rule about . . . I'm too wound up to talk about it. Don't worry about me, I'll be back Sunday afternoon. And I'll have gotten exactly what I want by then. Let Carrie know that I'm AWOL, would you?"

Who would have thought that she would be the only one home alone in her hotel room tonight? Carrie was a good girl at heart, and Rose was the most risk-averse person she'd ever met. And yet, they were probably getting off with some wine country studs right now, while she had only a bottle of wine and a dildo for company.

She'd acted completely out of character by turning her back on what would have surely been a night of hot sex with a very hot, very intense painter. Knowing it was ultimately the right course of action wasn't getting her off right now. Angry now, she flicked her dildo off the edge of the tub and watched it bounce a couple of times on the tiled floor. She was still hot and bothered, but nine inches of vibrating rubber was no substitute for Sam's long, hard, flesh-and-blood cock.

If she closed her eyes she could feel it slide inside her. The water hadn't cooled much, but she shivered in anticipation. Tonight, the time hadn't been right. But tomorrow would be.

AT 6 A.M. HER PHONE RANG, but she'd been up since five, shaving and moisturizing. Preparing. She picked up the receiver, but there was nothing but a dial tone. She smiled. Good. He was pissed off too. Probably hadn't been turned down in some time.

The smile stayed on her face as she made her way out of the

hotel and into quiet Main Street. She took a deep breath and realized that she felt more relaxed and happy than she had in quite a while. She loved the city, but taking a break from it every once in a while wasn't a bad thing either.

Especially if she was doing the breaking in Sam Marshall's bed.

He didn't bother to look up from his canvas when she emerged from behind a row of grapes. The white tarp was still on the ground, but today he'd exchanged his pencil and pad for oils. He had two canvases going side by side, and his hands were already covered with color.

He didn't utter so much as a "hello" or "good morning." Again, Vanessa couldn't help but admire the way he didn't waste words. She spent so much of her life with bullshitters—heck, she was one of the very best in the business—so Sam's silence was a rare treat. Without waiting for his direction, she pulled her thigh-skimming white sundress over her head, dropped her panties on top of the dress on a nearby chair, and lay down on her back with her arms as a pillow for her head.

"You always wear white," he said finally, still not looking at her. In spite of that, she'd never been more conscious of a man's attention.

"Angels always do."

Her eyes were closed, but she knew when he looked at her. It was the exact moment that the sun rose over the barn roof. Between the bright golden rays and the heat in his eyes, she felt warm all over.

For the next several hours, she relaxed into her job as artist's muse. Rather than being bored by her work, she enjoyed the challenge of it. He was right. Her muscles ached and her toes buzzed and she wanted to roll over, to move, to change position. Finally, even though her will was strong, her stomach rebelled with a loud growl.

She opened her eyes and turned her head. "Got any food around here?"

He started at her words. She was pleased by how absorbed he was with capturing her on canvas. She liked to think that if she'd been alive a couple hundred years ago, it would have been one of the masters immortalizing her.

"I forget food when I'm working," he said by way of an apology, but she didn't care about that, she just needed to eat. She stood up and slipped back into her dress, leaving her panties on the ground. He put down his brushes. "I picked up some pastries earlier. They're in the barn."

She followed him into the big, old wooden building, and it took a long moment for her eyes to adjust to the relative darkness. She sat down on a couch in the corner and grabbed a croissant, pulling off a flaky piece and stuffing it into her mouth.

He handed her a cup of coffee, and it was hot, strong, black. Just the way she liked it.

"You're a good model," he said, and you would have thought she'd won the Nobel Peace Prize for how much her heart swelled at his words. She took a moment to swallow down her unexpectedly emotional response along with a bite of pastry.

"It's difficult, but it feels good," she said.

She held his eyes as she said it, and they both knew that the time was coming. Soon. For more things that felt good. For both of them.

They ate in silence, but it was a surprisingly companionable silence. Albeit heavy with desire. But that, Vanessa sensed, was just the way things were between them.

Comfortable and yet terribly uncomfortable at the same time.

It was a delicious paradox, one she wanted to explore. At length. Too bad the weekend was so short. Then again, that's what made this all so exciting. It was a break from the normal.

She didn't know how she'd function if she were this aroused all day every day.

She grinned at the thought of being on the edge of an orgasm twenty-four-seven. Might not be bad, actually, she decided as she watched Sam flip through a box of paint tubes for more colors.

"Can I look at the paintings?" she asked, and he nodded absentmindedly.

"If you want." He really didn't seem to care either way, pulling a tube of paint out, studying it for a moment, then discarding it for another.

She liked that distracted thing Sam had going on. He was the polar opposite of her. She was a master of multitasking, he was so focused he lost sight of everything else. She was an always moving target, he stayed right where he was. Hot damn if they weren't going to fit together in the sack like puzzle pieces.

Figuring there was no point in waiting to see the finished product—might as well see what all of her cramping muscles were good for—she brushed the crumbs from her hands and brought her coffee cup outside.

What she saw made her gasp, and for the first time, she was oblivious to Sam's presence. Vanessa had a keen eye for art, and she knew at once that she wasn't the woman in the paintings. Her hips weren't that full, her breasts weren't that lush. And yet, he'd captured her essence in a way that no photo ever had.

The woman he'd painted was on the edge. Of what, exactly, it wasn't clear. But it was big. Really big. As if she were going to rise and leap off the canvas at any moment, into life. She'd been painted in shades of white—she didn't know there could be that many, that white could be black and red and orange—but all around the woman was a mass of color.

Vanessa was tempted to run a finger over the woman—over herself, she supposed—to see if she really would come to life.

"She's beautiful."

"I know," was his reply, and for the first time in her life she didn't know what to do. She stood there, hating her uncertainty but stuck in it at the same time.

Just as he'd helped the young waitress, he guided her into action. "Let's change things up," he said. She still stood there, and he added, "Naked again," so she stripped back off her dress, but this time she found herself sitting cross-legged, facing him, a thick bunch of newly picked grapes on her lap, covering her. He didn't touch her, but the way that he told her exactly where he wanted her arms, her hair, the grapes, made her feel as if he'd rubbed every inch of her skin with his hands. With his lips.

She inhaled a ragged breath and accepted that she, the unstoppable, imperturbable Vanessa Collins, very well might have gotten herself in over her head with a man. With every hour that passed, as the sun moved over the barn's roof to high in the sky and then back down behind an oak tree, her world turned increasingly inside out.

Soon, her stomach was empty again, and without thinking she reached down and popped a grape into her mouth. It was large and juicy, and her mouth couldn't contain all the sweet liquid. The juice dripped down her chin, falling to her chest, a lazy stream of purple-tinged liquid sliding down between her breasts.

The sun was still behind the oak tree, but her skin was on fire. She looked up, and Sam was no longer hidden behind his canvas. He was standing in front of her, and she felt so small, so tiny on the ground beneath him. The evidence of his arousal—an enormous bulge behind the zipper of his jeans—took what little breath she still had away.

Oh, God, she thought, not bothering to chastise herself for her girly-ness, *please let me be ravished.*

Without a word he was on his knees and his thumb was brushing away the lingering sweetness at the corner of her mouth. Instinctively, she turned into his hand, and then she was sucking on his finger. The throbbing between her legs intensified, and she wondered if she was going to come again, like this, with a bunch of Cabernet grapes on her thighs, Sam's thumb rasping against her tongue.

"Touch me," she said, and he knew exactly what she wanted—of course he did—because suddenly he had moved to sit behind her, his strong thighs pushing into her knees, and he was running his hands down her stomach. He hadn't yet touched her breasts, but there would be time for that later. All she could think about was the wetness between her legs and the way his fingers felt as they brushed slowly, so slowly down her skin, past her belly button, onto her smoothly waxed mound.

He stopped there, the tips of his fingers barely an inch from her clit. Desperate for him to push into her, she barely resisted the urge to buck up into his hands. He was in charge, and it was precisely where she wanted him to be.

His breathing came fast behind her and she wondered at his restraint, at how he managed to keep his fingers away from her open, ready cunt. She felt his free hand push the hair away from one side of her neck and then the delicious sensation of warm breath on her skin. Every muscle in her body tightened as his lips found a sensitive spot, and she knew she was going to come, his fingers an inch from her pussy, his teeth on her earlobe.

She arched slightly—there was no way she couldn't, she was completely gone now—and that was when he slipped his finger down that precious inch. He pushed into the wet folds, pressed against her clit, and everything exploded. She tilted her head back further to give him better access to her neck, to her shoulder, and as she convulsed he slipped one thick finger into her vagina, his thumb never leaving her clit as it swirled hard and deep against her. A second finger joined the first, and she stretched wide for him. Her hips moved into him and he was strong, so strong, as his palm pressed firmly back against her. Her nipples throbbed painfully, aching for him to squeeze them, to suck them.

When she opened her eyes, he was no longer sitting behind her. Quickly, he shifted them so that she was lying on the tarp again, her back pressed into the thick cotton. Sam hovered above her, his chest bare.

She couldn't stop her hands from roaming the hard, muscled planes of his chest. He was gorgeous, by far the most beautiful man she'd ever laid eyes on. Or hands. Her mouth found his tanned skin and he was groaning beneath her tongue, her lips. She had to give him the pleasure he'd given her. And even though she was counting the seconds until his cock was thick and deep inside her, she needed to do this first. For herself as much as for him.

In one quick move, she had him beneath her. "You're strong," he said, surprise evident in his voice, along with admiration.

"I know. I'll always surprise you." She ran her hands, the tips of her fingers, down his torso, down to the buckle on his jeans. "You should be naked when you're painting me," she said, and he smiled.

"I wouldn't be painting, then," he said, and she nodded.

"Jim Morrison managed to sing."

She knew he was envisioning her mouth around his cock while he painted, just as Jim Morrison had recorded his vocals while being blown by his groupies.

But Vanessa didn't have time for more banter because she had just pulled his jeans off, and her hand rested on the waistband of his boxers. Sweet Lord, he was big. And she hadn't even taken the cotton wrapping off.

And then she did.

His penis pushed at her, pushed into her lips, and she was running her tongue over his velvety softness. He was hot and hard in her mouth and she wanted to take him all the way down her throat as far as he would go. She couldn't get him in all the way, he was that big, but she tried. When her fingers came around to cup his balls, she forgot all about how she was going to blow him first, how she was going to make him come in her mouth.

She was too greedy for that.

And so she reached for the condom she'd stowed beneath the tarp that morning, only marginally surprised to find more than one condom under there. Great minds thought alike and all that. Swiftly, she slid it down his huge cock.

She wanted to ride him, to sink down on his shaft, hard and fast, but no matter how strong she was, he was stronger and she was on her back again. Beneath his heavy weight, again.

His eyes were black with passion, and he stared at her as he had since the moment she'd knocked on his door. And then it was all a blur, rough and fast and sweaty, as he thrust into her. She stretched wider and wider for him, and he was so hot and hard, and she was so wet, so sensitive that she felt herself coming again before he'd sheathed his whole length.

"Sam," she groaned as her hands found their way to the back of his head, threading through his blond hair. His lips were on hers and his hands cupped her ass, pulling her into him as he rocked harder and harder against her. Her hip bones collided against his and she knew she'd be bruised later but she didn't care, she just wanted him to keep pounding into her. She sucked at his tongue and his lips as he slid his shaft out, then in, then out again in time to her contractions. Finally, she came up for air and he was waiting, waiting for her to join him again.

Somehow, some way, he hadn't come yet. Vanessa didn't believe in the idea of the perfect man, but this was another of Sam's outstanding qualities. He could pleasure her and not fall apart himself.

He sat up and pulled her with him, her legs still wrapped around his waist. For a moment, they were motionless. Sam sat cross-legged, holding Vanessa on top of him as if she were a bunch of grapes.

Still hard and huge inside her, he ran his hands up from her hips to her waist, up the bottom of her rib cage, to just below the soft flesh of her breasts. She sucked in a breath and watched her nipples grow hard again. He wasn't touching her breasts, just looking with those hot eyes, but she felt as if there were a thousand tongues swirling over her tits.

"How do you do that?" she asked, and the corner of his mouth moved, though he didn't smile. His hands answered her as they moved to cover one breast and then the other. She closed her eyes as the sensations washed over her. And even though their hips were perfectly still, even though he wasn't pulsing inside her, even though his fingers weren't anywhere near her clit, she felt another orgasm building. She grew fuller and fuller with it as his hands massaged her breasts softly. He didn't kiss her, but he didn't need to. His gentle touch was her undoing this time—just as his rough taking of her had been minutes ago—and she arched her back into his hands and tilted her face back toward the sun as the orgasm overtook her. Her spasms were slow this time, but each one was bigger than the next.

He began to move inside her, movements so small that she wondered if she was imagining them in her pleasure. The slight pressure of his cock pushing into her, of it flexing inside her, of him coming beneath her, was enough to intensify her orgasm to the point of delirium. She couldn't have told him what her name was, or what she did for a living, or where she was.

All she knew was that he was inside her and she felt better than she'd ever thought to feel her whole life.

His hands never left her breasts. When she could finally open her eyes, when she had relearned to breathe and could remember what her name was and where she was, she looked up into his smiling face.

Vanessa knew she'd remember that smile forever.

5

Sam couldn't help his grin. Being with Vanessa was better than anything he could have ever imagined. But—and here was the big question that wiped the smile right off his face, even though she was naked and slick on his lap—was the most incredible sexual experience of his life worth losing his muse?

His mother had raised him to be a gentleman, and the gentlemanly thing to do was to tell Vanessa how beautiful she was, how special she was to him, how this was more than a weekend fling. She shifted on his lap and he smiled again. Good thing Vanessa would have known he was spouting utter bullshit, because he wasn't going to say any of that.

"First we'll eat," he said as he lifted her light weight off him and stood up, not the least bit bothered by his own nudity, but powerfully aware of hers. As always. "And then you'll pose for me again."

He wanted to skip right past food. Like most artists he was happy to forgo eating, sleeping, anything when the mood struck. But he couldn't exactly starve her, could he?

"No," she said as though reading his mind. "You'll paint. I'll go get food."

If he wasn't careful, he could really fall hard for a woman like her.

As she put her dress and panties back on, he didn't pick up any weird vibes. He didn't get the sense that she was disappointed by his lack of flowery post-sex compliments. Thank God. He'd never been good at that stuff.

She headed out through his vines without a word of good-bye, without checking to see what he wanted to eat, but he wasn't worried. She'd come back with something absolutely perfect for his palate. And he was confident that she wouldn't bolt on him. After what they'd shared, he had a feeling she was biding her time until round two.

But all of those thoughts were just his way of stalling. Of trying to forget that letting his penis overtake his brain might have ruined everything. Telling himself not to be a pussy, he zipped up his jeans and threw on his T-shirt. Barefoot, he headed back over to his paint-splattered easel. He moved the finished painting aside and put up a blank, white canvas.

For a moment, all he saw was white. Nothing else. No vision. No image. Nothing.

His heart raced and he nearly stumbled back into the red wall of the barn. It had already happened. He'd let himself touch her and he'd lost it.

Fear quickly turned to anger. Was this what the rest of his life was going to be? Finding a woman he desired, a woman who made his fingers itch to paint her, to stroke her, but never being able to do a damn thing about it?

Not a chance.

He picked up a paintbrush and began to fill the canvas with color. It was furious motion, one without direction. Vanessa's smell was on his hands, on his skin, and he couldn't help but be back on the tarp, with her riding him, her breasts in his hands, her mouth under his. His hands moved faster, and without conscious thought or intention the painting took shape before him.

It was astounding.

Reds and oranges and yellows exploded on the canvas. In the middle of it all were Vanessa's eyes, her curves, her strength, and her passion. He hardly breathed, didn't dare to stop as he created what he already knew would be his best work.

This painting was what he had worked for thirty-six years to achieve. His anger, his frustration, his love, and his lust—definitely his lust for Vanessa—were here for the rest of the world to finally see.

The sun must have moved in the sky, he must have been thirsty, or hungry, but he didn't notice any of that. He moved the canvas to the ground and picked up another. He could see so much now, so much was clear to him.

It was as if being with Vanessa had helped him tap into the deeper recesses of his creative subconscious, allowing him to tap into talent he'd never known he possessed.

Finally, he heard something behind him and remembered to take a breath. Vanessa stared at him, a bag of takeout forgotten in her hands.

"Where'd this come from?" she asked, and it was enough for him to know that he'd been right.

He turned away from his canvas, relief washing through him as he knew in his gut that his muse wasn't going anywhere, that it was there to stay this time.

He almost said "you," but he hated the way it sounded in his head, so he didn't answer her. He just said, "Let's eat," and she nodded, understanding that there were no words for it beyond a too-simple "you."

ↂ ↂ ↂ

VANESSA HAD BEEN GLAD to head out on her own to pick up lunch. Sex was just sex. That's what she'd always believed. More than that, it was what she'd always known. But somewhere along the way, as Sam had turned her body inside out with his hands, with his mouth, with his cock, she'd lost hold of her certainty.

Because sex had never been so good. So powerful. So all-consuming. It had only taken ten seconds for her to figure out that Sam Marshall was not only the best lover she'd ever had but also the one man who had a chance of breaking through her "no love" rule.

Life had taught her that men didn't stick around once their desire was slaked. Her father had been the best teacher around. And her mother had been his victim. As soon as she'd turned eighteen, Vanessa had gotten the hell out of that house, with all its lies and betrayals. She'd lived on her terms at Berkeley. No lies. No cheating. Because there was no love to lie about. And no one to deceive. Just men that she slept with on a casual basis.

The intensity of being with Sam, and the way it had richocheted out from her groin all the way up her chest to her heart, had been enough to make her consider leaving for sandwiches and not coming back. But she wasn't a coward. And, like she'd told him, she didn't run from a challenge. Plus, she wasn't leaving without the painting in the gallery window.

By the time she returned with a bottle of cool, crisp Chardonnay, chicken curry salad, artisan goat cheese, and freshly baked sourdough bread, she had convinced herself that modeling for Sam, that sleeping with Sam, was nothing more than a test of her will. One that she was certain she'd pass with flying colors.

Besides, even if she did something stupid like trying to envision a future with Sam, the fact was that things between them would never work in a million years.

He was a painter, she was a businesswoman.

He lived in the country, she thrived in the city.

He relied on passion to create art, she was only interested in passion if she was getting an orgasm out of it.

Which was why it was so unfortunate that the new painting he'd created since she'd been gone made her falter. No man had ever made her doubt her own mind before.

She'd opened her mouth too soon, hadn't been able to stop the words "Where'd this come from?"

He'd shrugged, but his gaze had been steady on hers in his silence, and she'd been glad that he hadn't felt the need to make up some poetic crap about her being the inspiration for his creative genius. She would have puked. And not only because she hated guys who tried to get in her pants with smooth words. Mostly, she would have been sick because she would have been afraid it was true.

She'd always been in control. Always. Her mother had spent hours, days, months weeping for her cheating husband. But to Vanessa it had seemed that her mother had been weeping not over a man but over her own helplessness. And so Vanessa had vowed never to be helpless. Never to give the reins of control to a man.

Vanessa's life was hers alone. She made herself happy and no one, except her girlfriends, maybe, relied on her for their happiness.

Sam was getting to her. Hard. First with his impressive cock. And now, with his breathtaking paintings. A seedling of resentment bloomed to life inside her. How dare he have such power over her. How dare he take it without her permission.

Not bothering with nice, she forced herself to look away from his magnificent work. "I've got to eat or I'll pass out. You still need me this afternoon, or are you all set here?"

Part of her wanted him to say *No, go ahead and leave,* to take care of the dirty work for her. But the other, much bigger part, couldn't hold back the pleasure at his "We made a deal. You pose, I paint, you get the girl in the front window."

She forked a bite of chicken curry into her mouth and couldn't hold back her pleasure at the sweet and tangy flavor. Sam uncorked the wine and poured it into small blue tumblers. She picked up the glass closest to her and drank it in one gulp.

"Good?" he asked, seemingly amused by her sudden bad temper.

"Fine," she snapped, even though she never snapped. It wasn't in her repertoire. She charmed, she schemed, she slipped in back doors wearing her signature little white dress, but she didn't snap.

Sam sat down on a plastic lawn chair next to her, against the barn wall. She wanted to smack his conceited smirk off his mouth. He thought he had her right where he wanted her, which proved that he didn't know anything about her at all.

Ten silent minutes later of a silence punctuated only by chewing and swallowing, the food was gone and Vanessa was ready to get back to work. Only this time, they were going to do things her way.

"I think it's time to mix things up." She walked over to Sam and pulled his shirt up his magnificent chest and over his head. He didn't stop her, but he didn't help her either. Damn, if she didn't like him even when he was being a know-it-all jerk.

"You're the model. I'm the painter." She unbuttoned the top of his jeans, and as she unzipped them, his hard penis sprang up against her fingers. "Although I don't know if I'm going to be able to find a big enough bunch of grapes to cover you."

His mouth curved up as he grew another inch before her. Using every ounce of will, Vanessa stopped herself from dropping to her knees to throat him, even though sucking him would have given her as much pleasure as it would have given him.

Later.

"You know anything about oils?" he asked as she pushed him over to the tarp.

"Lie down," she said. And then, "Not a thing. But it really doesn't matter."

He lounged on his back, his head in his hands, his ankles crossed, staring up at the sky as if lying naked in his vineyard with a raging hard-on was something he did every day.

"Is this how you want me?"

Again, it was an enormous strain to force herself to walk away from him when every cell in her body was screaming to slide down on his thick shaft. She picked through his can of horsehair brushes, picking up three that looked to be clean and fairly new.

"You can close your eyes or keep them open. I don't care. But don't move. And don't get in my way." His cock twitched in anticipation, and a small drop of fluid rose to the top. She wanted to touch his wetness more than she wanted to breathe, but she had a plan and she was sticking to it.

"I don't need to know anything about colors or oils or technique, because I'm not painting a picture." She paused just long enough for him to figure things out. "I'm painting you."

SAM NEARLY SHOT. He'd had his fair share of women in art school, and they'd messed around with body paints a time or two, but none of them had been Vanessa.

He watched her move toward him, lithe and tanned, and he couldn't help thinking that Marissa would never have done something like this. His previous muse had been content to lie still while he'd heaped adoration over her lush curves, whereas he got the sense that Vanessa could barely sit still on his cock long enough to come.

He smiled as she stood over him, one leg on each side of his hips. He'd seen her naked repeatedly since Friday night, but it still got him off to look up her short skirt like this. To see her white panties barely covering her smooth, hairless mound.

She smacked the heads of the paintbrushes into her left palm as if they were riding crops. By the look on her face—a cross between lust and power—he knew she was getting a kick out of dominating him. He'd never been the submissive type, but what the heck, he'd try anything once.

He couldn't resist messing with her, though, even if it was a slightly dangerous proposition. "You gonna get started soon, or should I take a quick nap first?"

Her nostrils flared. Bull's-eye. Nothing like pissing off a woman holding instruments of sensual torture.

"You're lucky I don't gag you right now to shut you up."

He barely fought the battle of holding back a grin. When was the last time a woman had made him laugh? Particularly one he wanted to do this badly.

"I was going to use these on your cock," she said as she stepped over him, turning toward his feet. "I was going to make you feel so good, just like you did to me. But now I've changed my mind. You're going to have to earn it." She dropped the medium and large brushes to the tarp, keeping only the thinnest, softest one. She brushed it lightly over the arch of one foot, and his toes twitched. "I'm not sure I'll ever get all the way up there," she added. "Unless . . ."

She let her words fall away as she bent her knees so the curve of her ass faced him. She moved the brush to his other foot, lightly running the fine hairs over the arch, then around to his ankles.

She was about as far from his usual erogenous zones as she could get, but his teeth were already clenched with desire. "Unless what?" he ground out.

She looked over her shoulder at him, her gray eyes flashing. "Unless you do exactly what I tell you." He was silent. There was no need to ask, she would say more in her own time. She moved the brush up the inside of one calf, and his hands fisted behind his head. "Don't you want to know what I've got in mind?" she asked, all innocence and pigtails and the most alluring woman he'd ever met all rolled into one.

"Sure," he said, feigning as much nonchalance as she was virtuousness and purity.

The brush found its way up one thigh to the base of his balls. More liquid found its way to the head of his dick and he knew that one quick touch of the tiny brush on his balls, on his penis, across his head, would be enough for him to blow.

"I don't want you to come," she said.

He went from lazy to irritated in a heartbeat. "Do you really think you have that much power over me?"

She smiled then, and he couldn't help but be seduced by it, even though he wanted to put both hands around her neck and shake her.

"I don't know," she said as the brush skirted around his shaft and dipped into the crevasse of his six-pack. "Do I?"

He sucked in a breath as she twirled horsehair over his nipples. In seconds he could have her flipped beneath him, her legs spread, his cock thrusting to the hilt, with her coming so hard she'd be seeing stars. But even as he lay beneath her in his own vineyard, with her using his own brushes on him, while she smart-mouthed all over the place and gave him ridiculous orders, he knew that her way was a heck of a lot more fun.

Smart woman. She'd figured out a way to be in control and

have him thank her for it. She had a gift for turning any situation to her advantage. He had no doubt she was indeed at the top of her professional game.

Still, he couldn't let her think she'd won. Even if she temporarily had. "Whatever," he said, as if it really didn't matter to him either way. "Just as long as this doesn't take long. We've got more work to do before sundown."

Her big eyes narrowed. Damn if he didn't love pissing her off. "Don't worry," she said, "it won't take long at all." She picked up the medium-sized brush and added, "Remember, you come, you lose."

Sam wasn't sure that was the case at all, but he didn't say anything this time. He let her work her magic.

He felt the first sweep of the small brush against his balls, followed closely by the larger brush as Vanessa slowly, deliberately worked them up his shaft, to the tip of his cock. Every part of him needed to come, but he couldn't let her win that easily. He knew she'd be disappointed, and sucker that he was, he didn't want to let her down.

"Have I mentioned how much I like winning?" she whispered as she bent down and licked at his hard, veined base, timing the sweep of the brushes with her licks.

Maybe another man could have toughed it out. There was probably some guy out there who could have fought this battle and won. But Sam wasn't that guy.

"There's only one problem with your plan," he said in as normal a voice as he could manage given the circumstances.

She stopped tasting, stopped painting. Crawling up over him, straddling his hips, her skirt pulling up tight over the tops of her thighs, she stared him down. "And what exactly would that be?"

His words were so soft that the breeze almost stole them. "I like it when you win," he said as he pulled her skirt up around her waist. Her hands fumbled over him as she rushed to push her panties to the side and drop the paintbrushes at the same time. He was in her, and he was glad, so damn glad she hadn't let him come, because he'd much rather be inside her like this. Somewhere in the back of his brain he remembered that they'd just met and better safe than sorry. He pulled out and reached under the tarp. Her sharp sound of protest cut short when she saw the condom in his hand. Grabbing the small, square package from him, she ripped it open with her teeth and shoved it onto his cock with a violence that nearly made him explode. But he forced himself to wait, wanting to be inside her, to feel her heat and her strength as she pulsed around him.

He shoved back inside her tight canal and flipped them over. She was still in control—she had been since the minute he'd set eyes on her—but he had to be on top, to drive into her as hard as he could.

Sam kissed her hard, then softer as his tongue found hers. All the while, his hips bucked and beat against hers and his fingers found her plump clit, so ready for his touch. He pushed his hand into her and she screamed into his mouth.

He needed to come more than he needed to breathe, but still he said, "Have I earned it yet?"

He felt her smile against his lips. "Yes," she said, and it was all he needed to let himself go. But even as he was losing it, she couldn't resist adding a "Just barely." In the middle of exploding into her, he smiled. And realized that he'd never smiled during an orgasm before.

6

FIFTEEN MINUTES LATER, Sam was back behind his canvases. Vanessa sat in profile, one leg up with her arms around it, the other bent and open. She popped grapes into her mouth one at a time, like a goddess of the vines, relaxing in her kingdom.

"What was her name?"

Sam stopped mixing paints. She was right. The time had come to take Marissa off her pedestal.

"Marissa. Marissa Robeiro."

"Where'd you find her?"

Vanessa's question seemed to hold no special interest. And yet, they both knew there was so much more behind her words, behind her curiosity. Still, he appreciated her approach. She knew when to be aggressive and she knew when to back down.

"She found me," he said, realizing for the first time that it was true. He hadn't been looking for a muse to take him over, but he had let it happen. "It was the end of the night at a show in San Francisco."

"You did well," she said, a statement, not a question.

"I did. Very. Everything sold in the first hour. The rest of the night was for contacts and cards and other galleries asking me what I was working on next." He paused to reset the scene in his head. "I was talking to the owner of the gallery, and when I looked up, she was there."

"You wondered how you could have missed her all night, when you wanted to drop everything to paint her."

"I can't remember anything after that. Somehow we made it back to Napa. For weeks all I did was paint her, sculpt her. Nothing else mattered. I didn't return phone calls. I didn't finish other projects I'd started. I didn't wonder how it was that she could have dropped everything, left her previous life behind to pose for me. I didn't wonder if there was someone else, a boyfriend, a husband."

"But she didn't offer anything. And she wouldn't let you touch her, would she?"

"No," he said, finally seeing his own stupidity for what it was. "I thought it was because she respected the purity of my art, of being my muse."

"But really she was just reeling you in."

He couldn't say anything to that. "I didn't realize what she was doing until she started getting into my business. She had a gift for opening doors, for making men believe her lies. But then she went too far, pushed too hard, reached too high. I wasn't ready for the kind of opportunities she craved. But by then, it was too late. I was already gone."

Vanessa dropped the remaining grapes to the ground and shifted to look him in the eye. "She was wrong about you, Sam. And you were wrong about her too. You never needed her. Not the way she wanted you to think you did. I won't deny that what you created while you were with her was amazing, because it is.

But that has everything to do with who you are, and nothing to do with who she is."

Her words were strong, forceful, but she followed them with a smile, and something inside of him started to crack.

"I'd like to think that I'm the reason you were able to create such magic today. But even I'm not that arrogant." She raised an eyebrow in a self-mocking way. "And that's saying something."

The crack grew bigger, and something broke open in his chest.

"Get dressed," he said. "Even though I'm sure spending an entire weekend on a tarp in my vineyard is really blowing your mind, I've decided to be your personal Napa Valley tour guide for the rest of the day."

She smiled again and took his hand as he helped her up. He didn't say "thank you" and she didn't say "you're welcome," but the words were there just the same.

It was a perfect afternoon. Maybe it was the delicious wines they tasted at a handful of gorgeous wineries and the blue, clear sky, the light breeze that blew through her hair, so different from the fog in the city. Maybe it was because the ghost of Marissa was finally gone. Or maybe, just maybe, it was because she was falling for Sam.

As the sun dipped behind the mountains, Sam took her to a five-star restaurant in the east hills, overlooking the valley floor. She'd been to plenty of extravagant, impressive restaurants. She'd been wined and dined from Paris to Rome to New York City. She knew Sam was successful, she figured he could easily afford it, but she was surprised by his choice.

Pleasantly so.

And even though they were still sitting in the valet zone of the parking lot, waiting for one of the young kids to take Sam's keys, tonight felt different. Not her usual five-star date experience. She couldn't help but wonder how different a lifetime with this man would be from everything she'd ever imagined.

Her startling thought of a future with Sam made her more crude than normal. "We look like shit," she said as he opened the passenger door of his truck and held out his hand.

"Correction. I look like shit. You look incredible."

She couldn't help but grin at that and had to hand it to the maître d' for not flinching when they stepped through the doors and into the throng of well-dressed, well-coifed diners. She should have known that Sam would be among friends here—hadn't he known everyone from one side of the valley to the next all day? The restaurant was packed and there were several couples waiting in the bar, but moments later she and Sam were seated at a table in the corner of the balcony, overlooking a glorious sunset falling down on the vines.

"You've been a nice surprise," he said when a bottle of champagne arrived.

She picked up the glass their waiter poured and took a sip, trying to figure out what she should say. She didn't want to give him the wrong impression that she was here to stay. To think she was going to cook his meals and have his babies.

"I don't do relationships," she finally said, deciding that blunt was the only option.

But Sam didn't seem particularly perturbed by her statement. "I already figured that out."

"That's one of the things I like about you. You're not an idiot like most men."

"Hey now, go easy on the compliments."

She grinned. "You get enough already. All day long people have been falling at your feet. And not only the women. I think you could convert most of the guys over to your team if you wanted to."

"Thanks for the confidence in my conversion abilities, but I'll take a rain check on that for now."

"I take it you don't have a publicist?"

He shrugged. "Never seemed to need one."

"Do you know how many artists there are out there who would kill to be in your shoes? Making a living doing what they love? Getting a name, building recognition without having to shout it from the rooftops?"

"I do know. And I know that I'm lucky."

"More talent than luck."

"But luck never hurts," he said, and she knew the conversation wasn't about his career anymore. It was about them.

"You've been a nice surprise too."

One incredible dish after another appeared on the table. They hadn't ordered, but Sam got the best out of everyone; she was certain this had to be the seven-course tasting menu.

"Who was he?" he asked as they dove in and polished off everything put down in front of them. She couldn't help but grin at his daring.

"There's never been a he," she said.

He leaned back in his chair and gave her a look of patent disbelief. "I find that hard to believe. You looking like that. With your brain. Your success." He lowered his voice. "You making love like you do."

She licked her lips, getting wet from nothing more than a six-word reminder of how much fun they'd had naked. "I'm not saying I haven't had a good time with a bunch of he's."

"That wasn't my question," he muttered.

She felt inordinately pleased. "Are you jealous of all the other men who've gotten to do me?" she teased.

"Sure I am," he said and her heart skipped a beat, shocked that he'd actually admitted it. Shocked that she liked that he cared.

"Oh," was all she could manage right then. "Anyway," she said, taking a large sip of champagne while she mentally shoved the new, flustered Vanessa off the wooden balcony, "I like my life. I've never wanted to change it for someone else." She looked him in the eyes. "No matter how good he is in bed."

"Message coming loud and clear," he said, but he was grinning and she knew he didn't believe her. He thought he was going to be the one to change her mind.

She'd been with men who'd thought that before. That they'd be the one to get her to settle for one cock for the rest of her life. But she'd never really thought it was possible. Until now.

Sam really was smart, however, and he steered the conversation away from other possible emotional minefields. She learned he'd grown up in the valley, that he'd thought he was going to be a contractor, which explained the big, rough hands she liked so damn much. He told her how surprised everyone was when he'd started painting.

She laughed at his stories, liking him more with every passing course. And when the questions came her way, she deflected them like she always did. But this time, she felt a pang of something she couldn't identify. She wanted to share her stories with him. As if she knew that he was interested in more than her body, in more than what she could do with her mouth, her hands, her vagina.

He was interested in her.

She'd never met anyone like him before. And even though horror movies were never nearly frightening enough, even though a dark night and a dimly lit street had never made her cower with fear, Sam's honest appreciation scared her to death.

After dinner they went back to his house. He stripped off her dress, her panties, and carried her to his bed. "I'm going to find out who you are," he said as he lay above her, "whether you want me to or not."

She should have left him right then. She should have gotten out of bed and told him thanks for the fun, but the only thing she wanted more than to turn tail and run was for him to take her to heaven one last time.

7

SAM WASN'T INTERESTED IN KINKY OR WILD. Right now he wanted to go slow, take his time. To love her right, the way she deserved to be touched, cherished. To explore the mystery that was Vanessa. She thought she was straightforward, but in fact he discovered something new at every turn.

He shifted onto his side, the top of his thigh barely touching the side of hers. The swell of her left breast curved into his chest. He didn't move his hands to touch her, he didn't bend down to kiss her.

He just looked.

"Haven't you seen enough?" she asked. "I've practically been naked since the moment we met."

She meant for her words to be challenging, but all he heard was the uncertainty behind them.

"I was a painter then," he said.

"And now?"

His eyes held hers. "I'm a man."

A flush washed over her tanned skin and she sucked her lower lip into her mouth. He watched the plump, red flesh disappear behind her teeth, and he ached to taste her.

"I'm not used to this," she said, and he admired her for admitting it. "When you were painting me it was—"

"Different."

She shifted under the weight of his gaze, turning to face him. He knew he'd sculpt her in clay from this memory. He couldn't stop his thumb from brushing lightly over her eyebrows, moving softly across her eyelids as she closed them, stopping on her lips, learning the texture. Soft and warm and wicked.

His hand moved over her chin, down to her throat, and he held it there, feeling her pulse race, then relax, beneath his touch. Being with Vanessa like this, stroking her skin, wasn't about sex.

And yet he'd never been so aroused.

His fingers brushed over her collarbone, finally finding the swell of her breasts. A part of him wished he could continue like this without giving in to how much he wanted her, but he was just a man. He leaned his head down, and she sucked in a breath as his hair brushed her chest.

Her nipple was warm and hard and sweet in his mouth. His tongue made lazy circles over the peak, and he felt her strong fingers thread through his hair, pulling him closer.

With his mouth busy, captivated, his hand continued its journey down the flat plane of her stomach, out to the curve of her hip, and then back in, to the center of her. She arched her hips into his hand and he slipped in, one finger sliding over her hard, slick clitoris. Her legs opened wide. He accepted her invitation, pushing one thick finger into her tight pussy. She moaned and his mouth got jealous of his hands, so he ran kisses down her torso until he found that patch of skin between her legs that he couldn't resist.

And then his tongue was there, licking, stroking, rubbing, and

she was twisting beneath him. He pulled her body closer and settled between her legs, her calves resting on his back. She moaned
again, but this time she was past desperation, and he sucked her
clit in between her pussy lips as his fingers drove slowly in and
out of her cunt.

She was coming now, so beautiful, so perfect, and Sam knew
that he loved her. Even as he mounted her, even as he drove into
her, even as she cried out his name and he took her lips in a bru-
tal kiss, he knew that she would fight against his love with every
weapon she could. And he would let her.

He wrapped his arms around her and pulled her solid warmth
close. This was the moment he would hold on to for as long as it
took. Eventually she would come around.

Until then, however long it took, he would not give up.

WAKING UP IN SAM'S BED was good. He was warm and hard, but
safe. His smell was spicy, dangerous, yet comforting. She wanted
to make her way down his body, one kiss at a time, but at the
same time she wanted to stay wrapped in his arms forever.

God, she was making herself sick. She knew better than to
think that she was actually in love with him. More like she was in
love with his cock. And his glorious mouth. Not to mention his
hands. His eyes weren't bad either. All he needed to do was look
at her and she turned into a quivering mess of orgasm.

This had been a weekend to remember, that's for sure, but she
was already chomping at the bit to get back to the city.

Okay, so that was a lie. She was surprised by how comfortable
she was with the pace of life in Napa. There was definitely something to be said about a life in the country. Even stopping to chat
every five minutes with another local, since Sam pretty much
knew everyone in the valley, had been fun. San Francisco was so
big that she hardly knew her neighbors.

It added up to one clear thing: She needed to get out of here. ASAP. Say thanks for a good time, cut ties, then leave as quickly as possible.

But he wasn't her worthiest adversary for nothing. Because he was one step ahead, anticipating her flight. Before she could give in and let herself relax into his strong arms one last time, he flipped her onto her stomach, her arms behind her back, her wrists held tightly beneath his strong grip.

The part of her that should have felt fear instead felt lust. Pure, brazen desire. She'd never let a man overpower her before. And none had ever dared try it. Until now.

Only Sam would know that being conquered was what she wanted. What she needed. She turned her head from the pillow to find a pocket of air, and he slipped something silky and cool over her wrists, binding them as firmly as his hands had a moment earlier. His hands left her arms and slid, roughly, up her rib cage to her breasts, smashed into the mattress by his weight. He cupped and squeezed her tits, and his breath blew hot on her neck as he said, "Has anyone ever taken your control away, Vanessa?"

His whispered words made her wet, so much wetter than she'd ever been. But she didn't answer. She couldn't admit that he was winning, even though he was. He could do anything to her now—anything—and she'd be the one begging for more.

His hands tightened on her breasts, and he bit down on her earlobe. "Answer me," he growled, and just as the words "No, only you" left her mouth, he slid into her, hot and hard and so big that she had to stretch to fit him. Again.

"Good girl," he said, and she tried to buck her hips back into him to mate with him. He pulled out, and she nearly cried out at the sudden emptiness.

"I thought you understood," he said, his voice low and hard and so damn seductive she was practically coming like that, with his hands on her breasts and her clit pressing into nothing more than his white cotton sheets. "You'll do what I tell you to. Nothing more."

Instinctively she fought him, using all her strength to try and wriggle out from beneath him, pulling at the bindings at her wrists. But he was strong, so much stronger than she was, and in an instant his hands were on her hips and he was holding her still, his cock poised at the entrance to her dripping cunt. Oh, God, all she needed was for him to press his thumb into her slit, to drive his huge length into her, and she'd be gone.

"I know you're a bad girl, Vanessa. And I like that." More blood swelled at the tip of her breasts, at her clit. "But sometimes even bad girls need to learn how to be good. How to say please. And thank you."

She couldn't help it, she had to say something. Something to let him know that controlling her wouldn't be easy. "And you think you're going to be my teacher?" Her words came out sarcastic and flippant, and she felt him smile behind her.

"Say please, Vanessa."

She shook her head no. And wiggled her ass against his hard-on while she was at it. To remind him that he needed her as much as she needed him.

"You like to make men beg, don't you?"

She smiled into the pillow. "They always do. You will too."

He moved his hand from her hip bone, in toward her belly. "Not today. Say please," he said again, and this time his fingers were an inch from her clit. Inside her head she was screaming "PLEASE!" and had to bite down on her lip to keep the word from pushing out her lips.

"I'm waiting," he said, nudging her legs further apart with his hard thigh. His free hand rode up her rib cage again to the base of her breasts. "You can have everything you want, Vanessa. Just say the word."

Her need for him broke her then. "Pl—" she began, the word getting lost in her gasp as, all at once, he rammed his cock into her, pressed the flesh of his thumb against her aching clit, and squeezed her nipple. Her orgasm hit her so hard that everything went black. She thought her stomach, her breasts would explode with the force of her pleasure, and she was glad for the pillow to mask her screams. His cock crashed in and out of her with a violence that she met thrust for thrust. The walls of her cunt squeezed him tighter and tighter as her orgasm crested, and as she fell back down to earth, as she remembered how to breathe again, he freed her wrists and flipped her onto her back. He tied her arms to the bedpost and she was his captive again.

His shaft was in her mouth and she sucked at him desperately, wanting to feel his hot seed shoot down her throat. He'd won and she'd been so glad to be beaten, but milking him with her tongue, with her lips, was her chance for redemption. But as quickly as he'd filled her mouth with his penis, he took it away.

"I know what you want, Vanessa. I'll always know," he said, and she forced herself to open her eyes, to stare straight into his green depths.

"You won't," she said. "You can't." But her protests sounded feeble. Because she already knew that he was right. He was the only man who could see her as she truly was. The only man who'd ever dared to try.

He ignored her weak objections, choosing instead to suck on her nipples, laving them one at a time until she was writhing again, utterly at his mercy. Just the way he wanted it.

"Right now, for instance," he said in a conversational tone, as if they were sharing scones over tea and not fighting each other for dominance in his bed, "you want me to spread open your thighs, don't you?"

She glared at him, or tried to, but it was hard to scowl when all she wanted was to scream "YES," to shove his head down to her pussy.

"Oh, yes," he said with a grin that bordered on evil. "I can see it in your eyes. You want me to lick your cunt with my tongue. Long, hard strokes. You want me to circle your clit, to make you so hot, so horny that all it takes is the lightest flick and you'll fall over the edge. Don't you?"

She couldn't glare anymore. All she could do was close her eyes and will herself not to beg him. He'd be so full of himself if she let him win. Again.

"I want to taste you, Vanessa," he said, and the heat in his voice made her open her eyes against her will. "But I don't think a good girl would let me do that, would she? A good girl wouldn't let me get her off with my tongue, with my teeth, with my mouth. A good girl wouldn't let me finger-fuck her until she came again, first one finger, then two, squeezing them so hard that I couldn't help myself and I had to slide into her pussy. A good girl wouldn't let me tie her to the bedpost so that I could take my cock out of her slick cunt and watch her suck it."

Her tongue shot out to wet her dry lips—he was amazingly good at this—and his hungry eyes devoured her. No one would win today.

Then again, maybe they both would.

"I'm not a good girl," she said, and when he grinned and said, "Thank God," she closed her eyes and let her legs fall open beneath his mouth, his teeth, his tongue. Just as he'd promised, he

sucked at her, then finger-fucked her, then followed his fingers
with his cock. But she never got the chance to taste him again, because once he was inside, there was no going back. For either of
them.

He untied her wrists in one deft movement, and she wrapped
her arms around his hard, wide shoulders, loving the play of
muscles beneath her fingertips. Her legs were already around
him, pulling him closer, tighter against her. Their bodies were
slick with sweat, with heat, and the sheets twisted beneath her
back as their passion raged further out of control. They came as
one, their bodies entwined, each claiming one another in an un-
forgettable kiss.

And in that moment, Vanessa knew that loving Sam like this
was the biggest mistake of her life. There would never be another
man as good as him.

Both in bed. And out.

Her orgasm barely finished, she pushed away from him,
pushed out of the bed and picked her dress up from the floor,
slipping it on over her sweat-slick skin.

"Leaving so soon?" he asked, looking down at her shoes, at her
feet that were already in them.

"It's been fun, Sam, but I think it's time for me to get my painting from the window and head back home."

She didn't know what she expected him to do, although
arguing with her would have been a start. Telling her he couldn't
live without her would have been good. Saying he couldn't paint
without her would have been nice too.

Because even though she was going to leave him no matter
what he said, no matter how much he begged, at least she would
have known that he'd been a tiny bit upset to see her go. Especially after the greatest sex known to mankind.

But he didn't do any of that. He didn't get out of bed. Instead he reached into the drawer on his bedside table and pulled out a key. He threw it to her, and she nearly fumbled it in her surprise.

"Go ahead and let yourself into the gallery. I've got to head over to the farmer's market for a plein-air demonstration."

Moments later, the bathroom door closed behind him and she was left standing in his bedroom, holding a key to his gallery. She couldn't believe it. She'd served as his muse, inspired him to greatness on canvas, and now he couldn't be bothered to make her a cup of coffee.

He was giving her exactly what she'd said she wanted: her freedom. And yet a part of her wished she could stay in bed with him forever.

It was a good thing that she wasn't the kind of woman who would ever let herself care about a man. Because if she had been, someone could have called what she was feeling heartbreak.

SAM FORCED HIMSELF TO TURN on the shower, to stand under the scalding hot water until he was absolutely certain that Vanessa had gone. It killed him not to chase after her, to beg her to give him a chance, to tell her he'd change everything to fit into her world.

But he knew better. He'd done that before and it hadn't worked. More to the point, it hadn't been right. Thank God Marissa hadn't stuck with him. She wasn't a tenth of the woman that Vanessa was.

He hadn't told Vanessa that he loved her before she'd left. There would have been no point in that. She wouldn't have believed him. Worse, she would have used those three simple words against him. She would have to discover it for herself, back in San Francisco. Over time she'd have to realize that they had something real, something special. That he understood her. And that a love like theirs was worth lowering her defenses for.

But he'd have to let her get there alone.

Only she wouldn't be alone. There'd be men sniffing after her everywhere she went. And he was certain she'd go home with at least one of them. That she'd try to erase him from her heart with another guy.

The vision of her with some jerk who didn't deserve her was almost enough to break him. The only thing for him to do was to keep at his work. He pulled on his paint-spattered jeans and told himself to get over it already. If he wanted to be with her, he'd have to be willing to deal with Vanessa as she was.

Frightened.

Bold.

Beautiful.

He headed out his front door to walk the two blocks to his gallery and studio. A part of him feared that he'd be dead to the world when Vanessa left, but it was just the opposite. The air had never smelled better. The sky had never been so blue. He'd never been this ready to paint.

She had brought him back to life.

Rounding the corner to his gallery, he braced himself for the empty space in the window, knowing that Vanessa would have already come and taken the painting. Instead what he saw took his breath away.

She'd replaced Marissa with herself. He smiled. He should have known she'd do that. Already, people were gathering at the window, commenting on the vivid colors, the passion. He wasn't ready to deal with them yet, so he ducked into the alley and grabbed a stack of blank canvases and an empty stand from the barn.

Months ago, when he'd agreed to do a plein-air painting

demonstration at the Napa Farmer's Market, he'd titled it Wine, Women & Seduction. That was some crazy foresight.

He quickly set up and mixed paints. He was usually slightly self-conscious when he had to paint in front of so many strangers. Today, they fell away into a background that he didn't see, that he wasn't aware of.

The only thing he could see was Vanessa. In his bed. In his vineyard. In his gallery. On his canvas.

8

ONE MONTH LATER Vanessa sat in her office, Marissa on the wall behind her. She didn't usually come in on Sunday—a day reserved for a good time, preferably in bed with some boy toy she'd picked up Saturday night—but she'd just returned from Sunday brunch with Rose and Carrie and hadn't been able to think of anything better to do. So she'd picked up a copy of the Sunday *Chronicle* and let herself into the bright, empty office. All of her employees were probably in the park with their husbands and babies or hungover after a late night of partying.

Vanessa felt too old, not to mention disinterested, to stay up all night anymore. As for the husbands and babies, well, they had never been in the picture.

As it was, there'd been enough gushing from her two best friends about their new men and how wonderful they were and how every second was better than the next. She had barely been able to eat her waffles. Her sugar and spice quota was full for the day, thanks.

That first week after they'd returned from Napa, she'd resisted the temptation to call Sam. Sure, Carrie and Rose thought they'd found their own Mr. Right. But Vanessa had been certain that she was the only one of the three of them who wouldn't end up with a broken heart. Just like always.

But then, one week had turned to two. Two had turned to three.

Rose and Carrie had fallen even more in love. And Sam hadn't called.

Vanessa hadn't been able to bring herself to sleep with any of the guys who'd taken her out. And then the invitation had come. Sam was having a show at a gallery less than one block from her office.

She'd grabbed the invitation out of her assistant's hands and locked herself in her office. He wanted to see her. He wanted her to come. To be there. With him.

But then she'd seen who'd actually sent the card. The owner of the gallery had been one of her first PR clients. He'd asked her to come. Not Sam.

She'd shoved the embossed card through her shredder. It had felt as if her heart had gone with it.

She hadn't mentioned Sam's show to her friends. They hadn't known that it was today. That she'd practically been counting down the minutes until it began.

Until it was over.

They knew her well enough to have kept Sam out of the conversation. Or maybe it had been because she'd bitten off their heads on the couple of occasions when they'd asked about him, asked about her weekend. Both Carrie and Rose had seen the paintings of her at his gallery, and Vanessa knew they had to have been talking about her behind her back.

That was perfectly okay with her, so long as she didn't have to say his name.

Or think about him ever again.

Vanessa wasn't a total bitch, so of course she was happy that they thought they'd found their soul mates. Rose, who never did anything without weeks of careful deliberation, had moved in with Jack immediately. But Vanessa knew San Francisco had never been a good fit for her. It was simply where her accounting degree had taken her. Already, Rose had started a bookkeeping business in Napa with the barest of help from her hot chef fiancé, who pretty much knew every business owner in town.

Just like Sam.

She shook the thought out of her head. What was the point of thinking about him? He hadn't claimed undying love for her that Sunday morning in his bedroom, like Carrie and Rose's men had. Not that she would have believed him anyway. Two people couldn't fall in love over the weekend.

Okay, so Carrie and Rose had. But they were the exceptions.

She turned her thoughts to Carrie, who was spending more and more time in Napa. She had secured her first commercial landscaping job at the winery next to Tyson's, and Vanessa knew that the strength of her work would quickly lead to more jobs.

Vanessa could see the future without her best friends around the corner to meet for drinks on a whim, and it was lonely.

Could she hear herself? Nice pity party she was throwing. She'd have to add that to her list of events to throw for clients. Besides, who was she kidding? She was never lonely. She'd always had a knack for meeting people, for making new friends.

Pissed off at what a sappy loser she was being, she flipped open the Calendar section in the *Chronicle*. She was going to take advantage of all the wonderful things San Francisco had to offer.

She'd go see a play or a lecture. Maybe there was a volleyball tournament at the marina, where she could put on some short-shorts and force herself to pick up a hottie.

But that was the problem. She could make new friends. She just didn't want to. Her real friends, Carrie and Rose, were important to her. It would be stupid to try and replace them with two strangers just to have someone to drink Cosmos with on Friday nights. Real relationships, not superficial ones, were important. Which brought her back to Sam. He was real. The most honest, passionate man she'd ever met.

And that was when Sam's smile hit her hard in the solar plexus, from the pages of the newspaper. The words below his photo assaulted her: "Sam Marshall's passion for his muse is breathtaking. His love for her is visible in every brushstroke, the kind of love we all wish we had."

HE'D BEEN SO SURE, so certain he'd been doing the right thing letting her go. His work had never been so fluid, so confident, and in the past thirty days, everything he'd painted had sold and been out the door before the paint had dried. But he hadn't wanted to part with his paintings of her—they were all he had left—so he'd doubled his prices. Then tripled them.

He'd made so much money that he could have bought a small castle.

But none of it mattered without Vanessa.

He'd asked the gallery owner to send her an invite. But there'd been no RSVP. He'd tried to tell himself she'd be there tonight, but he'd known it hadn't been true.

She'd meant what she'd said that night, up on the hill overlooking the valley. She didn't do relationships. She was happy with her life exactly as it was. Without him.

He parked his van in front of the gallery, knowing Vanessa's office was half a block down. He could set up camp there, refuse to leave until she agreed to see him. To talk to him. To love him.

Joe, the owner, came out to greet him, and Sam sucked it up and pulled himself together. He'd taken a risk, and it hadn't paid off. He had to face up to a future without her. Starting with tonight.

SHE WASN'T ABLE TO MAKE IT through the rest of the article. Her eyes were too wet to see clearly. Had she been a fool? Had she walked out on the best thing she'd ever had?

No, she tried to tell herself, he was like every other man. Out to get in her pants. Or, in his case, out to make money off the inspiration she'd provided.

Pain tore at her. Because she knew that she was utterly and completely full of it.

Sam hadn't used her. She'd used him. For a weekend fling. For an ego boost and hot sex and the power she'd had over him.

She had to see him. Even if he didn't want her anymore, even if she was nothing but a distant memory, she had to tell him the truth. She had to tell him that she loved him. Even though she was afraid to love. She wanted him to know that he was worth it. That she was willing to try to make the impossible work, if he had any feelings left for her at all.

She didn't remember to check her hair or her makeup as she pushed out of her chair and headed out to the street. The phone rang, but she didn't hear it. She was already halfway down the street when she realized she'd left her office unlocked. Momentarily undecided, she finally spun back and put the alarm on. Moving twice as fast for the delay, moments later she was knocking on the gallery door, peering in through the windows, trying to find Sam.

Joe answered the door. "Vanessa, it's been too long."

She didn't have time for pleasantries. "Is he here?"

"Sam?"

She nodded, unable to speak.

"He was, but he went out to grab a bite, I think."

"Oh."

"You want to wait for him to come back?"

"No," she said, but she wasn't sure, didn't care, if he heard her, because she was already walking away from the gallery, pushing past people to get back to her office, to hide there, to try and recover everything she'd lost. It was a sign. If he'd been there waiting for her, everything would have worked out. But he hadn't been.

He didn't love her.

"I should have told you I loved you."

Sam was there, right in front of her on the sidewalk. Tall and hard with those dirty, paint-spattered jeans she loved so much.

Her heart nearly pounded out of her chest at the surprise of seeing him again. Mostly, though, she felt joy. So much she was bursting with it.

He loved her.

"Saturday night, I already loved you. But Sunday morning, I let you go. I didn't tell you."

He loved her.

She didn't realize that she hadn't responded until he came a step closer, slowly, as if she were a wild animal that could flee at any moment.

"I love you, Vanessa."

He loved her.

The words fell from her mouth before she had time to think about them, to shape them into something better. Something witty or sexy. "You were right, Sam. You were right not to say it."

She pressed into him as he said, "I haven't been sleeping much.

Nothing's been right since you left, and I might be hallucinating and imagining what you just said. That I was right. I think I need to hear it again to let it sink in."

They were standing in the middle of the busy sidewalk, and people were having to travel around them, but it didn't occur to Vanessa to get out of the way, travel the final two feet to her office door.

This was one of the things she loved about Sam. Even when they were having the most poignant moment of their relationship, he was pushing her buttons, teasing her in the way that only he could.

"You were right," she said, and his eyes gleamed with something that looked like satisfaction. She wanted to kiss it out of him, to show him who was really the boss. But she couldn't. Not yet. Not until she came clean.

"If you had said, 'I love you,' I wouldn't have heard you, Sam. I couldn't have." Her voice faltered, and she didn't bother to hide it. She didn't need to hide when she was with him. "I lied to you. About my past."

If she'd expected something in his eyes to change—and she had—she'd been mistaken. The only thing she saw in them was love.

"You always told me the truth," he said. "Even when I didn't want to listen. You told me you had everything you needed. Everything you wanted. You said you weren't going to change for me. And I don't want you to. I would never ask you to."

"I know that," she said. "There was a he."

"Of course there was. You're beautiful. Brilliant. I'd be stupid to think that I was the first man you'd been with."

"No, not boyfriends. None of them matter. I'm talking about my father."

His fists curled. "I'll kill him."

"No. He wasn't like that."

His jaw loosened. "Thank God."

"He didn't love my mother. Or me." A bitter laugh escaped. "But he sure as hell loved everybody else he could get his hands on."

Sam shook his head. "Whatever he did to your mom, whoever he cheated with, it didn't mean he didn't love you."

But he didn't know what it had been like for her. He didn't know that she had spent her whole life trying to please him, to make him proud. Only to finally realize that she wasn't worth enough to her father to matter at all. Good or bad.

"He only loved himself. I'm a lot like him."

"Then you're the good part of him."

She laughed, but it was a harsh sound. "There wasn't a good part."

"He helped make you, didn't he?"

"You're full of it, Sam, but I still love you."

"I know you do."

And then she was in his arms, the only place she'd ever truly felt safe. The only place she'd ever felt loved. "I've always held myself back from love. I always thought it had to turn out bad. That I'd never find a man that I could trust." She looked into his eyes. "I'm not afraid anymore, Sam."

He smiled, and she fell all the way into him. "I know you're not."

"How come you know everything? I used to think I did, but now . . ."

His mouth was almost on hers, but before he kissed her, he pulled away and held her at arm's length. "Does this mean I'm going to have to take you down off of that pedestal I've put you on?"

She snorted. "Good one."

"I was tempted."

"Of course you were," she said in her patented smug voice.

"I made that mistake once. I'm not stupid enough to make it again. Not even with you."

"You're not obsessed with me?" she said with an exaggerated pout. "I'm not your every waking thought, your muse for life?"

"Too late. I'm already utterly obsessed."

"Good."

"And I always will be."

"Good."

"But you'll never stay on the pedestal for long."

"Screw you."

He grinned. "I hope that's an invitation."

"Of course it is." Finally, she unlocked her office door and pulled him inside, behind closed blinds. "Do you want me to take my clothes off?"